Vanishing act

Campion hurried forward to the opening in the yew hedge.

"Mr. Lobbett," he shouted, "answer us, please. You're scaring us."

The search went on in feverish silence.

Campion started off round the east side of the maze. The minutes passed quickly. Campion met Marlowe in the road which skirted the fourth side of the yew puzzle.

"It's absurd," Marlowe said. "We're getting wound up about nothing, of course. The whole darned place is as sound as an icebox. There isn't any way out except the one he went in by. He must be in there."

Mr. Campion seemed stupefied.

"We'll get round to the others," he said. "He'll probably be with them."

A light step on the road behind them made them swing around expectantly. It was Biddy.

"Albert," she said breathlessly, "he's gone. We've combed the maze, and there's not a trace of him. Not a glimpse—not a sound. It's as if he'd disappeared into the earth."

Agatha Christie

Death on the Nile
A Holiday for Murder
The Mousetrap and Other
  Plays
The Mysterious Affair at
  Styles
Poirot Investigates
Postern of Fate
The Secret Adversary
The Seven Dials Mystery
Sleeping Murder

Dorothy Simpson

Last Seen Alive
The Night She Died
Puppet for a Corpse
Six Feet Under
Close Her Eyes
Element of Doubt
Dead on Arrival
Suspicious Death
Dead by Morning

Elizabeth George

A Great Deliverance
Payment in Blood
Well-Schooled in Murder

Colin Dexter

Last Bus to Woodstock
The Riddle of the Third Mile
The Silent World of Nicholas
  Quinn
Service of All the Dead
The Dead of Jericho
The Secret of Annexe 3
Last Seen Wearing

Michael Dibdin

Ratking

Liza Cody

Stalker
Head Case
Under Contract

S. T. Haymon

Death of a God
coming soon: Death and the
  Pregnant Virgin
A Very Particular Murder

Ruth Rendell

A Dark-Adapted Eye
  (writing as Barbara Vine)
A Fatal Inversion
  (writing as Barbara Vine)

Marian Babson

Death in Fashion
Reel Murder
Murder, Murder, Little Star
Murder on a Mystery Tour
Murder Sails at Midnight
The Stalking Lamb
Murder at the Cat Show

Dorothy Cannell

The Widows Club
Down the Garden Path
Mum's the Word
coming soon: Femmes Fatal

Antonio Fraser

Jemima Shore's First Case
Your Royal Hostage
Oxford Blood
A Splash of Red
coming soon: Cool Repentance
Quiet as a Nun

Margery Allingham

Police at the Funeral
Flowers for the Judge
Tether's End
Pearls Before Swine
Traitor's Purse
Dancers in Mourning

MYSTERY MILE

MARGERY ALLINGHAM

BANTAM BOOKS
NEW YORK · TORONTO · LONDON · SYDNEY · AUCKLAND

MYSTERY MILE
A Bantam Book / published by arrangement with Doubleday

PRINTING HISTORY

*Doubleday edition published 1988
Bantam edition / December 1990*

ISBN 0-553-29013-4

Published simultaneously in the United States and Canada

Bantam Books are published by Bantam Books, a division of Bantam
Doubleday Dell Publishing Group, Inc. Its trademark, consisting of the
words "Bantam Books" and the portrayal of a rooster, is Registered in
U.S. Patent and Trademark Office and in other countries. Marca
Registrada. Bantam Books, 666 Fifth Avenue, New York, New York
10103.

PRINTED IN THE UNITED STATES OF AMERICA

OPM   0 9 8 7 6 5 4 3 2 1

To
P.Y.C. and A.J.G.
Partners in Crime

CHAPTER I

Among Those Present

"I'll bet you fifty dollars, even money," said the American who was sitting nearest the door in the opulent lounge of the homeward-bound *Elephantine,* "that that man over there is murdered within a fortnight. I'd say six weeks, only I don't like to rob you."

The Englishman at his side glanced across the sea of chairs at the handsome old man they had been watching. "Ten pounds," he said. "All right, I'll take you. You've no idea what a safe little place England is."

A slow smile spread over the American's face. "You've got no idea what a dangerous old fellow Crowdy Lobbett is," he said. "If your police are going to look after him they'll have to keep him in a steel bandbox, and I don't envy them that job. It's almost a pity to take your money, though I'm giving you better odds than any Insurance Corporation in the States would offer."

"The whole thing sounds fantastic to me," said the Englishman. "But I'll meet you at Verrey's a fortnight to-day and we'll make a night of it. That suit you?"

"The twenty-second," said the American, making a note of it in his book. "Seems kind of heathen celebrating over the old man's corpse. He's a great old boy."

"Drinking his health, you mean," said the Englishman confidently. "Scotland Yard is very spry these days. That reminds me," he added cheerfully, "I must take you to one of our night clubs."

On the other side of the ship's lounge the loquacious Turk who had made himself such a nuisance to his fellow passengers since they put out from New York was chattering to his latest victim.

"Very courageous of him to come down for the concert," he was saying, with all the satisfaction of one introducing a sensational subject. "He's a marked man, you know. I don't think there's any doubt about that. Four murders in his household within the past month and each time his escape was a miracle."

His victim, a pale young man who seemed to be trying to hide behind his enormous spectacles, woke out of the reverie into which he had fallen ever since the talkative Oriental had first tackled him and surveyed his persecutor owlishly. "Not that nice old gentleman over there?" he said. "The one with the white hair? Four murders in his house within a month? That ought to be stopped. He's been told about it, I suppose?"

Since this was the first remark with which the young man had favoured him, the bore jumped to the conclusion that he had inadvertently stumbled on a mental case. It was inconceivable to him that anyone should not have heard of the now famous Misfire Murders, as the Press had starred them, which had filled the New York papers for the past four weeks. While he was debating whether he would give up his carefully chosen seat for the concert by moving or stay where he was and put up with a lunatic, the young man spoke again.

"Who is the stormy old petrel?" he said.

His companion looked at him with some of the delight which a born gossip always feels upon finding an uninformed listener. His heavy red face became animated and he cocked his curious pear-shaped head, which alone betrayed his nationality, alertly on one side.

"That fine old man, typical of the best type of hard-bitten

New Englander," he began in a rhetorical whisper, "is none other than Judge Crowdy Lobbett. He has been the intended victim of an extraordinary series of crimes. I can't understand how you've missed reading about it all."

"Oh, I've been away in Nebraska for my health," said the young man. "He-man stuff, you know," he added in his slightly falsetto voice.

He spoke with the utmost gravity, and the old man nodded unsuspectingly and continued.

"First his secretary, seated in his master's chair, was shot," he said slowly. "Then his butler, who was apparently after his master's Scotch, got poisoned. Then his chauffeur met with a very mysterious accident, and finally a man walking with him down the street got a coping stone on his head." He sat back and regarded his companion almost triumphantly. "What do you say to that?" he demanded.

"Shocking," said the young man. "Very bad taste on someone's part. Rotten marksmanship, too," he added, after some consideration. "I suppose he's travelling for health now, like me?"

The Turk bent nearer and assumed a more confidential tone.

"They say," he mumbled, in an unsuccessful attempt to keep his voice down, "that it was all young Marlowe Lobbett could do to get his father to come to Europe at all. I admire a man like that, a man who's not afraid of what's coming to him."

"Oh, quite!" said the young man mildly. "A very distressing story, though. The neat piece of modern youthing with the old gentleman is the son you spoke of, I suppose?"

The Turk nodded.

"That's right, and the girl sitting on his other side is his daughter. Nice-looking youngsters, don't you think? That very black hair gives them a sort of distinction. Funny that the boy should be so big and the girl so small. She takes after her mother, one of the Edwardeses of Tennessee, you know. The beautiful Isopel Edwardes. The daughter is named after her. Someone was saying to me that she looked like Lillian Gish, but I don't see it myself."

"I don't see it either," said the young man. "But then I'm very short-sighted. As a matter of fact, I can't see the girl at all. When's the concert going to begin?"

The Turk smiled. He felt he had consummated the acquaintanceship at last.

"My name is Barber," he said. "Ali Fergusson Barber—a rather stupid joke of my parents, I have always thought."

He looked inquiringly at his companion, hoping for a similar exchange of confidence, but he was unrewarded. The young man appeared to have forgotten all about him, and presently to the Oriental's complete disgust, he drew a small white mouse from the pocket of his dinner jacket and began to fondle it in his hands. Finally he held it out for Mr. Barber's inspection.

"Rather pretty, don't you think?" he said. "One of the cabin boys lent it to me. He keeps it to remind him of his brother Haig. He calls it Haig, after him."

Mr. Barber looked down his immense nose at the little creature, and edged away from it.

The young man said no more, for already a very golden-haired lady with pince-nez was playing the Sixth Hungarian Rhapsody with a certain amount of acid gusto.

Her performance was greeted with only mild enthusiasm, and the Turk overcame his repugnance to the noise sufficiently to lean over and inform the young man in a noisy murmur that there were several stage stars travelling and no doubt the programme would improve as it went on. For some time, however, his optimism was unrewarded. "Turn" followed "turn" of uniform earnest but uninspired endeavour.

At length the fussy, sandy-haired young man who was superintending the performance with the discreet aid of a purser came forward with the announcement that Satsuma, the world-famous Japanese conjurer, was on board and had consented to perform some of his most celebrated illusions before the assembled company, and the audience's patience was craved while the stage was made ready for him.

For the first time Mr. Barber's companion seemed to take an intelligent interest in the proceedings and he joined enthusiastically in the applause which followed the announcement.

"I'm potty about conjurers," he remarked affably. "Haig will like it too, I fancy. I'm most interested to see the effect upon him."

Mr. Barber smiled indulgently.

"You are making jokes," he said naïvely.

The young man shot him a quick glance from behind his spectacles, but there was no hidden thrust intended in his words.

"I do a little conjuring myself," he went on confidentially. "And I once knew a man who could manage a spot of witchcraft in a small way. Nothing big, you know, but he could always produce a few potatoes out of the old topper, or a half bottle of Bass. He once got in some champagne that way, but it wasn't much of a brand. Hullo! what's going on up there?"

He peered at the platform with childlike interest.

Several enthusiastic amateurs, aided by an electrician, were engaged in setting up the magician's apparatus on the small stage. The piano had to be moved to make way for the great "disappearing" cabinet, and the whole audience watched curiously while the cables were connected and the various gaily-coloured cupboards and boxes were set in position.

The magician himself, it was obvious, was directing operations from behind a screen in the "wings", and at length, when the last scene-shifter had departed, he came forward and bowed ceremoniously.

He was tall for a Japanese, and dark-skinned, with a clever, cunning little face much too small for him.

Mr. Barber nudged the young man at his side.

"Old Lobbett doesn't let his troubles damp his interest, does he?" he rumbled, as he glanced across the room to where the old man who had been the subject of so much speculation during the voyage sat forward in his chair, his bright blue eyes alert and interested under his bushy white brows. His keenness and excitement were almost childlike, and after a moment or two, dissatisfied with his view of the stage, he left his seat and walked up to the front row, where he stood watching, plainly fascinated. The loquacious Mr. Barber's companion made no comment. He appeared to be engrossed in his small pet mouse, which he held up, apparently with the idea of allowing the little animal to watch the performance.

The magician began with one or two sleight-of-hand tricks, presenting each illusion with a witty topical patter which created a friendly atmosphere immediately.

"Very clever. Very clever," murmured Mr. Barber in his stentorian undertone. "They say those tricks are handed down from generation to generation. I think it's all done with mirrors myself."

His acquaintance did not reply. He was sitting bolt upright, staring at the stage through his heavy glasses.

Satsuma produced ducks, goldfish, pigeons, and even a couple of Japanese ladies, with amazing dexterity, and the distressing Mr. Barber beat his fat hands together delightedly, while far across the room old Lobbett also was clearly enchanted.

Eventually the magician came forward to the front of the tiny stage and made the announcement which always preceded his most famous trick.

"Ladies and gentlemen," he began, "it has only been by the kind co-operation of the electrical staff on board that I am now able to show you this most remarkable trick—the greatest I have ever performed."

He stepped back a pace or two and tapped the huge disappearing cabinet which had taken up the greater part of the stage during his entire act. He touched a button hidden in the moulding, and immediately the cabinet was illuminated until it glowed all over in a series of diagonal designs of light.

The Japanese beamed upon his audience.

"By the aid of this cabinet," he said, "I will make to disappear not just one of my assistants, but any one of you who will come up and help me." He paused to let his full meaning sink in upon his audience. "I will make them to disappear and to reappear," he went on. "And if, after the experience, any one of them can explain how the miracle was performed, then"—with a great gesture of solemnity—"I throw myself into the sea."

He waited until the polite laughter had subsided, and then went on briskly.

"Now. Who will come first? You, sir, you, perhaps?" he added, pointing out Mr. Barber, who was by far the most conspicuous person before him, with his obtrusive personality and rumbling voice.

The Turk shook his head and laughed.

"Ah! no, my boy. No. I am too old for these adventures."

The Japanese smiled and passed on. The pale young man in the spectacles jumped up, however.

"I'll disappear," he said, in his somewhat foolish voice. "I think Haig would like to," he murmured to the Oriental by way of explanation.

He went forward eagerly, but paused, as there was some commotion across the room. Judge Lobbett, in spite of his son's obvious disapproval, was already halfway up the steps to the small stage. He also paused as the young man appeared, and the two men stood irresolute until the magician, coming forward, beckoned them both on to the stage.

"One after the other," he said easily. "The first to come, the first to be served."

He helped the judge up as he spoke, and the pale young man leaped up beside them.

"I say," he said nervously, "would you mind if my pet went first?"

He held up the white mouse as he spoke, while the audience, thinking it was some intentional comic relief, tittered complacently.

Satsuma smiled also, but his English was not equal to the situation, and, ignoring the young man, he led Judge Lobbett over to the cabinet.

"Haig," announced the foolish-looking young man in a loud voice, "will be more than disappointed if he's not allowed to go first. This is his birthday and he's been promised the best and the first of everything. Surely, sir," he went on, turning to the old man, "you wouldn't deprive my young friend of his birthday thrill?"

Judge Lobbett contented himself by regarding the young man with a slow cold smile for some seconds, but the other appeared not in the least abashed, and the uncomfortable idea that he might be drunk began to permeate the audience.

Meanwhile, with a flourish from the orchestra, Satsuma touched the cabinet with his wand and the doors swung open, disclosing a safe-like metal-lined compartment whose grilled sides shone in the brilliant light.

"Now, ladies and gentlemen," said the magician, turning to his audience, "I shall invite this gentleman"—he indicated the older man—"to step in here. Then I shall close these doors. When I open them again he will be gone. You shall search the whole ship, ladies and gentlemen, the stage, under the stage—you shall not find him. Then I will shut the doors once more. Once more they will fly open, and this gentleman shall be back again as you see him now. Moreover, he will not be able to tell you where he has been hiding. Now, sir, if you please."

"What?" said the irrepressible young man, darting forward, consternation in his pale eyes. "Can't Haig go first? Are you going to disappoint him after all?"

The audience was becoming restive, and Lobbett turned upon the importunate one, mildly annoyed.

"I don't know who you are, sir," he said, in a low tone, "but you're making a darn nuisance of yourself. I'm genuinely interested in this experiment, and I think everyone else is. Go and play with your mouse on deck, sir."

On the last word he turned and stepped towards the cabinet, the doors of which stood open to receive him. The man who, by this time, was regarded by everyone in the room as a source of embarrassment, seemed suddenly to lose all sense of decorum.

With an angry exclamation he elbowed the unsuspecting old man out of the way, and before the magician could stop him deliberately dropped the small white mouse upon the glittering floor of the cabinet.

Then he stepped back sharply.

There was a tiny hiss, only just loud enough to be heard among the audience: a sickening, terrifying sound.

For a moment everyone in the lounge held his breath. With a convulsive movement the mouse crumpled up on the polished steel grille, where it slowly blackened and shrivelled before their eyes.

There was an instant of complete stupefaction.

The significance of this extraordinary incident dawned slowly. The men upon the platform to whom the thing had been so near stiffened with horror as the explanation occurred to them.

Marlowe Lobbett was the first to move. He sprang on to the platform by his father's side and stood with him looking down at the charred spot on the cabinet floor.

It was at this moment that the pale young man with the spectacles, apparently grasping the situation for the first time, let out a howl of mingled grief and astonishment.

"Oh! my poor Haig! What has happened to him? What has happened to him?" He bent forward to peer down into the cabinet.

"Look out, you fool!" Judge Lobbett's voice was unrecognizable as he caught the incautious young man by his collar and jerked him backwards. "Can't you see!" His voice rose high and uncontrolled. "That cabinet is alive! Your pet has been electrocuted!"

The words startled everyone.

An excited murmur followed a momentary silence. Then a woman screamed.

Concert officials and ship's officers hurried on to the platform. The noise became greater, and a startled, bewildered crowd swept up to the platform end of the room.

Judge Lobbett and his tall son were surrounded by an excited group of officials.

Satsuma chattered wildly in his own tongue, offering a thousand excuses which no one could understand.

The pale young man with the spectacles appeared to be on the verge of fainting with horror. Even the complacent Mr. Barber was shaken out of his habitual affability. His heavy jaws sagged, his greasy eyes grew blank with astonishment.

All the time the cabinet remained glowing with a now evil radiance, bizarre and horrible, a toy that had become a thing of terror.

The arrival of the chief engineer roused the general stupor. He was a lank Belfast Irishman, yellow-haired, lantern-jawed, and deaf as a post. He gave his orders in the hollow bellow of a deaf man and soon reduced the affair to almost a commonplace.

"McPherson, just clear the lounge, will you? I don't want anyone to remain but those intimately concerned. There's been a small accident here in the temporary fittings," he explained soothingly to the bewildered crowd which was being gently but firmly persuaded out of the lounge by an energetic young Scotsman and his assistants.

"There's something very wrong with the insulation of your cupboard," he went on, addressing the Japanese severely. "It's evidently a very dangerous thing. Have you not had trouble with it before?"

Satsuma protested violently, but his birdlike twittering English would have been unintelligible to the engineer even had he been able to hear it.

Meanwhile a small army of mechanics was at work. The chief entered into an incomprehensible technical discussion with them, and their growing astonishment and consternation told more plainly than anything else could have done the terrible tragedy that had only just been averted by the timely sacrifice of the unfortunate Haig.

It was impossible not to be sorry for the Japanese. There could be no doubt of the sincerity of his wretchedness. He hovered round the electricians, half terrified of the consequences of what had happened and half fearful for the safety of his precious apparatus.

After fifteen minutes or so of technicalities, Marlowe Lobbett, whose patience had been slowly ebbing, stepped up to the chief and shouted in his ear.

"I don't know if you've heard," he began, "but back in New York there have been several unsuccessful attempts upon my father's life. This affair looks very like another. I should be very glad if you could make certain where the responsibility lies."

The chief turned upon him.

"My dear sir," he said, "there's no question of responsibility. The whole thing's an extraordinary coincidence. You see that cable on the floor there?" He pointed to the exposed part of a cable resting upon the parquet floor of the platform. "If, in shifting the piano, the cabinet hadn't been moved a little so that the one place where the insulation had worn off the cabinet made a connection with it, the affair could never have happened. At the same time, if it hadn't been for the second purely accidental short, the other contact could not have been made." He indicated a dark stain on the polished grille of the cabinet. "But," he went on, fixing the young American with a vivid blue eye, "you're not suggesting that someone fixed the whole thing up on the very slender chance of getting your father in there, are you?" The chief was considerably more puzzled than he dared to admit. But since no harm had been done he was not anxious to go into the matter too thoroughly for the ship's sake.

Old Judge Lobbett laid his hand on his son's arm.

"This isn't quite the time to discuss this, my boy," he said. "Someone knew I couldn't resist a conjurer. But I don't think we'll discuss it here."

He glanced round as he spoke, and the chief, following the direction of his eyes, suddenly caught sight of the pale young man with the horn-rimmed spectacles who was still standing foolishly by the dismantled cabinet. The officer frowned.

"I thought I gave orders for the lounge to be cleared," he said. "May I ask, sir, what you've got to do with this affair?"

The young man started and coloured uncomfortably.

"Well, it was my mouse," he said.

It was some time before the chief could be made to understand what he was saying, but when at last he did he was hardly sympathetic.

"All the same, I think we can manage without you," he said bluntly.

The dismissal was unmistakable, and the pale young man smiled nervously and apologized with a certain amount of confusion. Then he crept off the platform like his own mouse, and had almost reached the door before young Marlowe Lobbett overtook him.

The young American had left his father and sister on the platform and came up eagerly. His dark-skinned face and piercing eyes gave him almost a fierce expression, and the pale young man in the spectacles had an impression of someone abounding in energy that was not solely physical.

"I'd like to thank you," he said, holding out his hand. "And," he added bluntly, "I'd like to talk to you. I'm greatly indebted to you, but I don't see quite where you come in on this. What's your game? Who are you?"

The pale young man looked, if possible, even more foolish than before.

"My game?" he said. "I don't quite know what you mean. I toss a few cabers, and tiddle a wink occasionally, and I'm a very fair hand at shove-halfpenny."

He paused.

Marlowe Lobbett was looking at him steadily.

"This is more serious for me than it is for you," he said slowly.

The pale young man grew suddenly very red and uncomfortable.

"I'm not bright," he said awkwardly. "But that's my affliction. I've got a card here somewhere." He took a handful of miscellaneous odds and ends out of his coat pocket, and selecting a visiting card from a collection of cigarette cards, stamps, sugar, string, and other things, handed it gravely to Marlowe.

"My trade card," he said, and added with more seriousness than he had hitherto shown, "if there's anything I can do for you, ring me up. I don't suppose we shall meet again on board. We bus conductors feel dreadfully out of place here."

Then, grinning fatuously, he bowed and disappeared

through the doorway out of sight, leaving the other staring after him.

The whole conversation had taken less than ten seconds.

Undecided whether the stranger was a genuine lunatic or not, young Lobbett glanced at the card in his hand. It was immaculate and beautifully engraved:

MR. ALBERT CAMPION

Coups neatly executed
Nothing sordid, vulgar or plebeian
Deserving cases preferred
Police no object

PUFFINS CLUB   THE JUNIOR GREYS

On the back a phone number had been scribbled:

Regent 01300

CHAPTER II

The Simister Legend

"REGENT Oh won thr-ree Oh Oh? You're thr-r-ough."

After half an hour's experience of the vagaries of the London telephone service Marlowe Lobbett heard the welcome voice of the operator whose triumphant tone suggested that they had both been through a difficult adventure together. For some time he could hear the telephone bell ringing in some far-off room in the great city which seemed to be huddling round his hotel as if it were trying to squeeze the life out of it.

At last he heard the welcome click at the far end of the wire and a thick and totally unexpected voice said huskily, "Aphrodite Glue Works speaking."

Marlowe Lobbett sighed. "I want Regent 01300," he said.

"That's right," said the voice. " 'Oo do you want?"

The young man glanced at the card in front of him, and a wave of disappointment overwhelmed him. He had cherished the idea that he could rely upon the man who had come to his father's rescue so successfully on board the *Elephantine.*

"No, it's all right," he said. "I only wanted to speak to a Mr. Albert Campion."

"Oh?" The voice became confidential immediately. "Could I have yer name, please sir?"

Very puzzled, Marlowe Lobbett gave his name. The voice became more deferential than before. "Listen carefully, sir," it said in a rumbling whisper. "You want Bottle Street Police Station. You know where that is, don't you?—off Piccadilly. It's the side door on the left. Right up the stairs. You'll see the name up when you come to it. No. No connection with the police station—just a flat on top. Pleased to see you right away. Goo'-bye, sir."

There was a second click and he was cut off.

The girl seated on the edge of the table by the instrument looked at her brother eagerly. She was dark as he was, with the same air of alert intelligence, but her features were softer and more delicate, and whereas he was tall and heavily built, with the shoulders of a prize-fighter, she was petite, finely and slenderly fashioned.

"Did you get him?" she asked anxiously. "I'm scared, Marlowe. More scared than I was at home."

The boy put his arm round her. "It's going to be all right, kid," he said. "The old man's obstinacy doesn't make it any easier for us to look after him. I was rather hopeful about this Campion fellow, but now I don't know what to think. I'll see if I can find him, anyhow."

The girl clung to him. "Be careful. You don't know anyone here. It might be a trap to get you."

The boy shook his head. "I fancy not," he said.

She was still not reassured. "I'll come with you."

Marlowe shook his head. "I wouldn't," he said. "It may be a wild-goose chase. Stay here and look after Father. Don't let him go out till I come back."

Isopel Lobbett nodded. "All right," she said. "But hurry."

The taxi route from the Strand to Piccadilly is not a long one, and Marlowe found himself outside the police station in the narrow cul-de-sac sooner than he had anticipated. The "door on the left", he decided, must be the unguarded dirty yellow portal which stood open showing a flight of wooden stairs, scrubbed white, leading up into darkness. He hesitated dubiously for some seconds, but finally walked in. After the first flight of steps he came upon a carpet, at the third there were pictures on the wall, and he began to have the uncomfortable impression that he had stumbled into some private house, when he suddenly came to a stop full before an attractively carved oak door upon which there was a small brass plate, neatly engraved with the simple lettering:

MR. ALBERT CAMPION, MERCHANT
GOODS DEPT

When he saw it he realized with a shock how forlorn he had expected his errand to be. He tapped upon the door with more vigour than he had intended.

It was opened immediately by the young man in the horn-rimmed spectacles himself. He was attired in what appeared to be a bathrobe, a stupendous affair of multicoloured Turkish towelling.

"Hallo!" he said. "Seeing London? I come next in importance after the Tower, I always think. Come in." He dragged his visitor into a room across the tiny passage and thrust him into a deep comfortable armchair by the fire. As he mixed him a drink he rambled on inconsequentially without allowing the other to get a word in.

"I have to live over a police station because of my friends. It's a great protection against my more doubtful acquaintances."

In spite of his agitation and the importance of his errand, Marlowe could not help noticing the extraordinary character of the room in which he sat. It was tastefully, even luxuriously, furnished. There were one or two delightful old pieces, a Rembrandt etching over the bureau, a Steinlen cat, a couple of original cartoons, and a lovely little Girtin.

But amongst these were scattered a most remarkable collection of trophies. One little group over the mantelpiece comprised two jemmies, crossed, surmounted by a pair of handcuffs, with a convict's cap over the top. There were also two signed photographs, one of which Marlowe recognized as that of a late Home Secretary, and the other, though it

conveyed nothing to him, subsequently proved to be an erst-
while governor of Dartmoor. Lying upon a side table, apparently used as a paper knife, was a beautiful Italian
dagger, the blade of which was of a curious greenish-blue
shade, and the hilt encrusted with old and uncut gems.

Campion picked it up. "That's the Black Dudley dagger," he said. "An old boy I met was stuck in the back with
that, and everyone thought I'd done the sticking. Not such
fun. I picked it up at the sale of his furniture for round
about fourpence. I suppose you've seen most of the sights of
London by now," he went on. "I must take you to the Crys-
tal Palace one day. Then there's my Great-aunt Emily. I've
often thought of running a good cheap char-à-bancs tour
round her."

Marlowe Lobbett did not smile. "You'll forgive me," he
said, "but can't we drop this fooling? I've come to you as a
last chance, Mr. Campion."

The boy's gravity was sobering, but his irrepressible host,
after a momentary expression of contrition had passed over
his face, began once more. "Rather—anything I can do for
you," he said affably. "I undertake almost anything these
days. But nothing sordid. I will not sell that tinted photograph of myself as Lord Fauntleroy. No. Not all your gold
shall tempt me. I am leaving that to the Nation. Patriotism,
and all that sort of rot," he added sententiously. "May I
offer you a slap-and-tickle?" he chattered on, proffering a
particularly dangerous-looking cocktail. "All my own work.
It contains almost everything except tea. Now, young sir,
what can I do for you?"

Marlowe accepted the drink. "I say," he said, "do you
always talk like this?"

Mr. Campion looked abashed. "Almost always," he said.
"People get used to it in time. I can't help it. I told you, it's
a sort of affliction, like stammering or a hammer toe. My
friends pretend they don't notice it. What did the police say
to you this morning?"

The last question was put so abruptly that Marlowe Lobbett had not time to conceal his surprise. "What do you

know about it?" he demanded. "How do you know that I visited your police headquarters this morning?"

Mr. Campion advanced with great solemnity and gingerly removed a tiny piece of fluff from his visitor's overcoat with his thumb and forefinger. "A police hair, my dear Watson," he said. "I noticed it as soon as you came in. Since then my brain has been working. I suppose they funked it?" he went on with sudden directness.

Marlowe glanced up. "They wouldn't guarantee his safety," he said.

Mr. Campion shook his head. "I don't altogether blame them," he said soberly. "Your own police in New York weren't handing out any insurance certificates, were they?"

"No," said Marlowe. "That is the main reason why I got the old boy over here. Our Big Noise over there told me that in his opinion they were playing cat-and-mouse with Father and that they'd get him just whenever they pleased. You see," he burst out impatiently, "it's mostly the old boy's fault. He won't stand for any reasonable restraint. He won't let the police look after him in their way. You see, he's never been afraid of—" He hesitated, and added the word "them" with a peculiar intonation. "And he's not going to begin now. He's not crazy. He just feels that way about it. You see what I'm up against."

"Not quite," said Mr. Campion thoughtfully. "How come, boy? How come?"

Marlowe stared at him in astonishment. "Do you mean to say you don't *know?*" he said. "I don't understand you at all, Mr. Campion. When you saved my father on the *Elephantine* surely you had some idea of what was up?"

"Well, naturally," said the owner of the flat airily, "but not very much. I met an old burgling friend of mine on board and he pointed out a fellow graduate of his, as it were, who had suddenly got very pally with old Hanky Panky the Magician. Like all professional men, we took an intelligent interest in the fellow's technique, and, well, I just borrowed friend Haig in case of emergencies. Do you know," he rattled on, "I believe that mouse was fond of me? He ate out of my hand. I am so glad it was a sudden death. By the way," he continued, with a desperate attempt at seriousness, "may I ask, without soiling my virginal modesty, was it because of my stupendous platform appearance that you came to me to-day?"

Marlowe Lobbett hesitated. "Not altogether," he admitted at last. "In fact, when I was talking to Chief Inspector Deadwood at Scotland Yard this morning and I found that they couldn't promise to protect the old boy without a regular police guard, which Father would never stand, I appealed to him as a man to tell me of someone to whom I could go."

Mr. Campion chuckled. "Good for him," he said. "Behold Albert Campion, C.I.D.—i.e. Cell in Dartmoor," he explained regretfully. "But it hasn't come to that yet. You know of course who 'they' are?" he said suddenly.

Marlowe Lobbett was becoming used to these lightning changes of mood. He nodded, his shrewd dark eyes fixed upon the spectacles which hid Mr. Campion's seriousness from him. "Simister." He spoke the word so softly that it sounded like a whisper. Mr. Campion was silent for some moments, and Marlowe Lobbett suddenly leaned forward in his chair.

"Mr. Campion," he said, "can you tell me about this man Simister? What is he? A gangster? A master crook? Is he a single personality at all? In New York they say his records go back for over a hundred years, and that no such person exists. According to them a powerful gang is using the word as a sort of trade name, if criminals can have such a thing. Tell me," he went on, "who is he? What is he? Is there any explanation?"

Still Mr. Campion did not speak.

"Is he a myth, a legend—like Jack the Ripper?" Marlowe continued, his tone only thinly concealing the intensity with which he spoke. "Does he exist?"

A laugh of unexpected bitterness escaped Mr. Campion. "My dear man," he said, "somewhere on this earth there is a man called Simister. Never doubt that for one instant. He may be a devil—a bogle—anything you like, but he's as real a power of evil as dope is. I'm not saying this to chill your youthful ardour," he went on, with an attempt to return to his old lightness of manner, "but it's most dangerous to underrate an enemy. This is all I know about him. I've talked to crooks and I've talked to policemen—I've even talked to members of his own gang—but I've never met anyone yet who has set eyes on him. Apparently he's a voice on the telephone, a shadow on the road, the gloved hand that turns out the light in the crook play; but with one big difference—he's never caught. There are thousands of amazing yarns told about him, and in not one of them does a hint of his face ever appear. They say no one ever escapes him."

Marlowe moved uneasily in his chair. "I've heard that," he said, "and that's why I've come to you—as a last chance, if you'll forgive my saying so. Can you do anything for me?"

Mr. Campion eyed him owlishly, but he did not give a direct reply. "There's one thing I don't get," he said. "Why your father?"

Marlowe Lobbett rose to his feet and walked up and down the room. "That's what gets me," he said. "It's nothing I can help. It's nothing money can undo. It's a sort of revenge."

Campion nodded. "I see," he said gravely. "Anything else?"

"I'm not sure," Marlowe spoke helplessly. "You see," he went on with sudden confidence. "I've found all this out with difficulty. It goes back a long time. When I was a kid of course I hadn't much idea of what Father was up to. I've only recently dug out the truth from him, and he won't admit much, even to me. Apparently the old boy has been fighting the Simister Gang all his life. He was the only weapon the police really had. When they got a gangster Dad gave it to him hot. He wasn't unjust, you understand, he was just hard where they were concerned. But he couldn't make any real impression on them. At first he simply tickled them; they didn't think him big enough to worry about, I guess. But quite suddenly—it was after the Steinway trial (he wasn't trying that, you know, he was just advising; that was after he had retired)—quite suddenly they went for him.

We've lived in terror for him for over six months," he finished quietly.

"Not a Mothers' Union Outing," said Mr. Campion appreciatively, and added more gravely, "Is that all?"

Marlowe Lobbett hesitated. He had an idea that behind the ridiculous spectacles Mr. Campion's pale eyes were watching him steadily. "Well, the rest is only conjecture," he said.

"Let's have it," said Mr. Campion.

Marlowe sat down again and lit a cigarette, which he did not smoke.

"Well, you must understand," he began hesitatingly, "my father has said nothing to me to give me this idea. I don't know anything for certain, but from several things that have happened lately I believe that he's got something pretty definite on the Simister Gang. You see," he went on abruptly, " 'advisory work' is such a vague term. I can't help feeling that it may mean that he's been devoting himself to investigations about these Simister people. He probably wouldn't admit it for fear of scaring us. For some time I think they just laughed at him, but then I believe the old boy tumbled on something. I've been trying to figure out what it could be, and it's just occurred to me, after what you said, that he might have stumbled on some clue or other as to the actual identity of this Simister fellow himself."

Mr. Campion took off his spectacles and his pale eyes regarded his visitor in frank astonishment. "Young sir," he said, "I hope for your sake that what you think is not true. If, as you said at first, the Simister Gang is after your father out of sheer temper, i.e. revenge, that's one thing. There's a chance for him. But if, as you suggest now, he's got a line on them, then I'm afraid that the fabulous sums spent in hiring Mr. Campion's assistance would be a mere waste of money. Consider," he went on—"what can you expect me to do? I tell you quite candidly, your only chance is to get the old boy into Brixton Jail, and that wouldn't be fun for him."

Marlowe Lobbett rose to his feet. "I see," he said. "I told you you were my last hope, Mr. Campion. I spoke quite frankly. My father will have a certain amount of police protection, you understand, but they said in effect what you did, only not so lucidly. Perhaps I didn't tell them so much."

Mr. Campion hesitated. "I'd like to have a whack at Simister," he said.

The young American turned to him quickly. "Well, here's your chance," he said. "It may be a forlorn chance, but after all, the mischief isn't done yet."

"My dear young optimist," said Mr. Campion admonishingly, "in effect you're saying, 'Here's a nice war; come and sit in it'."

He was interrupted from further comment by a tap at the outer door.

"The one-thirty," said Mr. Campion. "Excuse me."

He went out of the room and returned immediately with a racing edition of the *Evening Standard* in his hand. He was smiling. "Now I can dress," he explained cheerfully. "I had my shirt on the Archdeacon!"

His eye travelled down the stop-press column. Suddenly his expression changed and he handed the paper to his visitor.

"Well-known American's Narrow Escape," it ran:

Judge Crowdy Lobbett, the well-known American visitor, narrowly missed a serious accident when a taxicab mounted the pavement outside his hotel in the Strand and crashed into a show window this morning at twelve o'clock. No one was injured.

"My God!" Marlowe Lobbett started for the door. "They don't know where I am—I didn't leave your address. Isopel will be terrified. I must get along to them at once."

Mr. Campion had disappeared into his bedroom, which led off the smoking-room where they had been talking.

"Wait for me," he shouted. "I shan't be a second."

Marlowe Lobbett appeared in the doorway. "I don't quite get you."

"I'm in this," said Mr. Campion.

CHAPTER III

Mystery Mile

ON the grey marshy coast of Suffolk, fifteen miles from a railway station, and joined to the mainland by the Stroud only, a narrow road of hard land, the village of Mystery Mile lay surrounded by impassable mud flats and grey-white saltings.

The name was a local one, derived from the belt of ground mist which summer and winter hung in the little valleys round the small hill on which the village stood. Like many Suffolk hamlets, the place was more of an estate than a village. The half-dozen cottages, the post office, and the Rectory were very much outbuildings of the Mansion, the old Manor House, the dwelling of the owner of the Mile.

In olden times, when the land had been more profitable, the squire had had no difficulty in supporting his large family of retainers, and, apart from the witch burnings in James I's reign, when well-nigh a third of the population had suffered execution for practices more peculiar than necromantic, the little place had a long history of peaceful if gradually decaying times.

The families of retainers had intermarried, and they were now almost as much one kin as the Pagets themselves.

The death of the present squire's father, Giles Paget, had

left his young son and daughter the old house and worthless lands, with little or no money to keep them up, and some twenty or thirty villagers who looked to them as their natural means of support.

The Manor, hidden in the thick belt of elms which surrounded it, had but one lamp shining from the big casement windows. It was a long, low, many-gabled building, probably built round about 1500 and kept in good repair ever since. The overhung front sheltered rose trees under its eaves, and the lintels of the windows were low and black, enhancing the beauty of the moulded plaster surrounding them.

In the library, round the fireplace with the deep-set chimney seat, the squire and his sister were entertaining the rector. They had the air of conspirators as they sat bending forward in high-backed Stuart chairs, their faces turned towards the blaze.

The squire was twenty-three. Giles Paget and his sister Biddy were twins. As they sat together they looked startlingly modern against the dark oak-furnished room which had not been materially altered for centuries.

Giles was a heavily built, fair youngster whose sturdiness suggested a much larger man. He had a square-cut face, not particularly handsome, but he had, as Biddy remarked, "a patriotic look", a clean, wholesome, ingenuous expression which with grey eyes and a charming smile made him pleasant to meet and easy to talk to.

Biddy was a different proposition. Her hair was sleekly waved in spite of a fifteen-mile stretch between herself and the hairdresser, and it was as golden as the princesses' in the fairy stories. She was brown-eyed and was possessed of an animation unusual in a country girl. Tall as her brother, with a figure like a boy's, she had a more practical outlook on life than had been born into the Paget family for centuries.

Their visitor, the Reverend Swithin Cush, the rector of Mystery Mile, tenant of the ivy-covered Rectory and receiver of the eighty-pound-a-year living, sat and beamed at them. If the squire did not fit his manor, the rector made up for any deficiency. He was a great lank old man, with a hooked nose and deep-set twinkling black eyes surrounded by a thousand wrinkles. His long silky white hair was cut by Biddy herself when it got past his collar, and his costume consisted of a venerable suit of plus-fours, darned at knees and elbows with a variety of wools, stout land clogs, and a shining dog collar, the one concession he made to "the cloth". His only vanity was a huge signet ring, a bloodstone, which shone dully on his gnarled first finger. He had spent his life in Mystery Mile, and his fortunes were those of its owners. For nearly fifty years he had baptized, wedded, and buried the people of the isthmus. The village was conservative, not to say mediaeval in its religious opinions, and the old chained Bible in the little late-Norman church with the beacon tower was the only book of the law they considered at all.

The subject of discussion round the fire in the library was the paper Giles Paget held in his hand.

"St. Swithin, having drunk his sherry, can now see the telegram," said Biddy; "the first Mystery Mile has seen since Giles won the half-mile. That took twelve hours to come. This has beaten it by a short head. I don't know how Albert's going to get here, Giles; the Ipswich taxies don't like the Stroud at night."

The rector took the telegram and read it aloud, holding the paper down to the fire to catch the light from the flames.

LISTEN KIDDIES UNCLE HAS LET HOUSE STOP RING OUT WILD BELLS STOP SEND NO FLOWERS STOP ARRIVING NINE THIRTY STOP SHALL EXPECT FOOD AND RARE VINTAGES STOP OBEDIENTLY YOURS EVA BOOTH.

"If I know anything about Albert," said the rector, "he'll arrive on a broomstick. Half a crown is a lot to spend on a telegram. He must have come into money."

"Come *by* money," said Giles darkly.

Biddy sighed. "Think he has let the house?" she said. "I never dreamed he would take us seriously. I do hope we get something for it. Cuddy's third daughter's having another baby in September. That's another for the bounty. These ancient customs are a bit hard on the budget."

" 'The Lord will provide,' " said the rector regretfully, "is a tag which is not found in the Vulgate. But I have great faith in Albert."

Biddy chuckled. "St. Swithin," she said. "Albert is a fishy character and no fit associate for a dignitary of the Church."

The old man smiled at her, and his small black eyes twinkled and danced in the firelight.

"My daughter," he said, "out of evil cometh good. There is no reason why we should not sit in the shadow of the Bay Tree while it flourishes. Although," he went on seriously, "our very good friend Albert is a true son of the Church. In the time of Richelieu he would no doubt have become a cardinal. His associates are not solely criminals. Look at us, for instance."

Giles broke in. "Oh no," he said, "he's not a crook. Not exactly, I mean," he added as an afterthought.

"He's not a detective either," said Biddy. "As a matter of fact, he's really a sort of Universal Aunt, isn't he? 'Your adventures undertaken for a small fee.' Oh, I like Albert."

Giles grinned.

"I know you do," he said. "She's prepared a school treat for him in the next room, St. Swithin. One of these days she'll put us in a home and go off with him."

Biddy laughed and regarded them shrewdly out of the corners of her brown eyes.

"I might," she said, "but he's comic about women." She sighed.

"He's a comic chap altogether," said Giles. "Did I tell you, St. Swithin, the last time I saw him we walked down Regent Street together, and from the corner of Conduit Street to the Circus we met five people he knew, including a viscountess and two bishops? Each one of them stopped and greeted him as an old pal. And every single one of them called him by a different name. Heaven knows how he does it."

"Addlepate will be glad to see him," said Biddy, patting

the head of a sleek chestnut-brown dog who had just thrust his head into her lap. The dog looked self-conscious at hearing his name, and wagged his stump of tail with feverish enthusiasm.

Giles turned to the rector. "Albert said he tried to train Addlepate for crime before he gave it up as a bad job and brought him down to us. He said the flesh was willing but the mind was weak. I shall never forget," he went on, pulling at his pipe, "when we were up at Cambridge, hearing Albert explain to the porter after midnight that he was a werewolf out on his nightly prowl who had unexpectedly returned to his own shape before he had time to bound over the Coll railings. He kept old Webley enthralled in Norse mythology till five o'clock in the morning, when the old chap started seeing things and—"

The sound of a motor horn among the elms outside interrupted him. Biddy sprang to her feet. "There he is," she said, and ran out to open the door to him herself. The other two followed her.

Through the rustling darkness they could just make out the outlines of a small ill-lit two-seater, out of which there rose to greet them the thin leather-clad figure they expected. He stood up in the car and posed before them, one hand upraised.

"Came Dawn," he said, and the next moment was on the steps beside them. "Well, well, my little ones, how you have grown! It seems only yesterday, St. Swithin, that you were babbling your infant prayers at my knee."

They took him into the house, and as he sat eating in the low-ceilinged oak-panelled dining-room they crowded round him like children. Addlepate, grasping for the first time who it was, had a mild fit of canine hysterics by himself in the hall before he joined the others.

By common consent they left the question of the letting of the house until Mr. Campion should mention it, and as he did not bring up the subject, but chattered on inconsequentially about everything else under the sun, there was no talk of it until they were once more seated round the library fire.

Mr. Campion sat between Giles and Biddy. The firelight

shone upon his spectacles, hiding his eyes. Giles leaned back in his chair, puffing contentedly at his pipe. The girl sat close to their new guest, Addlepate in her lap, and the old rector was back in his corner, smoking a clay. Sitting there, the firelight making a fine tracery of his face, he looked like a Rembrandt etching.

"Well, about this Estate Agency business," said Mr. Campion, "I've got something to put up to you kids." His tone was unusually serious, and the two people who probably knew him better than anyone else in the world looked at him curiously.

"I know what you're thinking," he said. "You're wondering where the slow music comes in. It's like this. It so happened that I wanted a country house in a remote spot for a particularly peppy job I've got on hand at the moment. Your announcement that you'd have to let the ancestral home occurred to me, and I thought the two stunts worked in together very well. Giles, old boy, I shall want you to help me. Biddy, could you clear out, my dear, and go and stay with an aunt or something? For a fortnight or so, I mean—until I know how the land lies?"

The girl looked at him with mild surprise in her brown eyes. "Seriously?" she said.

He nodded. "More serious than anything in the world."

Biddy leaned back in her chair. "You'll have to explain," she said. "I don't want to miss anything if it's going."

Mr. Campion took Biddy's hand with awful solemnity. "Woman," he said, "this is *men's* work. You'll keep your little turned-up neb out of it. Quite definitely and seriously," he went on, "this is not your sort of show, old dear."

"Suppose you don't blether so much," said Giles; "let's have the facts. You're so infernally earnest that you're beginning to be interesting for once."

Mr. Campion got up unexpectedly and wandered up and down the room, his steps sounding sharply on the polished oak floor.

"Now I'm down here," he said suddenly, "and I see you dear old birds all tucked up in the ancestral nest, I've got an attack of conscience. I ought not to have done this, but since I have I'd better make a clean breast of it."

The others turned and stared at him, surprised by this unusual outburst.

"Look here," he went on, planting himself back in his chair, "I'll tell you. Now there's not a soul about, is there? Forgive the drama, but it's very necessary that I shouldn't be overheard. You read the newspapers, don't you? Good! Well, have you heard of Judge Lobbett?"

"The old boy they're always trying to kill?" said Giles. "Yes. You know I showed it to you this morning, St. Swithin. Are you in that, Albert?"

Mr. Campion nodded gravely. "Up to the neck," he said, adding hastily, "on the right side, of course. And I'm not sure that I haven't sunk in a bit farther than I thought. You know the rough outline of the business, don't you? Old Lobbett's stirred up a hornet's nest for himself in America and it's pretty obvious they've followed him here." He shot a glance at Giles. "They're not out to kill him, you know— not yet. They're trying to put the fear of God into him and they've picked an infernally tough nut. In fact," he went on regretfully, "if he wasn't such a tough nut we wouldn't have such a job. I'm acting for the son, Marlowe Lobbett—a very decent cove; you'll like him, Giles." He paused and looked round at them. "Have you got all that?"

They nodded, and he continued: "The old boy won't stand any serious police protection—that is to say he won't go about in an armoured car. He himself is our chief difficulty. At first I thought he was going to sink us, but quite by chance I stumbled on a most useful sidelight in his character. The old boy has got a bee in his bonnet about folk-lore —ancient English customs—all that sort of thing. Marlowe introduced me to him as a sort of guide to rural England. Said he'd met me on the boat coming over, as of course he had. Anyway, I've let him the house. There's a title of Lord of the Manor, or something that goes with it, isn't there?"

Giles glanced up. "There is something like that, isn't there, St. Swithin?"

The old man nodded and smiled. "There's a document in

the church to that effect," he said. "I don't know what good it is to anybody nowadays, though."

"Old Judge Lobbett liked it, anyway," said Mr. Campion. "It gives the place a sort of mediaeval flavour. But I'll come to that later. All that matters now is that the old bird has taken the place off your hands at fourteen quid a week. And if he knew as much as I do he'd realize he got it cheap."

Giles sat up. "You expect trouble?" he said.

Mr. Campion nodded. "I don't see how we can escape it," he said. "You see," he went on hastily, "I had to get the old boy out of the city and down here, because in a place like this if there're any strangers knocking about we know at once. Look here, Giles, I shall need you to help me."

Giles grinned. "I'm with you," he said. "It's time something happened down here."

"And I'm in it too," said Biddy, that expression of determination which the others knew so well appearing at the corners of her mouth.

Mr. Campion shook his head. "Sorry, Biddy," he said, "I couldn't have that. You don't know what you'd be letting yourself in for. It was only in a fit of exuberance that I went into it myself."

Biddy sniffed. "I'm staying," she said. "Judge Lobbett has a daughter, hasn't he? If she's going to be in it, so am I. Besides, what would you three poor fish do without me? We'll move over to the Dower House."

Mr. Campion turned to the rector. "Bring your influence to bear, St. Swithin. Tell her that this is stern stuff—no place for the tender sex."

The old man shook his head. "In the words of the poet, 'I do remain as neuter'," he said. "Personally, I always obey her."

Mr. Campion looked abashed. "You're making it very awkward for me," he said. "I'd never have done it if I'd dreamed that I was bringing you into it, Biddy."

The girl laid her hand upon his knee. "Don't be a fool," she said. "You silly old dear, I'm with you to the death. You know that."

Mr. Campion almost blushed, and was silent for an appreciable space of time. The rector brought him back to the subject on hand. "Let us be specific," he said. "No doubt you have your own dark secrets, Albert, but what are we expected to do?"

Mr. Campion plunged into the details of his scheme. "First of all," he said, "we've got to keep the old boy here. And that means we've got to keep him interested. St. Swithin, I rely on you for the archaeology and whatnots. Show him the village trophies. Get out the relics of the witch burnings and polish up the stocks. Make it all bright and homely for him. Then there's the doubtful Romney in the drawing room. Get his opinion on that. He's a delightful old cove, but obstinate as sin."

He hesitated. "What he's really interested in," he went on after a pause, "is actual folk-lore and superstition. Haven't you any prize yokels who know a few ancient wisecracks?—old songs and that sort of thing?"

Giles glanced up. "Plenty of those," he said. "Did I tell you, Biddy, I set George to cut down that dead thorn at the end of the home paddock this morning? When I passed by at lunch-time he grinned at me, as pleased as Punch—he'd been all the morning at it. 'How are you going, George?' said I. 'Foine, Master Giles,' he said, 'I can cut that down quicker than that took to grow.' When I said, 'So I should hope,' he seemed quite offended. We might pass him off as the original Old Saw himself."

"That's the sort of thing," Campion agreed. "But I warn you to go carefully. The old boy's no fool. This sort of thing's his hobby. You'd be surprised how much more the average American knows about England than we do."

The Reverend Swithin Cush coughed dryly. "There is enough here to interest a genuine antiquary for some time," he said. "How long do you expect him to stay? Is the length of his visit indefinite?"

Mr. Campion became suddenly vague. "I don't know," he said. "I've cracked up the place a lot, but he may give us one swift look and go home, and then *bang* goes little Albert's fourpence an hour and old Lobbett's sweet young life, most likely. Oh, I forgot. He'll be here the day after to-morrow. Can you be ready in time, Biddy?"

The girl sighed. "Just," she said. "It'll be a bit of a camp at the Dower House."

They sat discussing their plans until after midnight, when the old rector rose stiffly out of his chair.

"Biddy, I'll have my hurricane," he said. "You ought all to be in bed now if you're going to move to-morrow."

The girl fetched the storm lantern, and they watched him disappearing into the darkness—a gaunt, lonely figure, his white hair uncovered, the lantern bobbing at his side like a will-o'-the-wisp.

As they came back into the shadowy hall, Mr. Campion grinned, "Dear old St. Swithin," he said. "You've known him since you were muling and puking in Cuddy's arms, haven't you?"

Biddy answered him. "Yes," she said. "He's getting old, though. Alice—that's his housekeeper, you know—says he's gone all Russian lately. 'Like a broody hen,' she said."

"He must be hundreds of years old," said Albert. "There's an idea in that. We might pass him off as the origi-nal St. Swithin himself. Dropped in out of the rain, as it were."

"Go to bed," said Biddy. "The machinery wants a rest."

Up in the low-ceilinged chintz-hung bedroom the oak floor was sloping and the cool air was fragrant with laven-der, toilet soap, and beeswax. Mr. Campion did not get into the four-poster immediately, but stood for some time peer-ing out into the darkness.

At last he drew a small, much-battered notebook from an inside pocket and scribbled "St. S". For some time he stood looking at it soberly, and then deliberately added a question mark.

CHAPTER IV

The Lord of the Manor

"ALTHOUGH you're a foreigner, Squoire, which can't be helped, and therefore it ain't loikely that you'll be used to our ways, all the same we welcome you. We 'ope you'll take a good lesson by the last squoire, although of course you can't be what 'e was. Still we do 'ope you'll live up to the old ways and do all you can for us."

The speaker paused and wiped round the inside of his Newgate fringe with a coloured handkerchief. "Now let's sing a 'ymn," he added as an afterthought.

He was standing by himself at the bottom of his cottage garden, his face turned towards the meadows which sloped down sleekly to the grey saltings. After a while he repeated his former announcement word for word, finishing with an unexpected "Morning, sir," as a thin, pale-faced young man with horn-rimmed spectacles appeared upon the other side of the hedge.

"Morning, George," said Mr. Campion. "Going in for the talkies?"

George Willsmore surveyed the newcomer thoughtfully. He was a gnarled old man, brown and nobbled as a pollarded willow, with great creases bitten into his face, which was surrounded by a thick hearthbrush of a beard. As the oldest able member of the family of which the village was mainly composed, he considered himself a sort of mayor, and his rural dignity was enhanced by a curious sententiousness of utterance.

"You come upon me unawares," he said. "I was sayin' over a few words I be goin' to speak to the new squoire this afternoon."

"Really?" Mr. Campion appeared to be interested. "You're thinking of making a speech of welcome, George?"

"Summat like that," conceded the old man graciously. "Me and the rector was 'avin' a talk about the new squoire comin'. 'E was all for singin'. And me bein' churchwarden, seems only right, seems, I should do the greetin'. Him bein' a foreigner, 'e mightn't understand the others."

"There's something in that, of course," said Mr. Campion, who had followed the old man's reasoning with difficulty.

George continued.

"I put on some new clo'es. Seems like 'tis a good idea to look smart. I be a wunnerful smart old man, don't you think?"

He turned himself about for Mr. Campion's inspection. He was dressed in a pair of tight corduroy trousers which had once been brown, but were now washed to creamy whiteness, a bright blue collarless gingham shirt, and one of his late master's white waistcoats which hung loosely round his spare stomach. His straw hat, built on the Panama principle, had a black ribbon round it and a bunch of jay's feathers tucked into the bow.

"How's that?" he demanded with badly concealed pride.

"Very fine," agreed the young man. "All the same, I wouldn't make your speech if I were you, George. The squire doesn't come from these parts, as you say. I was coming down to have a talk with you about this business. Aren't there some customs, maypolings and whatnot, suitable for this afternoon?"

The old man pushed back his straw hat, revealing an unexpectedly bald head, the crown of which he rubbed meditatively with the edge of his hat.

"Not give the speech?" he said with disappointment. "Oh well, sir, I reckon you know best. But I'd 'ave done it right well, that I would. I do be a powerful talkative old man. But the time for maypolin's past," he went on, "and Pharisees' Day, that ain't come yet."

The young man sighed. "None of these—er—feasts are movable?" he suggested hopefully.

George shook his head. "No, you can't alter they days. Not for nobody," he added with decision.

Mr. Campion regarded the old man with great solemnity. "George," he said, "take my advice and make an effort. It wouldn't be a bad idea if you could think of some sort of turnip-blessing ceremony. You're a smart man, George."

"Aye," said the old man with alacrity, and remained in deep thought for some time. "No, there be nothin'," he said at last. "Nothin' but maybe the Seven Whistlers."

"Seven Whistlers?" said Mr. Campion with interest. "What's that? Who are they?"

The old man studied his hat intently for some time before replying. "Seven Whistlers, sir," he said at last. "No one knows if they be ghosts or Pharisees—that be fairies, if you take me. You 'ear 'em passin' overhead about this time of year. Whistlin'. Least, you only 'ears six on 'em. The seventh's got a kind o' whoop in it, trailin' away like a barn owl, terrible to 'ear, and when you 'ears that, that's the end of the world. Only no one's ever 'eard it yet."

"That sounds all right," said Mr. Campion. "But it doesn't get us more forrarder, does it, George?"

An unexpectedly crafty expression appeared upon the old man's venerable face. "Toime was," he said, "when the old squoire used to give a barrel o' beer for they Seven Whistlers. Just about round this time of the year it was, now I come to think on it." He paused and looked at Mr. Campion hopefully.

"For the Seven Whistlers?" said the young man dubiously.

The old man broke into hasty explanations.

" 'Twas so, only they Seven Whistlers they never came to

drink it, so it had to be drinked up by the poor, for fear of that goin' sour."

"I see," said Mr. Campion, who had begun to comprehend. "The poor, I suppose, were the villagers?"

"Aye. Anybody who were dependent on the squoire." George paused, and remarked after some consideration, "Master Giles and Miss Biddy most likely wouldn't know anything about it if you asked 'em. Doubt not they 'eard o' the Seven Whistlers, but not of the beer. You understand, sir?"

"Perfectly," said Mr. Campion. "It occurs to me, George, that you and I might get on very well together. You have the flair, if I may say so. You've got a brother, haven't you?"

"Oh 'Anry?" said Mr. Willsmore with contempt. "I'm the clever one. 'Anry is not. I'm the man for you, sir."

Mr. Campion regarded him gravely. "I believe you are," he said.

They remained deep in conversation together for some time.

When the young man walked back over the rough grass of the park and let himself into the old sunken garden of the Manor, he was considerably easier in his mind than before.

As he approached the house he was considerably surprised to see a long black Daimler outside the low oak door. He hurried forward. Biddy met him in the hall.

"Albert, he's a dear," she said. "They're in the library with Giles now. I've been looking for you everywhere. They've been here nearly an hour. We've shown them all over the house and they're just charming about it. The boy's awfully handsome, don't you think?"

"Nonsense!" said Mr. Campion. "You should see me in my new moustache. Quite the latest thing, my dear. Only ten-three. Illusion guaranteed. I'm being ringed for it. Mother need never know."

"Jealous!" said Biddy. "Come and see them."

He followed her down the stone-paved sweet-smelling corridor to where the library door stood ajar. The casement windows were open and the morning sun made diamond patterns on the polished floor. The lamp on the evening before had not done justice to the fine old panelled room with its heavy table, comfortable chairs, and many bookcases.

Judge Lobbett, still in his motoring coat, stood looking out across the lawn. The sun glinted on his fine old face, on the pictures let into the panelling, and on the sherry glasses on the table.

"It's a lovely place," he said, turning as Albert and Biddy came in. "Good morning, Mr. Campion. I congratulate you on your choice on our behalf." He turned to the young people. Biddy had crossed over to her brother and they stood together with their backs to the fireplace, looking wonderfully alike.

"Seems I'm turning you out of your homestead," he said bluntly. "Are you sure you want to let?"

Biddy smiled at him, her brown eyes meeting his gratefully.

"It's awfully nice of you to say that," she said, "but we've got to let. Did Albert warn you, you'll be taking over half our responsibilities as far as the village is concerned? We just couldn't do it as Dad did before the war. The money won't go so far. Being squire at Mystery Mile is rather like being papa to the village."

The old man smiled at her. "I'll like it," he said.

Biddy sighed. "You don't know what a relief it is to know that someone's got the house who really likes it."

Judge Lobbett turned to his daughter, a slim little figure wrapped in furs. "If you don't think you'll find it too quiet—"

Isopel glanced at him, and a faint scared smile passed over her face. "Not too quiet?" she said meaningly, and a sigh escaped her.

Meanwhile Marlowe Lobbett had crossed over to Mr. Campion and the two young men stood talking together.

"You weren't followed?" Mr. Campion spoke softly.

Marlowe shook his head. "I think they were waiting for us," he said. "Your policemen held up a car directly behind us. The chauffeur you found us is a genius. We got out of the city in no time. Anyone following us would have had an almighty job."

Biddy's voice broke in upon their conversation. "We'll leave the place to you now. You'll find Mrs. Whybrow's prepared everything for you. She's a wonderful housekeeper. You've all promised to come to dinner with us this evening, haven't you?" she went on, turning to Isopel. "The Dower House is only just across the park. Old Mr. Cush, the rector, will be there. In his Sunday clothes, I hope. You ought to meet him."

Isopel clung to her hand as they said good-bye. After the terrible experiences of the last few months this pleasant sleepy old house with its young untroubled owners was very comforting. "I'm so glad you're here," she said impulsively. The other girl shot her a swift comprehending glance.

"Don't worry," she murmured. "You don't know Albert."

As Mr. Campion and the Pagets walked down the gravelled drive and passed over the tiny village green where the pump stood to the Dower House they talked gravely.

The Dower House, built by a Georgian Paget for his mother, was a low red building covered with climbing roses. A high yew hedge hid it from the green, and all the main windows faced the other side of the house, looking over an old walled garden.

Mr. Campion looked greatly relieved. "Thank goodness the old bird fell for the house!" he said. "Naturally I couldn't get him to agree to take the place for any length of time before he'd seen it, but we couldn't have him running up and down to town setting our homicidal pal on his track immediately. What do you think of them, Giles?"

"Nice old boy," said Giles. "Not unlike the Governor, only American. Same direct way of looking at you and saying exactly what comes into his head. I didn't have much talk with young Lobbett, but he seemed all right. But oh boy! what a girl!"

Biddy and Mr. Campion exchanged glances. "Yuth! Yuth!" said she. "I like her. She must have been having a nerve-racking time."

Giles nodded. "I was thinking that," he said. "Time there was someone to look after her."

"That's the spirit," said Mr. Campion, adding with sudden gravity, "Biddy, I wish you'd clear out. Old Cuddy has lived at the Dower House so long she'll be able to look after us without any trouble."

Biddy shook her head. "You still expecting excitement?"

Mr. Campion nodded. "We can't escape it," he said. "Won't you go and leave us to it, old dear?"

Biddy was determined. "Find something else to be inane about," she said. "As I said before, I'm with you to the death."

Mr. Campion did not smile. "I wish you wouldn't say that," he said. "It puts the wind up me—all this harping on mortality. Whenever I see a white flower nowadays I think, 'Albert, that might be for you'."

"Would you say her eyes were blue or brown or a sort of a heather mixture?" said Giles.

CHAPTER V

The Seven Whistlers

THE drawing-room at the Dower House, small, cosy, and lined with white panelling, was lit that evening with candles only, and their flickering light was kind to the faded rose tapestry and the India carpet which had once been the pride of a great-great-grandmother of Biddy's. There was a fire in the old-fashioned grate, and the whole room looked particularly inviting when they came in from dinner in the tiny dining-room.

Swithin Cush and Judge Lobbett were still talking enthusiastically as they followed the young people and took their places in the wide circle of the hearth. They had delighted each other with a mutual display of archaeological fireworks all through dinner and were still engrossed in their subject.

The rector had appeared in his Sunday clothes in response to an urgent message from Biddy, and his venerable green-black clerical coat of ancient cut enhanced his patriarchal air tremendously. As he sat nearest the fire, his fine silver hair the least bit dishevelled by his enthusiasm, and his little dark eyes animated, it seemed difficult to believe that the Church which he served would so far forget him as to leave him the pastor of less than a hundred souls.

They had been discussing the Royal Letter which entitled

the incumbent of the Mansion to be styled Lord of the Manor. Old Lobbett was deeply interested, and the two elder men bent over the faded parchment, sharing their enthusiasm for the relic.

The other occupants of the room were less genuine in their light-heartedness. Biddy and Isopel sat side by side on the high-backed settee while the three younger men talked together on the far side of the fireplace. Even Mr. Campion's flow of persiflage failed to lighten the tension they all felt.

"By the way," said Marlowe, "we had a visit from a sort of deputation this afternoon. Two old fellows came up to see us, apparently representing the villagers, with an extraordinary yarn about free beer that was apparently doled out at this time of the year. It was something about 'Owl Friday', as far as we could gather."

Biddy and Giles exchanged glances. "I bet that's George," said Giles. "Disgusting old cadger!"

"That's right," said Marlowe. "George and a man apparently called ''Anry'. But George was the head man."

Biddy began to apologize. "They're dreadful," she said helplessly. "They're inveterate beggars. I hope you sent them away."

Marlowe shook his head. "The old boy rather liked them," he said. "It showed they were friendly, anyway. They were talking about old customs practically all the afternoon. At least, George was. 'Anry's comments were unintelligible."

"Henry's a bokel," said Biddy. "That was Father's word. It means half a barmy, half a yokel."

After a while the conversation died down and the little party sat in that pleasant silence which is induced by warmth and well-being.

Even Isopel's misgivings had been lulled by the quiet homely atmosphere. Giles had moved closer to her and sat frankly adoring.

Swithin Cush lay back in his chair, his long bony fingers folded in his lap, his signet ring glowing dully.

Judge Lobbett had closed his eyes. The firelight had reddened his face and softened the stubborn lines about his mouth. He looked a healthy, sober-minded old man.

Marlowe Lobbett leaned forward, his chin resting on his hands, his heavy lids drawn down over his dark eyes. For the moment he was lost in his own thoughts.

Even Mr. Campion seemed to have forgotten the existence of any cloud hanging over them all. He was looking at Biddy covertly from behind his spectacles, and there was no telling from his expression what his meditations might have been.

Outside the garden was very quiet, and through the open windows it was just possible to hear the far-off whisper of the sea. There was no definite sound save the crackling of the fire and an occasional sleepy twitter from the garden.

And then, from far away over the marshes came a sound, almost lost and diffused in the air—a soft, long-drawn-out whistle.

No one appeared to hear it, but Mr. Campion's pale eyes flickered behind his spectacles, and he shifted slightly in his chair, his ear turned to the window.

Within ten seconds the sound came again, a little nearer, more distinguishable. Still no one spoke in the warm peaceful room, but the atmosphere of security had vanished for one of the party at least. Again the whistle sounded, still far away, but appreciably nearer.

Suddenly Isopel looked up. "An owl," she said. "Did you hear it?"

Giles listened. "Yes, there it is again," he said. "It's flying this way," he added, as the sound was repeated, this time no farther away than the park.

Mr. Campion rose and walked over to the window, and it did not escape Biddy that he stood at the side of the sash, so that he could not be seen easily from without. For the sixth time the unearthly sound was repeated.

And then, while they were all listening, a curious sense of apprehension stealing over every one of them, a sudden blood-curdling wail was uttered somewhere within the garden, long-drawn-out like the others, but with a definite quaver in the middle.

"God bless my soul!" said Swithin Cush, sitting up suddenly. "What was that?"

Mr. Campion turned from the window. "That, if I am not very much mistaken," said he, "is a visitor."

Hardly had the words passed from his lips than a loose wire creaked uneasily somewhere over their heads and the next moment a bell pealed hollowly, echoing noisily over the small house.

No one moved or spoke. In the tiny hall outside they heard the sound of feet and the click of the lock as someone opened the door. Then there was a murmur of voices, a soft insidious tone mingled with the strident Suffolk accent. Then the door of the room in which they sat opened and old Cuddy, flustered and excited, appeared on the threshold.

She was a spare, scrupulously tidy old lady, with a round red face and a lot of combs in her scant hair. She wore a black apron over a particularly vivid magenta woollen frock with a high-boned collar of net round her throat.

She came in, carefully closing the door behind her, and striding across the room handed Biddy a card on a small brass platter. The girl took it in astonishment, Mr. Campion coming up behind her.

She read it aloud:

"MR. ANTHONY DATCHETT, PALMIST"

CHAPTER VI

The Man in Dress Clothes

"ANTHONY DATCHETT?" said Mr. Campion, reading over Biddy's shoulder. "Not a gate-crasher, I hope. I personally superintended all the invitations. He can't come palming at this time of night."

Giles looked relieved. "Oh, that's *the* palmist?" he said. "He must be rather a character. I met Guffy Randall at the Dog Trials last week; he was telling me about him then."

"A fortune teller?" said Judge Lobbett, joining in. "That's interesting. A gipsy?"

"Oh no, sir!" Old Cuddy was startled out of her respectful silence. "He's a gentleman, with a car as big as yours, sir."

"Yes, that's right," said Giles. "He's an extraordinary chap. Apparently he turns up after dinner at country houses and shells out the past and present for five bob a time. He'll give a more expensive reading if you desire it, I suppose. Anyhow, that sort of thing. Rather funny: he told Guffy Randall that a beautiful creature was going to throw him over and he was going to be pretty seriously hurt by it. Guffy was quite rattled. He didn't ride to hounds for a fortnight, and it wasn't until Rosemary Waterhouse broke off their engagement that he realized what the chap meant. He was awfully relieved."

Marlowe Lobbett laughed. "Let's have him in," he said, and glanced at Campion questioningly.

The young man in horn-rimmed spectacles was lounging against the back of the settee where the two girls were sitting.

"Since Owl Friday falls on a Wednesday this year," he said, "and that, I understand, means trouble anyhow, we may as well see him and hear the worst." And although Biddy glanced at him dubiously, there was no hint of anything but utter fatuity in his pale face.

Cuddy bustled off, still a little flustered. Once again they heard the soft insidious murmur in the hall outside.

Then the door with its faded tapestry portière swept open, making a quiet rustling sound. Everyone sat forward instinctively, and a sudden cold draught from the open hall door passed through the room.

On the threshold a man stood smiling at them, and as they looked at him the vague feeling of apprehension which had descended upon them when they had first heard the warning cry over the marshes now grew into a reality, and yet there was nothing in the stranger's appearance that was obviously alarming.

Small, slight, immaculately dressed in well-cut tails, he might have been any age. His face was covered with a reddish-brown curling beard; sparse and silky, it formed two small goat curls at the point of his chin, and above it his lips appeared, narrow and shapely, disclosing even teeth set in a smile that was somehow alarming.

The face would have been attractive had it not been for the eyes. They were small, slightly oblique, and of a pale indeterminate colour with extremely small pupils, so that at first glance it might almost seem that they had neither iris nor pupil. This illusion was helped by the candle light, and it was at once so startling and unpleasant that most of the people in the room dropped their eyes instinctively.

The stranger came forward, closing the door with a sweeping rustle behind him.

"I am so glad that you decided to see me," he said, and for the first time they heard clearly the voice that had been a murmur outside. It was low and soft, peculiarly insinuating, and yet not oily, not altogether unpleasing.

Mr. Campion regarded him speculatively.

"Perhaps I had better introduce myself more fully," the stranger went on. "My name is Anthony Datchett. I am an itinerant palmist—a fortune teller, if you like. It is my custom to tell fortunes for a small fee—" He paused and glanced round the room, his curious eyes resting at last upon Giles. "I should be delighted if one or two of you would consent to let me give a reading. If I do, I can promise you one thing. The truth."

He was still looking at Giles as he finished speaking, and the others were surprised to see the boy get up immediately and cross over to him. He was not mesmerized; there was no suggestion of any trance or coma, yet he seemed completely subjected to the stranger.

Giles held out his hands. "Tell me," he said.

The stranger glanced towards the deep window-seat at the far end of the room. "Certainly," he said. "Shall we go over there? I don't like an audience for my readings," he explained, smiling at the others. "It prevents one from being frank, I feel."

"The only man who ever told my fortune," said Mr. Campion, "was an income-tax collector, and he was stupendous."

The stranger turned. "Did he tell you about the Seven Whistlers?" he said.

No flicker of surprise appeared upon Mr. Campion's rather foolish face, and the stranger glanced round swiftly, but nowhere had the thrust gone home. He walked over to the window-seat with Giles beside him, and was presently engrossed in the boy's hand.

It was difficult to catch what he was saying, and Mr. Campion at all events made no effort to do so. He perched himself beside Biddy on the arm of the settee in a direct line between the fortune teller and Judge Lobbett.

"The time has come," he began, the fatuous expression

returning to his face, "when I think our distinguished visitors ought to hear my prize collection of old saws, rustic wisecracks, and gleanings from the soil. After years of research I am able to lay before you, ladies and gentlemen, one or two little gems. Firstly:

> When owd Parson wears two coats
> It be a powerful year for oats.

Consider the simplicity of that!" he continued with complete seriousness. "The little moral neatly put, the rustic spirit of prophecy epitomized in a single phrase. And then of course:

> Owl hoots once up in the rafter,
> 'Nother hoot be comin' after.

That needs no comment from me."

They laughed, eager to escape the tension of the last few minutes. At the far end of the room the murmur of the fortune teller went on steadily.

Mr. Campion continued. He chattered without effort, apparently completely lost to the rest of the world.

"I knew a man once," he said, "who managed by stealth to attend a Weevil Sabbath at Mould. He went prepared to witness fearful rites, but when he got there he found it wasn't the genuine thing at all, but the yearly outing of the Latter Day Nebuchadnezzars, the famous grass-eating society. He was awfully cut up. He ate a little grass and came home. He didn't see a single weevil."

He would have gone on had not Giles suddenly returned to the group. His expression was one of incredulous amazement.

"This is astounding," he said. "The chap seems to know all about me—things I hadn't told to anybody. Biddy, you must get him to tell your fortune."

Some of the uneasiness the occupants of the little room had felt at the arrival of their strange visitor began to disappear, but all the same there was no great eagerness on anyone's part to hurry over to the strange slight figure in the window-seat whose blank eyes seemed to be gazing at them all impartially.

It was at this moment that the attention of the whole party began to be focused upon the old rector. He had not moved nor spoken, but a change had taken place in his appearance. Biddy, glancing at him casually, was appalled by a look of great age which she had never noticed before. His jaw seemed to have sunk, his eyelids become grey and webby.

To their surprise he rose to his feet and walked a little unsteadily across the room to the fortune teller, who appeared to be waiting for him.

As the soft murmur began again Giles began to talk enthusiastically about his experience. "He's an amazing chap," he said quietly, lowering his voice so that the palmist should not hear. "He's got such extraordinary hands—have you noticed them? They don't feel like flesh. It's like being touched by silk gloves."

"What did he tell you?" said Campion.

"Well, it's a most extraordinary thing." Giles was childlike in his mystification. "He told me practically everything that has happened to me since I was a kid. But what really got me was when he said I was thinking of entering a horse for the Monewdon Show next month. I know, of course, that's fairly obvious. But he told me I wouldn't send my favourite mare as I'd intended, but I'd send a hunter. That's really most extraordinary, because I went down to look at Lilac Lady just before dinner and I made up my mind that I couldn't get her into really decent condition in the time. I was wondering if I wouldn't enter St. Chris, or let it go this year. I hadn't mentioned that to a soul." He laughed. "It's crazy, isn't it? He also told me the usual bunk—to beware of wagging tongues, and so on. He hinted at some sort of scandal, I thought. I didn't quite get it. I wonder what he's telling old St. Swithin."

He glanced over his shoulder to where the fortune teller sat upright in the window-seat, the candlelight making fantastic shadows on his unusual face. He was speaking in the

same subdued monotone, which they could hear quite
plainly without being able to distinguish the words.

They could not see the rector's face. He was bending
forward, his hands cupped before the stranger.

"He seems interested all right," said Marlowe.

Biddy laughed. "Doesn't he?" she said. "I do hope he's
promising him plenty of adventures. He has led such a good
quiet life."

"I doubt if he'd like it," said Giles. "Tranquillity has
always been St. Swithin's note."

"That seems to be the note of the whole place," said
Judge Lobbett, and sighed as if with content.

"Hullo, they've finished," Marlowe said suddenly, as the
old rector and the stranger came down the room together.
The fortune teller was smiling, suave and completely at ease.
Swithin Cush looked thoughtful.

Biddy turned to him smiling. "What sort of luck did you
have, St. Swithin?" she said.

The old man put a hand on her shoulder. "My dear, I'm
too old to have any fortune at all," he said. He pulled out his
old turnip watch. "I must go to bed," he remarked. "I know
you won't mind." He turned to Judge Lobbett. "We keep
early hours in the country."

He spoke the words absently as if he did not expect any
reply, and while the others gathered round the fortune teller
he returned once more to the girl. "Good night, my dear,"
he said. "Give my love to Giles."

She looked up at him without surprise. He often said
unexpected things; but as she did so she caught his eyes
before he had time to lower them, and for an instant she was
afraid.

The old man departed, taking his storm lantern from
Cuddy in the hall, although the night was fine and moonlit.

The fortune teller still dominated the room, and the old
man's going made very little impression. The stranger's
quiet, even voice was raised a little in surprise.

"I did not realize that it was so late," he said. "It was a
longer drive here than I expected. I can tell only one more
fortune. I will read the hand aloud so that you can all hear.

Let it be someone to whom I can promise nothing but happiness." He turned to Isopel. "Will you permit me to tell yours?"

The girl looked at him dubiously. During the past few months she had grown to distrust everyone, terrible experiences were still fresh in her mind, but with Giles at her side and Marlowe and Mr. Campion leaning over the settee behind her, it seemed ridiculous to be afraid.

The stranger took her hand in his own, and they noticed what Giles had meant when he had described them as "like silk gloves". The skin was fine and very white, the fingers long and pointed, with a natural polish on the nails, and when he turned his palm uppermost they saw with a little surprise that the natural fold of his hand made no permanent crease. The skin was smooth and unlined.

"I was right," he said, holding the girl's small hand out for inspection. "You have had troubles; they will end, though not perhaps as you expect. You will love, you will be loved. I see you in strange company at least twice in your life. The thing you remember most clearly," he went on with sudden intensity, "is lying on a bed of thick fur with the head of an animal looking down at you. Isn't that so?"

Judge Lobbett and his daughter exchanged astonished glances, and a smothered exclamation escaped Marlowe. Giles and Biddy glanced at their visitor inquiringly, and after some hesitation Isopel explained. "When I was a child," she said, "we were on a holiday in the Rockies. I got lost. A trapper found me and I stayed in his cabin for a few hours until Father found me. The trapper told me to lie down, and I rested on a heap of skins by the fire. There was a bear skin on the wall with a roughly stuffed head. I couldn't take my eyes off it. It was terrible, grotesque, and out of shape. It's one of my most usual nightmares. I don't know how you knew," she finished, staring at the fortune teller, her dark eyes widening as she realized the wonder.

The stranger smiled and went on. His voice revealed a peculiarly soothing quality, and he did not raise his eyes from the hand.

"You will have your dark hour," he said, "but it will

pass. There is serenity for you. Beware of strangers, although you will not marry one of your own people. Your domains will be wide, and your pastures rich in cattle, and you will know the peace which is the lowing of kine over small meadows when the hedges are gilt and the air warm with the last rays of the sun. That is your fortune. It is a pity that I cannot promise as much to you all."

He spoke the last words softly, and although his tone was unchanged, the soothing effect of Isopel's reading was completely spoiled, and an unpleasant flavour remained.

He made his adieux immediately afterwards, and Giles and Marlowe settled with him, paying the trifling sum he demanded with some surprise.

By common consent they all escorted the stranger to the door. A big saloon car with a uniformed chauffeur was waiting for him. He bade them a courtly farewell, stepped into the car, and the great headlights swept over the little green.

They watched the car disappear down the narrow road. As it passed out of sight the whistle that had heralded its approach sounded once more from the garden. "There's that owl again," said Isopel. "It seems to be flying away this time." They stood in the porch listening: the seven cries were repeated one after the other, each fainter and farther off than the one before, until a final long-drawn-out wail, hardly audible, reached Mr. Campion and Giles, who were still standing with Marlowe, the others having gone in.

"Seven," said Giles. "The Seven Whistlers. That means the end of the world, so they say."

"That means he's gone," said Mr. Campion with relief. "My respected friends George and 'Anry, with their five sons, have performed their spot of policing with great success. No one comes over the Stroud at night in future without our knowing on the moment. These blessed lads are posted every five hundred yards along the road. The moment a stranger passes any one of them—well, it's Owl Friday. Trespassers will be persecuted, you see."

They went back towards the door laughing. Biddy met them on the threshold. Judge Lobbett and his daughter were behind her, and a stout perplexed old woman who had evidently entered by the back way hovered at her side.

Biddy was pale and her brown eyes spoke unnamed terrors.

There was something in her hand which she held out to her brother.

"Giles," she said, "look at this. Alice has just brought it over."

The boy took the crumpled piece of paper and the big old-fashioned ring she gave him. It lay gleaming in his hand.

" 'Giles and Albert come over alone,' " he read slowly.

A look of horror suddenly dawned in his face.

"St. Swithin!" he said breathlessly. "His ring! He would never part with that unless—"

The words were silenced by a sound which reached them clearly through the open window, sharp and unmistakable. A gunshot on the night air.

CHAPTER VII

By the Light of the Hurricane

THE echo of the shot died away and stillness returned before full realization dawned upon them. Then the old woman screamed, a shrill stifled sound in her throat. They caught a fleeting impression of her face, still and horrified, as if carved out of red sandstone, her small black eyes dilated. She suddenly started for the door.

Mr. Campion laid a hand upon her arm. He was unnaturally quiet in his movements, his face expressionless.

"Wait, Alice," he said. "Giles and I will go first."

"Leave I go," said the old woman, wrenching her arm away. "Leave I go, I tell 'ee."

Biddy came forward. "Stay here, Alice," she said gently. "Stay here. He said they were to go alone."

Alice suffered herself to be led back into the room. Judge Lobbett stood between his two children, an inscrutable expression on his face. Isopel clung to him. Marlowe looked on gravely, ready to help when the occasion should arise.

Mr. Campion touched Giles upon the shoulder. "Come along," he said. They hurried out of the house together.

The Rectory lay across the green, standing back from the road down a long ill-kept gravelled drive lined with heavy shrubberies and tall trees. The house appeared to be in darkness as they approached, but the front door stood open under the ivy-covered porch.

Mr. Campion turned to Giles. "Let me go first," he said softly. "You never know."

Giles hung back unwillingly, but he did not attempt to remonstrate. Campion went on into the dark house alone.

In front of him a door stood open through which the room beyond was faintly visible.

He went in.

A moment or so later he reappeared on the porch. Giles caught a glimpse of his face in the moonlight.

"Come in, will you, old boy?" he said quietly, and Giles knew that the question which had been on his lips had been answered.

The two men went quietly into the house. The old rector's study was the only room with any light in it, and that was given only by the hurricane lantern which he had brought from the Dower House such a short while ago. It stood upon the heavy writing table shedding a diffused light over parts of the sombre place. It was a big rectangular room with a fireplace at one end and a bay window at the other and bookshelves ranged all along the intervening walls.

The desk was set parallel to the fireplace, and the rector's old chair with its dilapidated leather seat was pushed back from it as if he had just risen. The fire glowed dully in the grate.

Giles looked round anxiously.

"Where?" he began, and Campion pointed silently to a door corresponding to the one through which they had entered, on the other side of the fireplace. Giles recognized it as leading to the tiny robing-room which a thoughtful ancestor of his own had built off the study. The door was closed, and from under it there issued a thin dark trickle of blood on the worn brown linoleum.

Giles walked over and opened the door. He struck a match and held it high. The flickering light filled the tiny apartment for an instant and died out. His hand fell to his side. Then he shut the door unsteadily and turned to Campion. His face was very pale, and he moistened his lips with his tongue nervously.

"His old shotgun," he said.

Campion nodded.

"In his mouth—tied a string to the trigger. It's the usual way."

The boy sank down in the chair. "Suicide?" he said. "My God—old St. Swithin!"

Campion stood staring at the closed door. "Why?" he said. "In the name of all that's extraordinary, *why?*"

A step in the hall startled them both. Alice Broom, the old housekeeper, appeared on the threshold. Her black eyes fixed them questioningly.

"He shot hisself?" she burst out. "I saw the old gun was gone, but I never thought. Oh, dear Lord, have mercy on his soul!" She flopped down on her knees where she was and covered her face with her hands.

The sight of her helplessness brought Giles to himself. He and Campion lifted her up, and together they led her to the chair by the desk. She started away from it like a frightened sheep.

"Not in his chair. I'll not sit in his chair," he said hysterically. "The chair of the dead!"

The unexpectedness of her superstition breaking through her grief startled them oddly. They sat her down in the armchair by the fireplace, where she sat sobbing quietly into her cupped hands.

Campion took command of the situation.

"Look here, Giles," he said, "we shall want a doctor and the police. You haven't either in the village, have you?"

Giles shook his head. "No. We shall have to get old Wheeler over from Heronhoe. The nearest bobby's there, too. Campion, this is ghastly. Why did he do it? Why did he do it?"

The other pointed to a letter propped up against the inkstand on the desk, next to the lantern. It was addressed in Swithin Cush's spidery old-fashioned writing:

HENRY TOPLISS, ESQ.

"Who's that? The coroner?" he demanded. Giles nodded.
and again the incredulous expression passed over his face.

"He must have done it quite deliberately," he said. "I
can't understand it. You don't think that fortune teller—"

Campion put his hand up warningly. There was the
sound of feet in the hall.

The others had come over, unable to bear the suspense of
waiting any longer.

Biddy came in first, the others behind her. Her face was
white and twisted with anxiety. She glanced round the room
and her eye fell upon the closed door almost immediately.
With a little cry she advanced towards it. Campion darted
forward and drew her back.

"No, old dear, don't go in," he said softly. "You can't do
anything." The hand he held grew cold and the slender fingers bit into his flesh. For a moment she neither moved nor
spoke.

Campion put his arm round her until Isopel Lobbett
came up, and, slipping her hand through Biddy's, led her to
a chair by the fire.

Judge Lobbett and Marlowe came forward and Giles explained the situation to them as well as he could.

The old man was horrified.

"This is terrible," he said. "Terrible! I—" Words seemed
to fail him, and he stood silent for a moment, rendered completely helpless by the shock. Gradually his old practical self
reasserted itself. "Isopel," he said gently, "take Miss Paget
back to the Dower House and stay there with her, my dear,
while we see what's to be done here."

Campion joined the two younger men, who were talking
softly by the desk. "Giles," he said, "if you and Marlowe
would take a car and go in to Heronhoe and bring back a
doctor and the police, that's as much as we can do. Don't
disturb the servants if you can help it. I'll get Alice up to her
room. And then, if you don't mind, sir," he added, turning
to old Lobbett, "we'll wait for them here."

The two younger men jumped at the chance of doing
something, and hurried off.

Isopel and Biddy went back to the Dower House. Biddy

did not cry, but her face had not lost the strained twisted look which had been noticeable when she first came into the Rectory.

Campion watched her out of the doorway and then turned his attention to Alice. The problem of her disposal would have presented untold difficulties had it not been suddenly solved by the unexpected appearance of George. The old man had heard the shot while watching in the Dower garden and had followed Judge Lobbett over without daring to come in. However, at last, his curiosity exceeding every other emotion, he had ventured into the house.

Hat in hand, his eyes goggling, he listened to the curt explanation Campion gave him.

"Rector dead," he said, and repeated the words over and over again to himself, the horror and shock which he felt slowly becoming visible on his face.

"I'll take Al-us along," he said at last. "She's my sister. My wife'll take care o' she. She's looked after he so long this'll come like a shock to her, like."

He helped the old woman to her feet and guided her with awkward elaborateness out of the room.

"Good night, Master. Good night, Squoire," he said.

Campion hurried after him. "George," he said, "don't rouse the village, will you?"

The old man turned on him.

"No, sir. 'Tis best in time like this to keep the mouth shut till after police be gone."

With which unexpected remark he clumped off, his great boots clattering on the stones of the hall. Campion went back to the study and Judge Lobbett.

The old man stood by the fireplace, one hand upon the heavy oak mantel. He was evidently considerably shaken. There was a faintly bewildered expression upon his face and he was breathing heavily.

Campion lit the candles in the iron sticks on the shelf, and then sat down quietly on the other side of the fireplace and took out a cigarette.

"This is a bad business," said the old man suddenly; "a

terrible bad business. Death seems to follow me as gulls follow a ship."

Campion said nothing. He had thrown a log of wood upon the fire and the gentle crackling as the bark caught was the only sound in the big dimly-lit room. On the brown oilcloth behind him the thin stream of blood congealed slowly.

Judge Lobbett cleared his throat.

"Of course, you know," he began, "I'm not a fool. I know Marlowe's got you to bring me down here. I didn't say anything because I thought it might give them confidence if it didn't me. Besides, I like this sort of life. But if I'd dreamed that I should bring a tragedy like this into the lives of such kindly homely folk, nothing would have induced me to come here. I feel it can't be a coincidence," he added abruptly, "and yet there seems no doubt that it was suicide."

Campion, who had listened to this outburst without altering his expression, spoke quietly.

"It was suicide. No doubt at all, I think. He left a letter to the coroner."

"Is that so?" The old man looked up sharply. "It was premeditated, then. Have you any idea why he did it?"

"None at all." Campion spoke gravely. "This is the most astounding thing I've ever experienced. If I hadn't seen that letter I should have said it was a brainstorm."

Crowdy Lobbett sat down in the chair opposite the younger man and rested his elbows on his knees, his big hands locked tightly together. He looked thoughtfully at Campion without raising his head.

"I reckon you and I ought to understand one another before we go any farther," he said. "Of course I remember you on board ship. That was a very smart piece of work of yours, and I'm more than grateful. But I feel I've been following your instructions without knowing where I'm going long enough. I meant to have a talk with you this evening anyhow, even if this terrible thing hadn't made it imperative. Marlowe engaged you to look after me. I'll say I know that much. You're not a policeman, are you?"

"Hardly," said Mr. Campion. "I believe I was recom-

mended to your son by Scotland Yard, though," he added
with a faint smile. "I'm not quite a private detective, you
know. I suggested that you come here because I believe that
you'll be safer here than anywhere, and that your family will
run less risk."

Judge Lobbett looked at him sharply.

"You can't understand me letting Isopel into it, can
you?" he said. "Where else would she be safer than where I
can watch over her myself?"

Mr. Campion offered no opinion.

"Just how much do you know?" said Judge Lobbett unexpectedly.

The young man looked more thoughtful. "I know enough
to realize that it's not revenge pure and simple that they're
after you for," he said at last. "That's patent from common
or garden Holmic deduction. In New York they were trying
to frighten you. That points to the fact that you had a line
on them. Marlowe confirmed my ideas on that with a theory
of his own." He paused and eyed the other man questioningly. Lobbett signed to him to go on and he continued:
"Then I think they must have decided that, had you a definite line, you'd have used it before," he said. "They decided
to kill you. You escaped. One of the first things you did
when you got to London was to consult MacNab, the cipher
expert. That put the wind up them again. They want to
know what you hold first, then they want your blood. I
should say myself," he added, "that you've got a clue from
one of Simister's gang which you can't decipher yourself as
yet. Isn't that so?"

He sat back and regarded the older man speculatively.

Lobbett stared back at him in blank astonishment.

"I don't mind telling you," he said, "that when I first saw
you, Mr. Campion, I thought you were the biggest goddam
fool ever made; but I'm now beginning to wonder if you're
not some sort of telepathy expert." He leaned forward. "I'll
say you're right, and I may as well tell you MacNab didn't
help me any, but he was the first man I felt I could trust to
see what I had. I've got one end of the string, you see, but if
any of that crowd should get wind of what it is they'd cut it

higher up and then the one chance I've got of stopping this thing at the head would be lost for ever. As it is, the thing's no more use to me than so much junk. And I daren't and won't confide in any of you youngsters."

Mr. Campion looked at him critically. The determined expression on the judge's face and the obstinate lines about his mouth made the younger man decide in an instant that, upon this point at any rate, he would be as stubborn as a mule.

"You intend, I suppose," he said, "to stay here until you've found the solution to your crossword?"

Judge Lobbett nodded. "I certainly had that idea," he said. "But after the terrible affair this evening I don't know what to say." He glanced at Campion. "Look here," he said. "In your opinion what sort of chance have I got of getting my man if I stay here?"

The younger man rose to his feet. "One," he said, an unusually convincing tone in his voice. "You're in England, and I don't think it would be any too easy for our friend Simister to do anything on a very big scale. He couldn't get half his best people out of your country, for instance, so there's just one chance in a hundred that he'll do the job himself. The mountain may come to Mahomet for once; and in that case I doubt whether anyone is in any real danger except yourself."

Judge Lobbett nodded to the closed door behind the younger man. "Maybe so," he said, "but what about that?"

Campion remained silent for some moments, his hands thrust deep in his pockets.

"I fancy," he said at last, hesitating as if he were weighing every word, "that there's something more than ordinarily mysterious about that. Poor old boy!"

CHAPTER VIII

The Envelope

THE change in the drawing-room in the Dower House was extraordinary. The cosiness, the peace had vanished. The fire had burned down to a few red and grey coals, the candles had shrunk in their sticks, and the room was cold and desolate.

The two girls sat huddled together in the window-seat where but a short time before the man who now lay still and unrecognizable in the little robing closet across the green had crouched listening, his hands spread out before the stranger. Biddy was not crying; she sat up stiffly, her back against the folded wooden shutter. Her face was very pale, and the same twisted, suffering expression was still engraved upon it.

The other girl sat close to her, her small hand resting upon her knee.

"I can't tell you how unbelievable it is," Biddy burst out suddenly, keeping her voice down instinctively as if she feared to be overheard. "It's so unlike him. I didn't think he had a care in the world, and no greater worry than the attendance at the Sunday school. Why should he have done this horrible, horrible thing?"

Isopel could not answer her, and she went on again, still keeping to the quiet monotone.

"To think of it! He must have known when he said good night to me. He must have gone over there deliberately, written the letter to Mr. Topliss, sent Alice over here with that note, and then gone into that little cupboard all by himself and—oh—"

She leaned back against the shutter and closed her eyes.

Isopel nodded. "I know," she said. The lashes drooped over her dark eyes and a sombre expression passed over her young face. "For the last six weeks I've lived in an atmosphere like this. I'm growing callous, I think. At first, Schuyler, father's secretary. I'd known him since I was a kid. They found him in Dad's chair, shot through the head." She shuddered. "They must have shot him through the window from a block opposite. Ever since then it's been one after the other. Wills—the butler; then our new chauffeur, and then Doc Wetherby, who was walking down the street with Father. I was scared then. But afterwards, on board ship and at our hotel in London, I was so frightened I thought I should go out of my mind. And then when we came down here it seemed like an escape." She sighed. "That house of yours across the park, and this one—they were so quiet, undisturbed for centuries, it seemed that nothing terrible could happen in them. But now we've brought you this horror. Sometimes I feel"—her voice sank to a whisper—"that we've roused the devil. There's some ghastly evil power dogging us, something from which we can't escape."

She spoke quite seriously, and the gravity of her voice, coupled with the tragedy which had overwhelmed her, infected the other girl with some of her terror.

"But," said Biddy, struggling to regain her common sense, "St. Swithin killed himself. There's no doubt of that, they say. If it were a murder it wouldn't be so horrible. He must have gone mad. That's more dreadful than anything else to my mind. Oh," she said irrelevantly, "I wish Giles would come back."

A gentle tap on the door startled them both. Old Cuddy

appeared with a tray. The old woman's hands trembled and her round kindly face was mottled where the blood had drained away, leaving her weather-beaten skin to provide the only colour in her cheeks.

She had been told of the tragedy and had reacted to it in her own practical way.

"I've brought you both a cup of cocoa, Miss Biddy," she said. "A hot drink to warm your hearts."

She set the tray down beside them and without further words began to make the fire and refill the emptying candlesticks. They drank the cocoa gratefully. The heavy stimulant soothed their nerves and they sat quiet until far away over the silhouetted hedge tops they saw the faint glow of headlights against the sky. The light came nearer until they heard the car whisper past the house. Then all was black again.

"Who will they have got? The doctor and the sheriff?" said Isopel nervously.

Biddy shook her head. "It'll be Dr. Wheeler and Peck, the Heronhoe policeman, I suppose," she said; and quite suddenly she turned her face towards the shutter and wept.

In the study across the green Dr. Wheeler, a short, thick-set, oldish man with a closely clipped beard and a natural air of importance, set his bag down upon the desk and took off his coat.

Peck, the Heronhoe police-constable, red-faced and perspiring with unaccustomed responsibility, clutched his notebook unhappily.

Giles and Marlowe had followed them into the room and now stood gravely in the doorway. Giles introduced Judge Lobbett and Albert Campion.

The doctor nodded to them curtly.

"This is bad," he said. "Terrible. Not like the old man. I saw him only the other day. He seemed quite cheerful. Where's the body, please?" He spoke briskly.

Giles indicated the door of the robing-room. "We've left him just as he fell, sir. There was nothing to be done. He—he's practically blown his head off."

The little doctor nodded. "Yes, quite," he said, taking the

affair completely into his capable hands. "We shall need some light, I suppose. Peck, bring the lantern, will you?"

His deference to their susceptibilities was not lost upon the others, and they were grateful.

The closet door swung open and the doctor, stepping carefully to avoid the stream of blood, went in, the constable walking behind him, the lantern held high.

Some of the horror that they saw was communicated to the four who now stood upon the hearthrug waiting. Dr. Wheeler reappeared within a few minutes, Peck following him, stolid and unmoved.

The doctor shook his head. "Very nasty," he said quietly. "Death must have been absolutely instantaneous, though. We must get him out of there. We'll need a shed door, and if you could get a sheet, Giles— How's Biddy?" he broke off. "Is she all right? Over at the Dower House? I'll go in and see her before I go."

Giles explained that Isopel was with her, and the old man, who had known the brother and sister since they were children, seemed considerably relieved. Campion and Marlowe went through the dark stone kitchens of the Rectory. They let themselves into the brickyard, and lifting a toolshed door off its hinges, brought it carefully into the house. Giles was upstairs in search of a sheet: they could hear him stumbling about on the uneven floors.

With the constable holding the light, they assisted the doctor to lift the gruesome sightless thing on to the improvised stretcher. The doctor had thrown a surplice that had been hanging on the wall over all that remained of the old man before Giles returned with the sheet.

They laid the stretcher on a hastily arranged trestle of chairs at the far end of the room. Campion swung the great shutters across the windows, and then without speaking they trooped off to the scullery to wash.

Peck was particularly anxious to avoid troubling the Pagets and their friends any more than was absolutely necessary, and when he once more produced his notebook it was with an air of apology.

"There's just one or two things I'll have to make a note

of," he began, clearing his throat nervously. "You'd say the gun was fired by the deceased 'imself?"

"Oh, yes, no doubt about that." The doctor was struggling into the coat Giles held for him. "You'll go to Mr. Topliss, Peck? Tell him I'll 'phone him in the morning."

"Mr. Cush left a letter for Mr. Topliss," said Campion, pointing to the big yellow envelope on the desk. The policeman moved forward clumsily to take it, and the doctor sighed with relief.

"I expect that'll make it all very simple," he said. "I was afraid from the look of things there might be a lot of tedious questioning for you all. This'll probably mean only a formal inquest. Maybe Peck and I can save you even having to attend."

The constable slipped the letter into his pocket. "I'll ride out to Mr. Topliss first thing," he said. "There's just one thing, 'owever, if you don't mind. Where was you all when the shot was fired?"

"All together," said Giles, "in the drawing-room at the Dower House just across the green there."

"I see," said Peck, writing laboriously. "And the housekeeper, Mrs. Broom, where was she?"

"She was with us," said Giles. "She brought a message from St. Swithin—I mean Mr. Cush."

"Oh?" said the constable with interest. "What was that?"

Giles handed him the slip of paper and the countryman held it to the light. " 'Giles and Albert come over alone,' " he read with difficulty. "Albert—that'll be you, sir?" he said, turning to Campion.

"Yes," the young man nodded. "As soon as we got the message we heard the shot."

"I see. And that was when you was over at the Dower House? That makes it seem very deliberate, don't it, sir?" said Peck, turning to the doctor.

"There's no doubt that it was deliberate." The medical man spoke emphatically.

"And you two gentlemen found the body, I suppose?" said Peck, coming to the end of his entries with relief. "No idea of cause or reason, sir, I suppose?" he added, turning to Giles.

"None at all," said Giles.

"Mr. Topliss's letter will explain all that, be sure," said Dr. Wheeler, pulling on his gloves with an air of finality. "I'll go over to your sister now, Giles."

At this juncture the question of who was to remain with the body of the old rector became a pressing one. Giles and Campion sat down one on either side of the fireplace and prepared for the vigil, and would have stayed there alone in spite of Marlowe's generous offer to remain with them, had not Alice, the old housekeeper, appeared in the doorway.

She had got over her first outburst of grief, and the stolid stoicism of the countrywoman who accepts birth and death, spring and winter in the same spirit had come to her rescue. Her red face was set and unmoved.

"You go to your bed, Master Giles," she said. "I'm staying." She waved aside his protestations. "I looked arter him in loife. I'll look arter him in death," she said. "He's old," she explained quaintly. "He wouldn't loike nobody but me. Good night to you."

They accepted their dismissal.

Campion was the last to leave, and some thought of the old woman alone with the horror passing through his mind, he turned to her and whispered a few words of warning.

She looked at him, faint surprise showing in her small eyes. "I shan't be afeard o' him," she said. "What if there's blood? 'Tis his, ain't it? I looked arter him since I were a young woman, but no doubt you meant well. Good night."

He followed the others out into the drive. They walked in silence over to the Dower House, where the doctor was soothing the two girls in his brisk professional manner.

Old Lobbett moved quietly over to Campion. "I'll take my girl up to the Manor," he said. "Marlowe will send the chauffeur down to drive the doc back. I guess we won't intrude on you people any longer. Get Miss Paget to go to bed. There's nothing like sleep. Time for talking in the morning."

With the departure of the Lobbetts the affair assumed a more intimate aspect. Giles sat with his arm round Biddy. Campion stood on the hearthrug, one elbow on the mantel-piece.

The doctor and Peck departed with the reassurance that all needful arrangements would be made. Once more the headlights swept over the green and disappeared.

The three young people faced one another.

"Now," said Giles explosively, "what in the name of creation does it all mean?"

Biddy turned to Campion appealingly. "What does it all mean, Albert? How did it happen? You know him almost as well as we did. Why did he do it?"

Campion thrust his hand into his coat pocket and produced a bulky yellow envelope and handed it to them.

It was addressed, "For Giles, Biddy, and Albert Campion", and was marked in the corner "Confidential".

"This was lying on the desk beside the note for the coroner," he said. "I thought it best to keep it till we were alone. You open it, Giles."

The boy tore open the flap with unsteady fingers and drew out the contents. There was a second envelope marked "Giles", a folded paper for Biddy, and something hard wrapped in a piece of notepaper for Campion. Giles handed them out gravely.

Biddy glanced at her message. There were only two lines. The old man's writing was shaky and almost illegible.

Tell Albert about our longest walk [it ran]. God bless you, my dear.

She handed the slip of paper to Campion, an expression of utter bewilderment on her face. "He must have suddenly gone mad," she said. "How horrible—over there in the dark."

Campion took the message from her and stared at it. Then he shook his head.

"He wasn't mad, Biddy. He was trying to tell us something, something that he didn't want anyone but us to know.

Perhaps this will help us." He began to unwrap the little package which bore his name. He drew off the paper and a murmur of surprise escaped him. He held out the little object in the palm of his hand.

It was a single ivory chessman, the red knight.

CHAPTER IX

"In Event of Trouble . . ."

"WHAT does it mean?" Biddy sat back in her chair, her eyes fixed upon the little ivory figure in Campion's hand, some of the superstitious horror which she felt visible on her face.

Giles was startled also. "I recognize it, of course," he said. "It's one of his best set—the ones we seldom played with. What do you think, Albert? It looks as if he went crazy, doesn't it?"

Campion dropped the chessman into his coat pocket. "Suppose you read your letter?" he suggested. "That'll tell us more than anything."

Giles ripped open the thick envelope he held in his hand. "Of course," he said, "I'd forgotten it."

To everyone's surprise he drew out two sheets of closely written paper upon which the ink was dried and black. The latter had evidently been written some time before. Giles began to read it aloud, his young voice husky and curiously impressive in the chill little room.

"MY DEAR BOY:
"If ever you read this letter it will be because I shall have committed a crime the magnitude of which I

realize fully. If, however, it does come to this, I ask you to believe that it was because I preferred to go to my death with my health and sanity than to weary out a tortured existence in which I should be a burden to you all, and a wretchedness to myself.

"I have known for a long time that I was a victim of a malignant and incurable disease, and my increasing fear has been that it would enfeeble not only my body but my mind. I ask you and Biddy to forgive me. I shall leave a note for the coroner which should relieve you from any ordeal in the court. However . . .

"This is underlined," said Giles.

". . . *in the event of any serious trouble* arising directly after my death, send Albert Campion to my old friend Alaric Watts, the Vicar of Kepesake in Suffolk, who will know the correct procedure in this situation.

"Something is crossed out here," said Giles, holding the paper up to the light. "The 'this' has been put in afterwards. As far as I can see it looks as if he had first written 'in so terrible a situation'. Then it goes on, getting very wobbly towards the end.

"In any case I do most particularly ask your forgiveness and your prayers. My temptation was great. I succumbed to it. All my love to you, my children.
                                        ST. SWITHIN

P.S.—My will, bequeathing my few belongings, is in my desk.

"That's all," said Giles.

Biddy broke the silence. There were tears in her eyes, but she spoke firmly. "Albert, the whole thing's a mistake; it's not true."

Campion looked at her thoughtfully. "How do you mean?" he said.

"I mean"—Biddy's voice rose a little—"St. Swithin was no more ill than you or I. He's hiding something, or shielding someone, or—" Her voice died away into silence.

Campion took the letter from Giles and spread it out on the table in front of him. "It's been written a long time," he said, "before we'd heard of the Lobbetts. Not long after your father died, I should say."

Biddy was sitting bolt upright, her eyes shining. "That doesn't alter it," she said. "St. Swithin's never been ill in his life. I've never heard him complain even of a headache. He's been moody lately, a little strange, but not ill. Besides, why did he choose such a curious time to kill himself? Just after that—that man was here."

This was the first mention of the fortune teller that the three had made. It seemed as if they had all instinctively shied away from it. Now that Biddy had brought it to light it had to be faced.

The brother and sister looked at Campion. He sat regarding them, his pale eyes grave behind his spectacles.

"My dear old birds," he said, "you've got me pipped. I don't know him. I've never heard of him. I've never even dreamed of anything like him. But when he turned up this evening he had me quaggly with fright. You say you've heard of him, Giles?"

The boy nodded. "Yes. From all over the county. I told you about Guffy, and a man who had a place round by Hadleigh spoke of him. He's been going for several years, I believe, off and on. He turned up at Maplestone Hall on Christmas Day and was a great success. That's when Guffy saw him."

"Maplestone Hall?" said Campion, looking up. "Wasn't there a bit of a row there a month or so ago? I thought I read something about it."

Giles nodded. "A libel case or something," he said. "Something fishy, anyway. Guffy had some rambling yarn about it."

Biddy leaned across the table and put her hand on Campion's arm. "Albert," she said, "that man killed St. Swithin."

"But, my dear old girl," he protested gently, "we saw him driving away. His headlights didn't stop for an instant. We had watchers all along the road and the seven whistles came quite clearly. Besides, it was obviously a suicide. There's no getting away from it."

"Oh, I *know*." Biddy spoke impatiently. "I know. I'm not saying that poor old St. Swithin didn't shoot himself over there in the dark, but it was that man who really did it. That terrible man with the little red beard. He told him something. While we were all sitting here laughing round the fire, watching him over there on the window-seat, he said something that made St. Swithin go right out and kill himself. I know it, I'm sure of it."

Campion hesitated. "It's too far-fetched," he said.

"Do you think he was just an ordinary fortune teller?" Biddy's tone implied her opinion of the theory.

Campion shook his head. "Oh no, I don't believe that for a moment. That bird, whoever he was, was up to some most fishy stunt. Oh no," he went on thoughtfully, "he was no ordinary gipsy's warning. That neat little exercise in telepathy was a stout piece of work. A chap like that could earn a fortune on the music halls. And yet, what did he get at Maplestone Hall last Christmas? Certainly not fifty quid. And what did he get to-night? About fourpence. Oh no, he was up to some really nasty nap and double. I can't help feeling that he came to spy out the nakedness of the land and the impoverished state of our Albert's intelligence." His hand closed over Biddy's and he smiled at her wryly from behind his spectacles. "Dear old St. Swithin was too small game for him, I think, Biddy."

"Then do you believe this?" Biddy tapped the letter lying on the table.

For some time Campion was silent. "Not altogether," he said at last, and turning, added with apparent carelessness, "Where is Kepesake, Giles?"

"About twenty miles across country. It's not far from Bury. It's a tiny little village on the Larksley Estate. The story goes that an ancient Larksley, setting off to some war or other, left it to his mistress as a keepsake. I remember old Watts. He used to come over here and preach sometimes. He's an authority on Church history or something, I believe. Quite a nice old boy."

"I think," said Campion, "that a visit is indicated. 'In the event of any serious trouble' sounds ominous, without leading us anywhere."

"And the red chessman?" said Giles.

Albert Campion drew the ivory knight out of his pocket and set it on the table before them. It was small, beautifully carved, and of a slightly unusual pattern, the horse's head being much more realistic than in most pieces. It was stained a bright scarlet and stood vivid and beautiful upon the polished walnut table. Giles picked it up and turned it over and then weighed it in his hand.

"It's too light to contain anything," he said. "Besides, that's such a fantastic idea. I'm afraid he was quite right, Biddy. The old boy had some disease that was affecting his mind and suddenly it sent him clean crazy."

"That won't wash." Biddy spoke vehemently. "Just look at the facts." She ticked them off one by one on her fingers. "St. Swithin lives here all his life, never ill, never really worried. And then, after Father died, we noticed that he was getting a little older. Alice said he'd 'gone broody'; thoughtful, she meant. Well, as far as we can judge, about the time we noticed this slight change in him, he wrote this letter. So far it all fits in, you think?" She was speaking passionately, her brown eyes wide and eloquent. "But it doesn't—really. If St. Swithin had actually thought he was ill he would have gone straight to Dr. Wheeler. He believed in doctors. When he got that lump on his foot that he thought might be gout he was off to Heronhoe within the hour. The Shrine of Aesculapius he used to call it, you know."

"How do you know he hasn't been to Wheeler?" Giles objected.

Biddy shot a withering glance at him. "How could he, without us knowing? I should have had to drive him if he'd gone, and if Wheeler had come within a mile of the Rectory the village would have been full of it. That man—that man with the horrible red beard—I'm sure he is the real explanation. That chessman means something. The very fact that he sent it to Albert proves something. He's brighter than we are."

Giles looked at Campion. "You think that fortune teller chap came here because of Judge Lobbett?" he asked.

Campion nodded. "It doesn't seem unlikely."

"And yet," Giles persisted, "you said yourself that he was a brilliant man. Could he be an ordinary spy? I never heard that Guffy Randall's fortune teller had a red beard. Straight, Campion, is there a chance that he could be Simister himself?"

Campion raised his head and his pale eyes did not waver.

"Well, there's always a chance, isn't there?" he said. "You see," he went on after a pause, "a snapper-up of unconsidered trifles like myself usually hears about a gentleman like that. He gets talked about in the profession, if you understand. I have never heard of this man before. That's why I wondered."

He got up and walked over to the fireplace and kicked a smouldering log in the grate. "That's all there is to it for tonight," he said. "There's nothing else to be done as far as I can see. Unless—" he swung round, a frown upon his face— "I'd forgotten. Of course. Perhaps the most important thing of all. Your message, Biddy. What did it mean?"

For an instant she looked at him blankly. In the excitement of the moment she had forgotten the last of the three curious bequests. She took up the slip of paper from her lap, where it had been lying.

"Tell Albert about our longest walk. God bless you, my dear."

"Your longest walk? Where was it? Where did you go?" Campion spoke eagerly, coming across the room to her and looking down into her face. "This may explain everything. Oh, what a fool I was!"

The girl strove to compose her mind. "We've gone for so

many walks," she began desperately. "We've walked all over the place together. We got lost on the saltings one night. Alice came out to meet us with a hurricane. That must have been the time," she went on suddenly. "We reckoned we'd done fifteen miles." ·

Campion shook his head. "That doesn't tell us much. What else happened? Where did you go?"

The girl struggled to remember. "We crossed the Stroud and went off on the farther saltings," she said slowly. "We went on for miles until we came to a belt of quick mud. Then we turned back. I remember it now. The sky grey and the water the same colour, the drab mud with the saltings brown beside it and the dykes cut out in red. Then there was the great pool of 'soft'. That was all."

Campion was looking at her intently. "Think, Biddy," he said. "Think, my sweet. Was that all? How did you know when you came to the quick mud, for instance?"

"Oh, there was a board up, you know. There always is." She spoke carelessly, but then an expression of horror spread over her face. "Oh, I see now," she said breathlessly. "The board said 'Danger', Albert."

CHAPTER X

The Insanity of Swithin Cush

GILES and Judge Lobbett walked one on either side of Dr.
Wheeler out of the long room at the thatched *Dog and
Pheasant,* and down the flint road towards the green and the
Dower House.

It was still early. The inquest had taken scarcely half an
hour and the village was still discussing the affair in the
taproom.

The morning was very sunny, although it was cold for
late May and the last of the May-blossom trembled in a chill
wind. The whole of Mystery Mile looked as if it were decked
out for a country wedding. The *Dog and Pheasant* itself was
covered with large white cabbage roses, and the green was
knee-high and full of buttercups.

Giles walked along, his hands thrust into his pockets, his
chin on his breast. He walked slowly, his long strides keeping pace easily beside the shorter steps of the older man.

Dr. Wheeler talked volubly. The case had interested him,
and he found Judge Lobbett the best of audiences. The
American had the great gift of being interested in everything
with which he came into contact, and the doctor, whose
profession did not bring him up against many intellectual
men, was only too anxious to give his opinions.

"A significant case," he was saying. "I don't like parsons as a rule. Too little to think about makes them narrow. But Swithin Cush was an entirely different proposition, don't you know. I've known him ever since I came to this part of the county thirty years ago. I attended him once only that I remember. A strained tendon in his foot or something. But a more healthy, hearty-living old man I never saw. And yet he gets an idea into his mind, imagines all sorts of things, and then goes and blows his head off one fine day without with-your-leave or by-your-leave. We're beginning to know more about the power of the mind every day."

Judge Lobbett shot a bright sidelong glance at him.

"Then there was absolutely no trace of any disease?"

"Not at all, sir." The doctor spoke emphatically. "Just as I told Topliss in the court there. There was no reason why he shouldn't have gone on living perfectly healthily for another twenty years. And yet it's one of the most common forms of delusion," he went on. "I always put it down myself to the fact that the emotion of fear acts more noticeably on the digestive organs than on any other. Therefore once a man is thoroughly afraid that he has a malignant growth, he'll have plenty of physical corroboration to help convince him. What a pity! He had only to come to me, and I could have reassured him. He never complained to you, Giles, I suppose?"

The boy shook his head. He was hardly listening to the doctor's explanations. This sane matter-of-fact elucidation of the mystery, which he would have believed so willingly had it not been for the contents of the long yellow envelope which Campion had brought over from the Rectory, now had very little meaning for him, based as it was on only half the facts. He could not help feeling that it was an explanation that St. Swithin himself had devised.

A faint smile passed over Judge Lobbett's face. "Your inquest reminded me of the sort of thing we still have in the West. Everybody knew everybody else and there was a sort of general apology all round for having to go into an unpleasant business. What would happen if you had a murder case?"

The doctor looked vague. "Oh, I suppose the procedure would be a little more strict," he said. But he spoke without conviction. It was evident that in his opinion the chances of anything so unlikely happening in his little corner of Suffolk were sufficiently remote.

"Poor Biddy!" he went on suddenly. "She won't take this easily, I'm afraid. They were great friends, she and the old man. He did his best to take your father's place, Giles."

Giles did not reply, and Lobbett nodded.

"My girl's with her over at the Dower House," he said. "They get on very well together, those two." He stooped and threw a stone for Addlepate, who had waited in the bar for Giles during the inquest and now gambolled foolishly in the dust.

"Remarkable what a durned fool that dog is," he observed, as the mongrel darted off in pursuit, changed his mind halfway, and finally collapsed in the road, falling over his own feet.

An unexpected grin appeared upon the doctor's face. "That's so," he said. "I had to save his life once by artificial respiration. Biddy's very fond of him, don't you know. She was throwing some bread to the ducks on the horse pond and this crazy animal went in and tried to imitate 'em. Well, ducks keep their heads under water for some time, don't they? Swim upside down, in fact. He was just on drowned when she got him out."

Addlepate, who was now barking furiously at a dead mole, suddenly forgot his enthusiasm and returned to walk sedately behind them, his nose very close to the road. The doctor looked back at him.

"The silly part about that is," he said, "that I don't believe he can smell a thing."

Lobbett laughed. "He's Campion's dog, isn't he?" he said.

The doctor nodded. "They say like dog, like master," he observed dryly.

As they reached the Dower House they saw Mr. Campion's little car standing outside the gate. The young man himself was bending over the open bonnet, flushed and heated. Marlowe and Biddy stood with Isopel in the porch watching him.

"Hullo, he's back!" said Giles, hurrying forward to where Addlepate was already prostrated before the car, all four legs waving in the air.

As the two older men advanced more slowly towards the group a figure emerged from the thatched post office and village shop and hurried towards them. The newcomer, although in his shirt sleeves, was unexpectedly and unsuitably well dressed. He wore wide pin-striped trousers, a snugly fitting black waistcoat, patent-leather shoes, and an immaculate white shirt with a stiff collar. For the rest, he was a large white-looking man with fair hair so closely cropped that he appeared almost bald.

This was Mr. Kettle, the village "foreigner": that is to say, he was not a Suffolk man, but had been born, so it was believed, as far away as Yarmouth, a good forty miles off. His excessive politeness to the "Gentry", as he insisted upon calling them, and his gentle superiority to the "Locals" (also his own term), made him at once the chief topic of conversation and the most unpopular man in the village community. He lived with his daughter, a sour-faced young woman, white and flabby as himself, and between them they managed not only the post office but the only shop for six miles.

He came through the long grass of the green at a dignified amble and bounded on to the road two or three paces ahead of the judge and the doctor.

"Letters, sir," he said breathlessly, disclosing a Norfolk accent of the worst type, over which a certain veneer of "refeenment" had been spread. "The second post 'as just come. And popping my 'ead out of the door, sir, I said to my daughter, I said, 'There's the new squire'." He laid an unpleasant unction on the last word, and his attempt to curry favour was sickeningly transparent. He gasped again for breath, and hurried on. "And my daughter, sir, she said, 'Take it over to him, Dad'. And so I did."

He handed the square white envelope to the judge as he finished speaking and stood squelching his white hands together, a ridiculous smirk on his face.

"We 'ave a very nice little shop 'ere, sir, and any time you're wanting anything up at the Manor 'all, sir, we shall only be too 'appy to send it up. Any time of the day or night, sir."

The judge, who had listened in some bewilderment to this oration, his ears unaccustomed to the two distinct accents, the one affected and the other natural, felt in his pocket, having come to the conclusion, in common with so many other visitors to Europe, that the safe rule is, "When in doubt, tip".

Mr. Kettle, who had determined to be obliging at all costs, refused the coin magnificently. "Oh no, sir," he said. "Only too 'appy to do anything for you. Any time of the night or day, sir." And turning, he ran off through the long grass, flapping his hands against his sides as he ran.

As the doctor went to join the others Lobbett opened his letter. They were gathered round Giles.

"Yes, 'Suicide during temporary insanity,' " he was saying as the doctor came up. "Topliss was very decent, I thought. It didn't take very long. Alice was there, very cut up. George's wife took her home. I've brought the doc in to lunch, Biddy. How long has Albert been back?"

"Only about ten minutes." It was Campion himself who spoke. "The bit of sardine tin that keeps my carburettor from leaking into the mag has slipped its bootlace. I shall be a minute or so. Some of the rigging has come adrift."

Giles went over to him, and together they bent over the miscellaneous collection of hairpins and string that seemed to make Campion's car go.

"Well?" he murmured. "Did you see him—Alaric Watts, I mean?"

"Yes," said Campion, producing a small fountain of petrol from the carburettor, "but there's no lift in the fog in his direction. He was very grieved at his old pal's death, but that's about all. He knows no more than we do."

"That means, then," said Giles, "that St. Swithin was really insane when he wrote us."

"Yes," said Campion thoughtfully, "either that or else—"

He glanced at his friend over the top of his spectacles. "Or else the 'serious trouble' has not yet arisen."

Giles did not reply. Campion straightened his back and stood looking after the others, who, at Biddy's invitation, were disappearing into the house.

"Giles," he said suddenly, "do you like that American chap?"

"Marlowe? One of the best. I like him immensely. Biddy and I were talking about him this morning. She admires that type, you know."

"That's what I mean," said Campion. "Now if I were to grow a beard," he went on with apparent seriousness, "what colour would you suggest? Something with lure, to cover all this up?" He indicated his face with a gesture. "Let's go in, shall we? I hate to be out of anything."

They reached the morning-room, where they were all gathered, drinking sherry as an aperitif. Judge Lobbett was speaking as they entered.

"I'm real sorry about this. I forgot every word about my letter to this firm. That picture got me interested, and as Miss Biddy had suggested it I wrote to them asking for the expert to be sent, directly before we all came over here that night. The things that happened after that put it right out of my mind." He put a typewritten letter down upon the table. "This note says their expert will arrive here by car to-morrow afternoon. I can easily put him off. I should feel it kind of ungracious to have him around at a time like this."

"Is that about the pseudo-Romney?" Biddy came forward. "Because if so, please don't let this—this terrible thing make any difference. St. Swithin never disobliged any-one in his life and I know he'd hate to do it now. I feel he'd never forgive me if I let it make any difference to anyone's plans."

She spoke quietly, but with such sincerity and conviction that it made it impossible for the old man to refuse her.

Giles nodded. "That's true," he said. "Biddy's right about St. Swithin. How I feel about it is: we can't do any-thing. Let's get away from the horror of it if we can." He paused, and added reflectively, "If you're going to have an expert, there're some rather curious old chairs in the north attic. Father and I used to have great arguments about them. He always swore they were Stuart products and I always thought they were early Victorian junk. I'd like to know if I was right or not."

Marlowe was dubious. "A chap who knew all there was to know about Romneys might not know anything about furniture, don't you think?" he suggested.

His father picked up the letter. "It says here, 'The famous international expert, Mr. A. Fergusson Barber'!"

"Eh?" said Mr. Campion.

Biddy turned to him with interest. "Do you know him?"

Mr. Campion sighed. "I've met him," he said. "He was on the *Elephantine*. As far as pictures are concerned he may be the Big Bezezus himself, but as a guide, philosopher, and friend he's a menace."

Marlowe grinned. "He's a bore?"

"A bore?" said Mr. Campion. "He's worse than a movie star's confessions."

CHAPTER XI

The Maze

THEY were having tea on the lawn at the Manor the following day. The weather had turned warm and the innovation was a pleasant one. Judge Lobbett had insisted that his "landlords", as he called them, should be present when the art expert arrived. The old man was anxious to do all he could to dispel the gloom which had settled over the Dower House, and since Giles himself had expressed the desire to carry on as usual, he was all the more eager to help.

Mr. Campion had accompanied the twins as a matter of course, and Addlepate escorted them. He was interested in the Lobbetts, cherishing a belief that strangers were more easily prevailed upon to feed him out of hours than the friends who prescribed his daily diet.

They had sat long over their tea and it was almost six o'clock when they arose. The sun was dropping behind the house, the last blaze of yellow light shone over the garden, gilding the green leaves and warming the pale browns of the tree stems. The old house looked mellow and resplendent in the haze. The air was very warm and clear and the sound of clanking water pails and the lowing of cows sounded distinctly from the yard on the other side of the stables a quarter of a mile away.

Some of the peace and contentment of the evening settled upon them. They spoke softly and lazily, and Mr. Campion permitted himself some relief from the rigorous restraint placed upon his natural methods of self-expression during the past few days.

"Isn't it lovely?" Isopel spoke enthusiastically.

Campion followed her gaze round the wide shrub-encircled lawn, through the high trees to the park land beyond.

"Charming," he said. "I knew a man once, though, who said the country wasn't the country without paper bags. He was a millionaire at the time, having made all his money in the jellied-eel business. The only country he knew was Burnham Beeches and Epping on a bank holiday. When he had made his fortune and bought a big estate in Surrey he wasn't at all satisfied with it. The staff was in an awful stew until one of the secretaries imported half a ton of orange skins, a few peanut shells, and a gross or so of paper bags. That transformed the place, and the old boy's lived there very happily ever since. It's all a question of ideals, you know."

Judge Lobbett rose from his deck chair. "How about a walk round the estate?" he said. "George tells me there's a maze over on the east side of the park."

"So there is," said Giles. "Though I'm afraid it's not in very good condition. It hasn't been clipped for the last year or so."

"It's still there, though," said Biddy. "Shall we go and have a look at it?"

"Talking of mazes," said Mr. Campion, "I knew a man once who did a remarkable spot of Rip Van Winkleing at Hampton Court. A gardener found him and mistook him for a haycock, his beard had grown so, and—"

"Shut up!" said Giles. "I can't stand it, old boy. Imitate something if you must be funny."

"Spurned!" said Mr. Campion affably. "But I'd like to see the maze. Perhaps there'll be an opportunity for me to recount my witty little anecdote later on."

They trooped off over the lawn to the narrow paved walk which, enclosed by low hedges, led through the park land to a second and larger orchard and kitchen garden on the east side. At the far end of a wide strip of grass in which fruit trees stood they saw the maze before they reached it—a great square of yew, the dense bushes, which had once been trimmed as square as a marble block, now overgrown and uneven.

"It's quite big," said Biddy. "It stretches down the rest of the field on one side, and there's the road at the end. We used to play here a lot when we were children, but I don't know if I could find my way through it now."

She turned to find herself speaking only to Mr. Campion. Judge Lobbett had gone on a little way in front with his usual interests, and Giles and Isopel lagged behind. Marlowe had not come with them.

When she saw him her expression changed. She linked her arm through his. "You haven't found out anything— about St. Swithin, or the red chessman?"

Campion's arm gripped hers. "Biddy," he said softly, "promise me. Never, never, never say anything about the red chessman to anyone. Never. Promise me."

She looked at him sharply, a suggestion of fear in her eyes. He smiled at her reassuringly. "Don't worry, old dear. Nothing to get the wind up about. But you must give me that promise."

He did not attempt to disguise the seriousness of his tone.

"I promise," she said, "and Giles—?"

"That's all right," said Campion; "he's wise. He won't even mention it amongst ourselves."

They walked on a little way in silence.

Mr. Campion allowed his vacuous expression to fade for an instant. "I say, Biddy, can you ever forgive me for getting you into this?"

She shot him one of her sharp inquiring glances. "Then you think St. Swithin had something to do with this—this other affair?"

Mr. Campion did not look at her. "How could he?" he said. But he spoke dully and without conviction.

"Is this the entrance?" Judge Lobbett's shout made them both look up. The old man was standing against the yew hedge, his light flannel suit outlining him sharply against the sombre background.

"That's right," Biddy shouted back. "I'm afraid you'll have to push your way through, here and there. Do you want to know the key?"

"No, I'll find my way myself." He disappeared into the green walls on the last word. "It's going to be easy," he called, his voice only slightly muffled by the hedges.

"My own tour," said Mr. Campion, "which our impetuous friend has missed, will be personally conducted by the greatest living authority on Barratry, Trigonometry, and the Kibbo Kift. I shall charge a small fee—"

"Good heavens, he's at it again," said Giles, coming up with Isopel. "Where's Mr. Lobbett? In the maze?"

"I shall charge a small fee," repeated Mr. Campion, ignoring him, "for my service. This will include tea, a free presentation plate, and a bootiful voo of the ruins. Part two of my lecture will be for adults only."

"Dad's very quiet," said Isopel. "I bet he can't find his way and won't own to it."

"We'll see," said Giles, and shouted, "Found the centre, Mr. Lobbett?"

"I'm just on it." The reply came back from the middle of the dense square of yew. "It's not very overgrown. There ought to be a lot of birds' nests here."

"They're not fond of yew," Biddy remarked.

"I don't believe it's got a middle," came the judge's voice. "Are you coming?"

"Righto." It was Giles who called back. "But the key is, turn to the left whenever possible."

Mr. Campion looked at him coldly. "Cheating," he said. "Don't forget the old college, Brother. What would the boys of St. Agatha's say? Remember our proud school motto, '*Floreat Fauna*', which being translated means, of course, 'Grow, you little beasts'."

Giles was about to retort when Biddy, who had been looking in the direction from which they had come, interrupted him.

"Oh, look," she said. "He's arrived."

They looked round to see Marlowe coming down the path towards them, and beside him, smiling, self-important, and talking volubly, was Mr. Fergusson Barber.

An expression of dismay appeared on Isopel's face. "Oh, I remember him now," she said. "He was the bore at our table on the *Elephantine*. Look at Marlowe."

The others smiled. The young American's disgust was evident. His keen dark face wore a dubious look, and he made no attempt to interrupt Mr. Barber's flow. The expert carried a large flat picture case under his arm, but it did not hamper the freedom of his gesticulations.

"Hullo!" Campion murmured to Giles. "He's brought some pictures to sell. I bet he says they're Cotmans. Whenever I see a leather case like that I say, 'Hullo. The Great Defunct has been at it again.'"

By this time Marlowe and the expert were upon them. Mr. Barber bowed gravely to the ladies, and recognizing Campion, greeted him as a brother.

"We meet again, my friend," he rumbled. "You think I don't remember you," he continued in the same gusty bellow, "but I never forget a name or a face. Nothing ever escapes me. No, no, don't remind me. You told me your name just as you were leaving, I remember. Ah, yes, I have it. Mr. Memorial—Albert Memorial."

Everyone looked at Campion accusingly. That gentleman seemed not in the least abashed.

"How absurd of me," he said. "I gave you my address by mistake. My name is Campion. Albert Campion. You see how the error occurred."

Although his gravity was perfect the others were not successful, and the Oriental glanced at them suspiciously. Biddy reddened, and kicked Mr. Campion gently to relieve her feelings.

"You want to see Judge Lobbett, don't you?" she said, turning to Mr. Barber. "He's exploring the maze. I'll call him."

Mr. Barber appeared interested. "In the maze?" he said. "Ah, yes, I see now. He is in the bush, as the Australians say."

"Well, we're all a little bit up the garden this afternoon," said Mr. Campion.

Marlowe introduced the others hastily, and Giles inquired politely if the visitor had had a good run down.

"Magnificent!" Mr. Barber threw out a fat hand. "I did not realize it was so far. That is why I am a little late. Then I was held up by a police trap just on the far side of the road that joins this place to the mainland. I saw no sense in it. I told the policemen so. On a main road, yes, but at the beginning of a tiny village which leads nowhere, there is no point in it. Unless, why, of course"—his face broadened into a grin—"I understand. They are there to protect Judge Lobbett."

As soon as he had spoken he realized the bad taste of his remark. He opened his mouth and was about to make bad worse by apologizing when the situation was saved by Mr. Campion.

"Had you got your licence?" he said. "It means rather a lot to us," he went on with embarrassing earnestness. "Police funds are rather low, and we need a good fine or two to set us on our feet again. Even a five-bob touch would help," he added wistfully.

Mr. Barber laughed uproariously. "What a joke, what a joke!" he said. "I was all right. I could not be touched, in either sense of the word. I too make jokes," he added, a little proudly.

"Well, where is Dad?" said Marlowe. "He must have had enough of the maze by now. Hullo, Dad! Half a minute!"

His voice sounded clearly over the still sunlit garden. There was an echo at the point where he stood, and his own words came back mockingly across the fields. There was no reply.

"He's foxing," said Isopel. "He's got lost."

"Let's go in and get him out," said Biddy. "I bet he hasn't found the centre."

"But he must have done," said Giles. "I shouted the key to him. Call again, Marlowe."

"Here, Dad! seriously"—Marlowe's voice rose. "Here's a visitor to see you. You must come out."

Once again the echo was his only reply.

A faintly scared expression flickered into Isopel's eyes. "I suppose he's all right?" she said.

Her alarm passed from one to the other of them. The smile left Campion's face, and he hurried forward to the opening in the yew hedge.

"Mr. Lobbett," he shouted, "answer us, please. You're scaring us."

They listened with more anxiety now, a growing presentiment of danger becoming more and more firmly fixed in their minds.

"He does not answer," said Mr. Barber idiotically.

Biddy hurried forward. "Come on, Giles," she said. "We can find our way through the place. I'll go straight to the centre, you go down the blind alleys." She disappeared into the green fastness, Giles at her heels. The others congregated at the mouth of the maze, listening breathlessly. Isopel called suddenly, her voice shrill and appealing.

"Daddy! Daddy! Answer me."

Marlowe's face grew very pale, and he put his arm around the girl.

"This is crazy," he said. "He must be there. There's no other way out, is there?"

"I don't think so." Campion spoke with unaccustomed seriousness. "A maze never has a second door."

Biddy's voice silenced him. "I'm here at the centre," she said. "There's no sign of him, Giles."

"Half a moment," the boy's voice answered her. "No luck yet. Try that false exit from the centre."

The search went on in feverish silence. Mr. Campion, who had hitherto been standing rather foolishly before the entrance to the maze, now turned to Marlowe and Isopel. "You go round to that side," he said, "and I'll cut round this. He may have found some opening."

"What shall I do?" said Mr. Barber.

"You stay here and give us a call if you see anyone come out," said Campion, and started off round the east side of the maze. He climbed the hedge with some difficulty and scrambled along the ditch by the field. The minutes passed quickly. Campion met Marlowe in the road which skirted the fourth side of the yew puzzle. Their expressions betrayed their lack of success.

"It's absurd," Marlowe said, as if in answer to some unspoken question. "We're getting the wind up about nothing, of course. The whole darned place is as sound as an icebox. There isn't any way out except the one he went in by. He must be in there. He's playing the fool with us. I guess he doesn't realize how jumpy we are." The words were belied by his tone. In spite of the evidence of his own eyes, which proved to him that there was no second way out of the maze, he was afraid.

Mr. Campion seemed stupefied. Had the situation been less serious his expression of utter bewilderment would have been comic.

"We'll get round to the others," he said. "He'll probably be with them."

A light step on the road behind them made them swing round expectantly. It was Biddy. Her face was pale, her brown eyes dark and startled.

"Albert," she said breathlessly, "he's gone. We've combed the maze, Giles and I, and there's not a trace of him. Not a glimpse—not a sound. It's as if he'd disappeared into the earth."

CHAPTER XII

The Dead End

"IT's no good hanging about the maze any longer." Biddy spoke helplessly. "He can't be here."

She and Isopel were standing in the entrance to the yew puzzle. Mr. Campion had dashed down to interview the police trap on the far side of the Stroud. Giles was still searching every corner of the maze with dogged obstinacy, and Marlowe with the servants was scouring the grounds. Mr. Barber, a stolid expression of surprise upon his face, was seated bolt upright in a deck chair upon the lawn, his leather case upon his knee, considerably bewildered by the whole affair. Addlepate, as upon all other occasions when he might conceivably have been useful, had entirely disappeared.

Isopel had grown very pale. She looked more like her brother than ever. Her features seemed to have become sharper and her eyes larger in the last ten minutes.

Biddy was frankly flustered. She had spent all her life in the country, and the rapid sequence of startling events which had begun with the arrival of the Lobbetts and now showed no prospects of ending, had shaken up her placid nature until she had become mentally dizzy.

"But it's impossible," she said, her voice rising a little on the final word. "He *can't* have gone. It's like magic."

Isopel shook her head and her lips moved silently. She seemed to be struggling for words.

"They've followed us—here. I knew we couldn't get away from them. I knew—I—"

She put out her hand as if to save herself, and Biddy, catching a glimpse of her face, moved forward just in time to catch her before she collapsed.

Faced with a problem with which she could deal, Biddy's practical nature reasserted itself. She let the other girl down gently into a sitting position and thrust her head between her knees. A shout to Giles brought him stumbling out of the maze.

He let out a short nervous exclamation when he saw the girl on the grass, and came running towards them. He looked at Biddy with eyes full of horror.

"Good heavens, she's not dead, is she?" he said.

"Of course not, you fool," said Biddy, whose nervousness had turned into irritation. "Pick her up and carry her into the house. She's only fainted. Poor kid, she's frightened out of her life. And so am I, Giles. Where on earth is he?"

Giles did not appear to be listening to her. He was looking down at the white-faced girl whose head lolled so heavily against his shoulder, and whatever he was thinking, he did not confide it to Biddy. He carried Isopel into the house and set her down on her bed, where he left her to his sister's ministrations, then went back stolidly to the maze, which his own faith in cold reason would not allow him to leave.

He stepped into the dark bushes and found his way along the narrow paths, going over and over ground that he had already searched. The grass was sparse and rank in the sunless ways, and altogether so beaten down that it was impossible to discover any tracks. He went on searching systematically, and at length, pausing in a cul-de-sac on the west side, he remained for some time regarding the hedge before him speculatively. One of the yew trees was dead and there was a decided hole near the ground, leading into the ditch that skirted the hay field which flanked the garden. He scrambled through it himself: it was a comparatively simple matter. The discovery relieved him to a certain extent, for although it did not lead him materially nearer to the solution of the puzzle, it eliminated that element which Biddy had called "magic" and which had been so abhorrent to his prosaic mind.

The ditch in which he found himself was dry and had recently been cleared. He could see up and down it unimpeded, on his left as far as the road and on his right to the end of the field, some two hundred yards distant. The hay was ready for cutting, and as he stood in the ditch it waved above him higher than his head. It would be perfectly possible for a small army to have hidden in the wide dry ditch without being seen from the road, but there was no evidence of a struggle of any sort.

Unsatisfied, Giles returned to the maze the way he had come. He searched the cul-de-sac carefully. The light was going, and it was getting dark between the high yew hedges. He was afraid to move about too much lest he should destroy any traces there might be. At length, however, he paused and squatted down upon his heels. A cigarette which had burnt itself out where it had fallen lay undisturbed upon the grass, the long grey ash unscattered. The smoker had evidently thrown it down or had knocked it out of his mouth the moment he had lit it.

Giles hesitated, and left it where it lay. He had no great faith in himself as a detective. He mentally resigned the secret of the maze to Mr. Campion, in whom he had a perfect and childlike faith. He walked out cautiously and pushed on towards the centre, looking about him anxiously for any further sign of the judge or his captors. But he was unsuccessful, and he reached the middle without further discoveries. The stone bird bath with its decoration of bulbous amorelli was covered with creepers and moss. It had evidently been undisturbed for years. There was not even a pathway round it. The grass, seizing upon the sheltered but airy space, had grown high, and there was no track through it.

While he was standing there undecided he heard Campion's voice shouting from the roadway, "Hullo! Anyone in there?"

He called back eagerly, "Any luck?"

"Not a trace. It's the durndest mad thing I ever struck." It was Marlowe who answered. "And you?"

"I don't know," said Giles. "Come down the ditch at the side of the hay field and I'll show you." He turned back and went to meet them, stepping carefully through the cul-de-sac and squatting down in the opening by the dead yew. Presently they came along, stumbling through the ditch, Campion in particular slipping about considerably on the uneven ground.

"See this?" said Giles. "This is the only way anybody could get in or out, bar the entrance, as far as I can see, and I've gone through the place with a comb. There's a cigarette here too. You'd better come in and have a look."

They scrambled through the hedge, making the hole considerably wider.

"That's the judge all right," said Mr. Campion, as Giles pointed out the cigarette. "He must have lit it and dropped it. That doesn't help us much, though. We all know he was in here. The question is, how did anyone get him out without his making the least sound or putting up any struggle? There's no sign of a row here, you see, and we didn't hear a whisper."

"And we haven't told you the most extraordinary thing of all yet," said Marlowe. "There were only two old cops there—neither of them a hundred per cent, but not altogether dumb—and they swear that not a car, vehicle, or pedestrian has left Mystery Mile since four o'clock this afternoon. And that's not all. I've been up to George's brother, 'Anry, who's been sitting outside the inn at the corner of the road there, and he swears that he hasn't seen a soul except Mr. Barber, who stopped to ask him the way and seems to have impressed him considerably."

Giles stared at him. "Then he must be on the estate," he said, and the thought seemed to relieve him. "He couldn't have lost his memory or something, could he? Has he ever gone off like this before?"

This attempt to attribute the affair to a natural cause was a new idea. Marlowe seized it hopefully. "No," he said, "he hasn't. But this trouble hanging round put the possibility of that sort of thing clean out of my head. Suppose he had a brainstorm or something? The things he's been through lately would be enough to bring it on. He might easily have gone wandering off on his own somewhere. Couldn't we turn out the village and have a hunt for him? I can't believe that he could stay lost for long in a little place like this."

"Of course," said Giles slowly, "there's the estuary, you know. Could they have got him off in a boat?"

"That won't be difficult to trace," said Mr. Campion. "Two or three men with a prisoner would be noticed in a place like this. When was high tide, Giles?"

"That's what I was thinking," the boy replied. "It was high tide about five. It must have been still well up at the time he disappeared. We'll get the village out, anyway. They're certain to know if there have been any strangers around. There are only about six rowboats in the place, now I come to think of it. It's such a long way to the water across the saltings. I say," he went on abruptly, "don't you think we'd better tell all this to Isopel? About the idea of a brainstorm, I mean. She came over faint out here about twenty minutes ago, and I carried her in. She's with Biddy now, but I feel that if we could reassure her, even a little bit, we ought to."

They were filing out of the maze as he spoke, and they turned towards the house.

"Of course," said Marlowe, "the staff's hunting round the place now. We may hear something any minute."

It was only then that the others realized the strain under which he was labouring. "Something's bound to turn up," said Mr. Campion reassuringly. But his pale face was expressionless and there was a trace of alarm in his eyes.

They found the house in considerable commotion. Biddy came running out to meet them. After they had reported their discoveries to her, and she had satisfied herself that no more could be done at the moment, she turned to them.

"I've shoved some cold food on the table. You'd better

eat it. I'm trying to make Isopel eat, too. Perhaps if you all
sit down you'll be able to think of something. Nothing's
even logical at present."

As they went into the dining-room they were startled to
see the smiling Mr. Barber rise out of the window-seat.

"Oh!" said Biddy, surprised into frankness. "I'd forgotten all about you. I'm so sorry."

"Not at all." Mr. Barber spoke complacently. "I will wait
until Mr. Lobbett can see me. You see," he went on confidentially, "I have here something that I think will interest
him." He tapped the leather case significantly. "The works
of Cotman are only now beginning to be fully appreciated.
But since their worth has become known the samples of this
genius have naturally become rare. I think I may say that
the discovery of a hitherto unknown painting of his Greta
period is an event, the importance of which can hardly be
overestimated. Now"—with a magnificent gesture he proceeded to unlock the silver catches—"you shall judge for
yourselves."

The expressions of bewilderment which had appeared
upon the faces of his audience gave place to those of incredulity as they realized that his mind was on some picture or
other that he had come down with the intention of selling.

Marlowe stepped up to him. "You'll forgive us," he said.
"I thought you understood. My father has mysteriously—"
He jibbed at the word "disappeared". "I mean we can't find
him."

Mr. Barber smiled and spread out his hands. "It does not
matter," he said. "I will wait."

Marlowe lost his patience. "Don't you understand?" he
said. "We don't know where he is."

Mr. Barber's reproachful smile did not vanish. "I have
come down to value the other picture," he said. "There will
be no compulsion to buy my Cotman. I think I will wait,
having come so far."

His cheerful non-acceptance of the facts was too much
for them. Giles repressed a violent desire to shout at him.
Marlowe turned away helplessly. "Oh, wait then," he said,
and quite obviously dismissed the man from his mind.

Mr. Barber bowed and sat down again, nursing his precious case.

Addlepate's single sharp imperative bark, demanding entrance, startled them all. "Curse him!" said Giles, getting up out of force of habit to open the door. No one looked at the little dog as he came padding in. They were eating mechanically, almost in silence, waiting for the coherent frame of mind which Biddy had foretold.

"Oh, down, darling, down!" Biddy spoke irritably as the only creature in the room faintly interested in food pawed her arm.

"Ah," said Mr. Barber conversationally. "The dog. The animal sacred to the English."

No one took any notice of the opening, but Giles glanced moodily at the little mongrel, vaguely seeking inspiration there.

His reward was sudden and startling. Folded through the ring of the dog's collar, and indubitably placed there by human hand, was a small twist of paper.

Before he could speak, Campion had seen it also. He called the dog over to him. They watched him fascinated as he unwound the strip of paper and spread it out upon the tablecloth.

They left their seats and crowded round him, leaning over his shoulder. It was a page torn from a notebook, and the few words were scrawled as if the sender had written under great difficulty. Marlowe read out the message in a shaking voice:

"Am safe if blue suitcase is not lost.

"I don't quite get this last bit," said Marlowe. "The paper's got crumpled. Oh, wait a bit—yes, I see it now.

"Keep the police out of this. Safer without."

They exchanged frightened glances.

"Is it your father's writing?" It was Giles who spoke.

"Yes, that's his hand all right. The leaf's torn from his

notebook, too, I think." Marlowe raised his eyes and looked round at them, bewilderment and incredulity mingling on his face. "Not a sign of anyone on the roads, not a trace of a stranger in the place, and then out of the air—this," he said huskily. "What do you make of it? I feel I've gone mad."

CHAPTER XIII

The Blue Suitcase

IT was very nearly dawn before the last of the yellowing hurricane lanterns which had been bobbing over the saltings and in every nook and cranny of Mystery Mile all night took the path across the park and came to a stop outside the big kitchen door at the back of the hall. There were ten of them, carried by the entire male population of the village, with the exception of two old men who were bedridden and a few small boys.

They were an untidy red-faced crowd, considerably wearied by their night of search, but intensely interested in the proceedings.

The distinction between the two main families, the Willsmores and the Brooms, was sharply defined: the Willsmores, lank dark people with quick beady eyes and a knowing expression; the Brooms, sturdier, more stolid, with large red bovine faces, and every variety of fair hair from red to yellow.

Cuddy, who had come over from the Dower House to help Mrs. Whybrow, the Manor housekeeper, bustled about preparing tea or mulled beer for each newcomer.

The outer kitchen where they were assembling was one of those great stone outbuildings without which no East An-

glian house is complete. It was tacked on to the rest of the
Manor and was stone-floored with a great brick fireplace
whose chimney was built out into the room. The trestle tables had been pushed back against the whitewashed walls,
and forms and settles dragged round the roaring fire.

Mrs. Whybrow was a housewife of the old school, and
black hams of her own curing hung from the centre beam,
high above their heads. The beer barrel was in the room,
and the great kettles of boiling water steamed on the wide
hearthstone.

The housekeeper and Cuddy were sisters; both old
women had entered the service of the Paget family when
they were girls, and they considered themselves quite as
much a part of it as any of the household. As they hurried
round now, doling out the great white mugs of beer and
hunks of home-made bread and yellow cheese, they looked
marvellously alike with their greying hair and their stiff
white aprons crackling as they moved.

George and 'Anry were well to the fore, as became
George's dignity. They sat side by side. 'Anry was the
younger by a year or so. He was considerably less proud of
himself than his brother, and was afflicted with a certain
moroseness, which, coupled with his natural inarticulate
tongue, made him something of a man of mystery in the
village. He was a simple old fellow with a goatee instead of a
fringe, which he eschewed out of deference to George, mild
brown eyes, and, when he permitted it, a slow and rather
foolish smile.

Mr. Kettle, the postmaster, who had come in after the
others with a great show of exhaustion, sat some little distance away from the crowd. He drank his beer from a glass,
a circumstance which seemed to make the beverage more
genteel to his way of thinking. He also wore a bowler hat,
and had wrapped himself up in an immense grey-and-white
striped scarf.

" 'E looks like an owd badger," remarked George in an
undertone to 'Anry. The observation was quite loud enough
to reach Mr. Kettle, but he remained magnificently aloof
and offered no retaliation.

One of the Broom boys, a great sandy-haired lout with the beginnings of a beard scattered over his chin like golden dust, repeated the jest, and the party tittered hysterically while George preened himself. Wit, he considered, was one of his strongest points.

"If yow'd a' found summat o' the foreigner instead o' 'tending yow was barmy, yow'd ha' summat more to tell Mr. Giles when he come in," said Cuddy sharply, forsaking her company accent for her native sing-song. "I heard him and Mr. Marlowe comin' in a minute ago."

A gloom fell over the party as they recollected the matter on hand.

"I had I owd dog on ut," remarked one of the Brooms, a great hulking cross-eyed fellow with a red moustache. "'E didn't find nobbut. 'E kept leadin' I back to I own house."

"'Owd dog go by smell," said George contemptuously, and once again there was laughter.

Cuddy banged a china mug down upon the table, her kindly old face paling with anger. "I'm ashamed o' the whole lot on yow," she said, her voice rising. "Don't none of yow realize that the foreign gentleman's lost? An' yow set here guzzling and laughing yow'sel's sillier'n yow was before."

"'E ain't a foreigner," said George. "'E talks same as I do."

"Anyone as don't be born 'ere is a foreigner, ain't they?" said the man with the red moustache, squinting viciously at Mr. Kettle.

"T'other gentleman wot come s'afternoon was a proper foreigner," said 'Anry, speaking entirely without the aid of George for one of the few times in his life. "'E couldn't 'ardly understand what I said to un. 'E got riled with I. I couldn't 'elp laughin'."

"Yow'll 'elp ut this minute," said Cuddy quickly. "Here come the house folk." Her sharp ears had caught the sound of Giles's voice in the passage, and the talk died down immediately, so that there was perfect silence in the kitchen when the wooden latch clicked, and Giles, followed by Marlowe, came into the room.

They too had been out on the saltings all night. Marlowe, who had clung to the idea that his father might have been the victim of a sudden loss of memory or brainstorm of some kind, despite the extraordinary message which Addlepate had brought in, had insisted on searching every corner of the place.

The two young men looked pale and worried as they pushed their way into the group.

"Anything to report?" Giles's voice slipped down a tone or two and there was the suspicion of a country accent in some of the words he used. "Now," he went on, "anyone who's seen anything unusual about the place, speak up right away. Let's hear about it."

There was silence in the room. The group shifted uneasily and glanced uneasily at one another.

"Us ain't seen nothin'," said George. "It do be a wonder." He spoke with a certain amount of satisfaction. Giles was nettled.

"It's no wonder you couldn't find him, George," he said. "He can't have disappeared into thin air, though. There must be some trace of him about the place."

"I could find 'im if annybody could," said George. "I be a wunnerful smart old man. But neither me nor 'Anry, we didn't see nothin'."

"I'm afraid the man's right, sir." Mr. Kettle's unpleasant voice was raised from his corner. "I myself 'ave been over all the principal means of exit from the estate and there is no trace as far as I can see. As you know, sir, we are practically an island, only more cut off, if I may say so, on account of the mud at low tide. You can depend upon it that we have done our best. Ever since I left my little shop, sir, at eight o'clock, I have walked—"

"Yes, yes, I know. That was very good of you," said Giles brusquely. He disliked Mr. Kettle quite as much as any of the village. "But the question I'm trying to get at is, have there been any strangers seen on the estate since yesterday morning?"

There was silence again in the big kitchen, and then

'Anry suddenly became violently agitated. He grew very red, and struggled for his words.

"Master Giles—I seen un. In a car wi' great red wheels. 'E stopped I and 'e said to I, 'Where's the big 'ouse?' and I said to 'e, suspicious-like, 'What do yow want ut for?' and—and—"

"Oh, you're talking about Mr. Barber," said Giles. "We know about him, 'Anry. He's in the next room now."

George nudged his brother self-righteously. "You be a fool, 'Anry," he said, wagging his head complacently. 'Anry cast his eyes down and looked supremely uncomfortable.

"How about boats?" said Giles. "Did anybody see a row-boat or any other kind round here between six and seven yesterday evening?"

"No, sir." It was George who spoke, and the others agreed with him. "We was nearly all on us t'home, you see, sir," explained one of the Willsmores. "We was gettin' our tea 'bout that time."

"You was out, George," said 'Anry.

George nodded. "I were. I were down by owd mist tunnel, Master Giles, right lookin' on the water, as you might say. And I didn't see nothin', like I would 'a' done 'ad there been a boat there. Come to think," he went on reflectively, "I come right round from t'lower meadows, so if there'd been a boat a-pullin' away from the shore I couldn't 'elp but see ut. No, sir," he finished, "I doubt there wasn't no boat left 'ere last night."

"Half a minute," said Marlowe. "What's the mist tunnel?"

George answered. "That be a pocket, as you might say, sir. A bit of a dip, like, in the salting. The mist do lie there. Summer and winter, 'tis always the same. It be a wunnerful place for snares. It used to be, I mean," he corrected himself as he caught Giles's eye upon him, "afore young squoire forbid snarin'."

"And you were down there, you say?" said Marlowe, "and you didn't see a soul?"

"Nothin'," said George. "Nothin' anywheres."

He passed his mug to Cuddy without a word. She took it

from him and set it in the big stone sink which ran all along one side of the room.

The old man left his seat and walked gingerly over the stones towards her. "That warn't for washin'," he said. "I've been tellin' of Master Giles, and tellin' of makes I thirsty."

Marlowe turned to Giles. "It's no good," he said. "They don't know anything. We'd better get back to the others. Those girls ought to get some sleep if possible."

They left the crowded kitchen and went back into the library, where Biddy lay dozing in a chair. She started up when they came in. "Any luck?" she said eagerly.

Their faces told her their news.

"Where are the others?" Giles glanced round the room.

"In the garden. As soon as it got light Isopel wanted to go out searching again. Albert wouldn't let her go alone. Mr. Barber went to bed. I put him in the honeysuckle room. Isopel and I thought it was the best thing to do."

Giles crossed over to the window and looked out: it was just light. There was still a greyness over everything, and the air was fresh and sweet. He caught sight of Isopel and Campion coming up through the trees towards the house. Campion was bending forward, looking at the girl, and Giles fancied he heard her laugh. There was nothing unusual in it; most people laughed with or at Mr. Campion, and yet he felt surprised, almost resentful. The situation had no funny side that he could see.

They came in two or three minutes later. Isopel was grave as before, but Giles's resentment against Campion grew. He had certainly succeeded in reassuring her where he himself had failed.

"See here," said Marlowe, "this thing's getting more and more peculiar every way you look at it. I must admit our crowd of sleuths aren't over-gifted, but it is their own back gardens they've been searching, isn't it? There's no boat been seen about, and none of those belonging to Mystery Mile are missing. Nor were any of them out yesterday."

"You know," said Biddy, suddenly sitting up, "what we're all doing is to ignore that note Addlepate brought in.

It's so extraordinary we've refused to accept it. Whatever it is, let's face it. There're three suppositions: either Mr. Lobbett has really been kidnapped and managed to scribble a few lines to warn us, or else he went quite mad and wrote it because he imagined the whole thing, or else someone else wrote it to put us off."

"She's right, you know," said Marlowe. "We've been jibbing at that note. But Dad wrote it, sure enough. And on a page of his own notebook, too. I remember it now. I'd like to believe," he went on slowly, "that Dad had written that sanely, even though it meant that he had fallen into their hands. But I can't believe it, because there's no sign of them. You don't tell me a stranger wouldn't be noticed on a place like this. A carload of men strong enough to get Dad away would be the most conspicuous thing in the scenery for miles. He must have crawled out of that maze alone, fixed the note on the dog's collar—heaven knows when—and then disappeared as if he'd dropped into a quicksand."

As he spoke the others started, and Mr. Campion and the twins exchanged glances. The explanation which had occurred to all of them at some time during the search had not been mentioned by any of them. As in many other places on the east coast, there were several spots of "soft" in the black mud which lay round Mystery Mile, and in these quick patches it was quite possible for a man to be sucked under and completely buried within a few minutes.

No one cared to suggest this possibility. Marlowe drew the sheet of paper from his pocket. " 'The blue suitcase,' " he said—"that's quite safe, isn't it, Isopel?"

The girl nodded. "Yes. Biddy and I brought it down here. We thought it would be safer." She smiled wryly. "I don't envy anyone trying to steal it. It weighs about a hundredweight. It's over in that corner." She pointed to the far end of the room, where the heavy leather suitcase with a blue canvas cover stood beside a bookcase.

"That's it," said Marlowe. "That's the one he was so anxious about all through the voyage. I think we'd better open it."

Isopel looked dubious. "I don't think he'd like it, Marlowe."

"I just can't help that." The boy spoke emphatically. "I've got to find out what this whole thing is about. We can't stand any more of it. If I ever get Dad back here again he's going to be so surrounded with police that a gnat couldn't get at him. That's all there is to it."

He strode across the room and took the case by the handle. The weight of it surprised him, and instead of lifting it he dragged it into the centre of the room. The others watched him, fascinated, as he dragged off the blue canvas cover and disclosed a leather-bound steel case with a lock that ran all one side of the box.

The boy looked at it doubtfully. "Now we're sunk," he said. "There's no key, of course. Father had that with him."

Giles and Biddy glanced at Mr. Campion, who was standing modestly in the background.

"It'll take a locksmith to do this," said Marlowe, "or a crook," he said bitterly.

Once again the brother and sister looked at their friend inquiringly. He came forward, looking slightly uncomfortable.

"This sort of thing looks awfully bad," he said. "I never show off in the ordinary way."

"Do you mean you can do it?" Isopel's look of wide-eyed astonishment brought a faint colour to Mr. Campion's cheek.

"Perhaps if you would all turn your backs—" he murmured, taking out a small piece of wire and what appeared to be a penknife from his pocket.

"You're not going to do it with that? It's only got two blades," said Biddy, staring at the knife, her curiosity overcoming her anxiety.

"Inaccurate," said Mr. Campion. "Two blades *and* a thing for taking nails out of horses' hooves. Whenever I see a horse hoof I take out this natty little instrument and—" As he was talking he was bending over the delicate lock, his thin fingers working with unbelievable rapidity. "I prod," he went on, "and prod—and—*hup!*—out she comes! *Voilà!*"

A sharp click accompanied the last word as the spring lock shot back. Their whisper of admiration was mingled with a certain amount of embarrassment. It was difficult to dismiss the notion that such remarkable skill in this particular direction was somehow discreditable. However, all such misgivings were forgotten as Marlowe slipped down upon his knees before the case to raise the lid.

As he lifted the heavy steel covering he disclosed a layer of newspaper. The others pressed round eagerly, hoping for at least some glimmer in the mystery which surrounded them.

Marlowe drew off the paper carefully and a murmur of surprise escaped them. Filling the entire case, and neatly stacked in half-dozens, were some forty or fifty, gaudily bound children's books. It looked like the supply for an infants' school-prize day.

Marlowe stretched out his hand and drew out a book gingerly as if he suspected it to contain some hidden explosive. He turned the leaves over: it was entitled *Robinson Crusoe Told to the Children,* and appeared to be perfectly genuine. They took out one book after another, turning over the pages of each. They were all in the same binding, some new, some patently second-hand, and appeared to be the complete output of a library called "The Kiddies' Own."

They were little green books profusely decorated with designs in gold, and pasted on the front of each was a coloured illustration of the story within. They consisted mostly of famous tales, simplified and bowdlerized for young people's consumption.

Campion and the others turned each copy over, hunting vainly for any mark in the margin or message scribbled on the flyleaves.

They hardly spoke, but went on steadily scouring every volume, until at last with the bright sun pouring in upon them through the open window they sat back and looked at each other in bewilderment and dismay. The most exhaustive and methodical search had revealed only that no copy differed to any great extent from its fellows, that they were, in fact, the most ordinary and uninteresting collection of children's books in the world.

Marlowe looked at Campion helplessly. "What do you make of it?" he said.

Mr. Campion glanced round at all of them. They were looking at him appealingly, asking for an explanation. He threw out his hands. "My dear old birds," he said, "I think I'm losing my speed. This finds you where it leaves me at present—high and dry. It all looks like good clean reading to me."

CHAPTER XIV

Campion to Move

MR. CAMPION was hidden in the high-backed Queen Anne chair in the faded drawing-room at the Dower House, and Biddy did not notice him at first when she came bustling in.

It was not until she caught sight of his long thin legs sprawled out across the hearthrug that she realized that he was there. She pounced on him immediately and spoke with conviction.

"Albert, if you don't call in the police and get rid of Mr. Barber for the Lobbetts this very day I shall have a nervous breakdown or hysterics or something. I can't bear it."

He sat back in his chair and grinned at her.

"You won't," he said. "You've got more real nervous stamina than all the rest of us put together."

Biddy did not smile. She remained staring down at him, a peculiar intensity in her eyes.

"You're a beast, Albert," she said. "I used to be awfully fond of you. I'd never seen you at work before. Now I think you're callous and—oh, and horrible!"

She was speaking hurriedly, her voice very near tears.

"There's Isopel and Marlowe nearly ill with grief and anxiety about their father for the last two days," she hurried on, "and all you do is to organize silly little searches over the island and advise them not to call in the police. You're making so little fuss about it that that idiot Barber doesn't even believe that Mr. Lobbett has disappeared."

Mr. Campion did not speak. He sat huddled in the corner of his chair, blinking at her behind his spectacles.

"Well, what are you going to do?" Biddy looked down at him angrily.

He rose to his feet, and walking up to her suddenly put his arm round her neck and kissed her vigorously. She gasped at him, astonishment predominating over every other emotion.

"What—what are you doing?" she expostulated, breaking away from him.

"Rough stuff," said Mr. Campion, and walked out of the room with unusual dignity. In the doorway he paused and looked back at her. "You'll be sorry when you see me in my magenta beard," he said.

Still puzzled, flustered and annoyed, she watched him from the porch as he crossed the green and entered the park gates.

Mr. Campion swaggered consciously until he was well out of sight of the Dower House, when his shoulders drooped; he walked more slowly, and he allowed himself a profoundly mournful expression, which persisted until he reached the Manor.

Marlowe was waiting for him.

"I've got it all set, as we said last night," he said. "There's one snag in it, however. Mr. Barber wants to come up with us. He's taken some photographs of the Romney and he wants to get a second opinion on them. He insists on driving us up. What shall we do?"

Mr. Campion seemed not in the least put out. "That's a good idea," he said. "Perhaps we can lose him in Town. I don't know about Isopel, but Biddy seems to have taken a dislike to him."

"Isopel's shown signs of strain, too," said Marlowe. "They've had to listen to him more than we have. Do you feel confident of this trip to the city?"

"It all depends on what you mean by 'confident'," said Mr. Campion. "I certainly feel that we shall have more chance of finding out where we are, through a few well-placed inquiries in Town, than we shall if we sit here and wait for something else to happen. If we leave Giles in charge he'll look after the girls quite as well as ever we could. He's hot dogs on the England, Home, and Beauty Act. I think if we get rid of Mr. Barber for them that'll be about the best thing we can do."

"Giles knows all about it then?" said Marlowe.

Mr. Campion nodded. "I put a bit of sugar on his nose and said 'Trust', and away I came."

Marlowe grinned. "They're charming folks," he said. "I've got the greatest admiration for Biddy."

He paused abruptly, but Mr. Campion made no comment.

He did not appear to have heard, and the conversation did not continue, for at that moment Mr. Barber appeared, bustling out of the doorway to the waiting car. He was smiling and self-engrossed as ever, and the leather case was still under his arm.

He was a little too fastidiously dressed. His rough brown tweed suit fitted snugly to his pear-shaped form, and his short wide feet were half hidden by speckless fawn-coloured spats.

"My friends, I have kept you waiting." He apologized profusely. "I hope you have persuaded Mr. Campion to be of our party, Mr. Lobbett. I am a chauffeur *par excellence,* I assure you. I drive, as you say, as well as the devil. I shall run you to London, take you where you will, and at six or seven o'clock I shall be ready to drive you back again."

Marlowe's jaw dropped. "But I thought, Mr. Barber," he said, "that you had seen all you wanted to of the Romney?"

Mr. Barber's bushy eyebrows rose. "But no," he said, "I am just begun. Besides, you must remember, I am acting for your father. Until I see him I shall not consider that I have carried out my commission. You see"—he tapped his leather case mysteriously—"I have something here that I know will interest him."

Marlowe glanced at Mr. Campion, who sighed but offered no comment, and the three climbed into the car, Campion hatless and without a coat. Biddy saw them flash past the Dower House, and her resentment against Mr. Campion grew as her curiosity was piqued.

Mr. Barber lived up to his word. His driving was really remarkable. His two passengers sat at the back of the car and alternately marvelled and trembled as he turned round at terrifying speeds to make foolish comments on the scenery, or to bellow inane stories at them while the hedges were blurred and indistinct by the sides of the road.

They reached London before lunch in spite of their late start, and Mr. Barber, who had his own ideas of what was the most important place in the city, drew up with a flourish outside Simpson's.

Lunch with Mr. Barber proved to be a greater ordeal than a journey in his company. Freed from the restraint of being a guest, his behaviour became skittish. He playfully threw a piece of bread at a man several tables away whom he fancied he recognized, and was childishly amused when he discovered his mistake. He also pocketed a fork as a souvenir, an incident that horrified Mr. Campion, at whom the Oriental winked delightedly. He continued in this sportive fashion throughout the meal, and as they came out into the Strand disclosed to the bewildered Marlowe that the loose pockets of his ulster contained at least four crescent rolls which he had secreted.

"Not a bad bag," remarked Mr. Campion appraisingly. "How's the time going, by the way?"

The Oriental put his hand into his waistcoat pocket and felt for the immense gold watch he usually carried. The change in his expression was ludicrous. His heavy jaw fell open, his eyes goggled.

"My watch—my watch—it's gone," he said. "I must have dropped it in there." He turned and hurried back into the restaurant with extraordinary agility for so cumbersome a man.

Mr. Campion watched him disappear into the glass-covered foyer, then he turned to Marlowe with a sigh of relief.

"He'll be no end of a time looking for it," he said. "I put it under the tablecloth. Come on." And before the other had realized what had happened he had piloted him out into the roadway and hailed a taxi.

"I'm afraid you got rather a curious impression of my place last time you came," said Mr. Campion, as they climbed the stairs. "I didn't expect you, and I'd made up my mind I wasn't going to take on the job anyway."

"Do you just walk out of this place and shut the door?" said Marlowe with interest. "I didn't see a janitor here. Who looks after you?"

"Oh, you didn't meet the family," said Mr. Campion. "I forgot. They'll both be in." He threw open the oak door as he spoke, and Marlowe followed him into the fantastic little room in which they had first discussed the whole thing. It was scrupulously neat and extremely comfortable, but there was no sign of a human being.

However, after standing silent for a moment or so, the young American became aware that someone was watching him with intense interest. He felt the scrutiny of a quizzical and speculative eye. He spun round nervily to find himself confronted by a venerable and wicked-looking jackdaw, who balanced himself sedately on the high back of a chair and regarded the visitor, his head cocked on one side.

"That's Autolycus," said Mr. Campion. "My chaplain. A brilliant chap, but, like our friend Barber, a kleptomaniac. I don't know where my major domo is."

He went out to the doorway and called, "Lugg!"

There was a heavy step in the passage, and the next moment the largest and most lugubrious individual Marlowe had ever seen appeared on the threshold. He was a hillock of a man, with a big pallid face which reminded one irresistibly of a bull terrier. He was practically bald, but by far the most outstanding thing about him was the all-pervading impression of melancholy which he conveyed. He was somewhat unconventionally clothed in what looked remarkably like a convict's tunic, apparently worn as a house-coat over an ordinary suit.

Campion grinned at him. "Still in your blazer?" he said pleasantly.

The man did not smile.

"I thought you was alone, sir," he said, revealing a sepulchral voice. "I put it on, sir, when attending to the bird's cage," he remarked to Marlowe. "It may interest you to know, sir," he added, once more addressing his master, "that during yer absence 'e's laid an egg."

"No?" said Mr. Campion. "Don't you believe it, Lugg. He pinched it from a pigeon to deceive you. He's pulling your leg. I've known Autolycus for years. He's not that kind of a bird." He turned to Marlowe. "Autolycus and I are always trying to cheer Lugg up," he said. "We prepare little surprises like this for him. Now, Lugg, suppose you mix us a drink and tell us the news. By the way, Marlowe, you've met Uncle Beastly before. He told you he was the Aphrodite Glue Works once, but that was only his fun. Lugg," he went on, his manner changing, "I want you to get Mr. Crayle for me."

Lugg paused, the decanter in his hand. "It can't be done, sir," he said, for the first time something approaching a glimmer of cheerfulness in his face and voice.

"Oh, and why not? Haven't we paid the phone bill yet?"

"Worse than that, sir. Mr. Crayle 'ad an accident at Manchester only last week. Five years, sir. Carelessness, it looked like to me."

"Damn!" said Mr. Campion. "That's a nuisance, Marlowe. Who's carrying on the—er—business, Lugg?"

"'Is wife, sir. Everything was in 'er name." The major domo relapsed into his usual melancholy. "Shall I get on the phone to 'er, sir?"

Campion remained thoughtful. "I don't like dealing with women," he said at last. "They've got no moral sense. I want some information about one or two people. There's a fortune-teller chap who works country houses, who has awakened my interest. But most particularly I want an authority on the American side. Who do you suggest, Lugg?"

"Well, in my opinion, sir, though you won't take it, I'm sure"—the tone was once more aggrieved—"if I was you,

I'd apply to Thos Knapp. It's wonderful wot 'e picks up, one way and another."

Mr. Campion's pale face flushed. "I'll be hanged if I do," he said with unusual heat. "There are some people at whom even I draw the line. As I've told you before, Lugg, we do not associate with Mr. Knapp. The fact that you are—er— old college friends doesn't make it any different."

"Wot did I tell you?" said Mr. Lugg, unexpectedly turning to Marlowe. " 'E won't be guided by me. Keeps me as a pet about the 'ouse, 'e does."

"I know," said Mr. Campion suddenly. "Our old friend Stanislaus. Get me on to the Yard."

"Imperialism," muttered Mr. Lugg bitterly. But he took up the telephone and gave the magic number. His voice assumed a husky, confidential tone.

"Mr. Ash—Mr. Tootles Ash to speak to Detective-Inspector Stanislaus Oates, _if_ you please. 'Ullo, sir, yes, sir, it's me, sir. Very nicely, sir, thank you. Very nicely, sir, too, sir. Laid an egg, sir. Oh _no,_ sir. Mr. Tootles is 'ere, sir."

Mr. Campion took the receiver.

"Hullo, Stanislaus," he said cheerfully. "How's the son and heir? Another tooth? Wonderful! I say, Stanislaus, do you know anything about X224? No, no friend of mine, you know that." He was silent listening for some moments. Then he shook his head and smiled faintly. "No, old bird. If it were really half as risky as you say I-couldn't drop it." He laughed. "All right. Send no flowers. Say it in marble. But no information?" he went on, and there was intensity beneath the lightness of his tone. "You'd come clean? You see what it means to me." He frowned. "Damned elusive party! You're right! Well, ever heard of a chap called Datchett?" His face became animated as he listened. "That's him!—a chap with a curling red beard . . . Blackmail? Why don't you get him? Oh, I see . . . What had he got on Mrs. Carey at Maplestone Hall? Eh? Yes, of course he was in it, you ought to know that . . . Yes, well, go all out for him, and when you get him, bring up the subject of the Reverend Swithin Cush . . . I don't know; that's what I want to find out. X224? Yes; well, it might lead you to that in the end.

Righto. All the best. Oh—they say 'Delila's' a good thing
for to-morrow. Take care? Nonsense, old boy. I shall be
dining with you and the girl-wife before the month is up. Ah
well, you're all in the army now. So long."

He rang off. "Well, that's something," he said. "I think a
concise history of our friend old Baa Baa Blacksheep might
be a good idea. And the man who can probably tell us more
about him than anyone is the best old Sherlock of them all
—old W. T. Get me on to young Mrs. Challoner, will you,
Lugg?"

Within a few minutes he was chatting affably. "Hullo,
Norah. Angel Face speaking. Where's Jerry? Up north? Is
the old man there? Will he give me a moment or two? I
want information rather badly . . . You're an angel. I'll
hang on." He was silent for some minutes: then a respectful
expression appeared on his face. "Hullo, is that you, W.T.?
Hewes speaking. Sorry to disturb your millennium, but in
your adventurous youth did you ever come across a man
called Fergusson Barber? I should say he's an Armenian or
a Turk of some sort. He might be a dealer . . . Oh, was he?
Even as a young man? You remember him well? Kleptomaniac? I rather gathered that myself."

The old detective's voice sounded so clearly over the wire
that some of the words reached Marlowe, who had listened
to the conversation with growing astonishment.

"Will steal anything of small value," he said. "Seems to
have a passion for bread . . ."

Campion took up the conversation, and for some time the
listener could not follow the talk. When at last he rang off,
Campion sighed. "Barber seems a funny old cuss," he said.
"It seems that W. T. met him over an affair at the Lord
Mayor's banquet. If you pinch the cutlery at a restaurant it
doesn't matter much, but start taking home souvenirs from
the Mansion House and no one is amused. Apparently the
old chap has establishments all over the place. Dabbles in
every sort of dealing and collecting. W.T. says he has a
harem, but spreads it about over the earth. He was very
shocked about it. If we weren't so busy he might be quite
amusing. But now," he went on, the old anxious look re-

turning to his eyes, "to the one really fundamental and serious matter in hand—your father. Lugg, who can tell us anything about the Simister crowd?"

Mr. Lugg raised his eyes in pious horror. "Now I warn yer," he said, his voice becoming plaintive, "I warn yer. You're ignorant compared with me. You don't know. They're a nasty lot, leave 'em alone. Yer own mother couldn't give yer better advice."

"My hat, I wouldn't like to hear her advice on this question," said Mr. Campion, scandalized. "Come on, pull yourself together. What can we do?"

"I shall wear a black band round me 'at for yer," said Mr. Lugg. "The funeral cards'll cost a bit, 'avin' all your different names on 'em."

"Mon, you're makin' a fearrful exhibition o' yersel," said Mr. Campion. "I think perhaps we will have a chat with Mr. van Houston."

"Very good, sir. 'E calls 'imself ' 'Omer, the society photographer,' now." Lugg took out a dilapidated notebook and looked out the number.

Mr. Campion took the instrument, and a long and animated conversation ensued in what was apparently a French argot. Marlowe could not follow it.

"Eh, bien m'sieu, je vais vous offrir mes profondes remerciements—Jusqu'au nez—Au 'voir," he finished, and hanging up the receiver, returned to Marlowe. "That sounds most promising," he said, "but it's hardly cheerful. Apparently there's great activity in certain quarters. Van Houston, who usually knows everything, is extraordinarily vague. He hates to be discovered in ignorance, however, so that probably means that only half of what he says is true. Still, he's a very well-informed chap. I don't think he'd play the fool with me. I think we're on the right tack. Lugg, has anyone of the fraternity been away recently, except for the usual reasons?"

Mr. Lugg considered. "Now you come to mention it, sir," he said, "I was talkin' about that down at the club only last night. There's been a notable absence among the really

nasty customers lately. Ikey Todd an' 'is lot. Very significant, I thought it."

"Very," said Mr. Campion. "Did you hear any other
funny stories at this club of yours?"

"Well, since you're being nosey, as you might say," said
Mr. Lugg affably, "I did 'ear that that dirty little Chink,
Ropey, is back in the country, *and* they say on to a very
good job."

"Ropey?" said Mr. Campion questioningly. Then a slow
expression of disgust passed over his face. "Not the man
who—"

Lugg nodded. "That's 'im. The chap they call the Tor-
turer. ' 'Tis an infamy that such a bloke as you should live,'
said the Beak. You know 'im."

"Yes, I do," said Champion, ignoring Lugg's effort at
local colour. "I say, I don't like that. I mean, that chap was
a—" He glanced at Marlowe. "Well, we won't go into that.
He may be nothing to do with us." His voice did not carry
much conviction, however.

Marlowe looked at him dubiously. "I haven't got much
of all this. What does it all amount to?"

Mr. Campion considered. "We've got daylight on one or
two interesting points," he said. "In the first place, we know
who Mr. Datchett is. He's a blackmailer, though what he
had on poor old Swithin Cush is more than I can possibly
imagine. I think he must have been a spy in his spare time.
Then we've placed Mr. Barber, but that doesn't help us any.
And last, and most important, we've discovered that there is
a move on amongst those gentlemen who can be hired for
any really unpleasant job. So Simister isn't working altogether with his own men. He must be doing this as a kind of
side line to protect himself. The attacking army isn't a very
bright lot. I don't know about the brains behind it. On the
whole the prospect looks brighter than I expected to find it."

There was a tap at the outside door, and Lugg went to
open it.

"Say I've gone to Birmingham for my health," said Mr.
Campion.

Lugg returned in an instant, however, an orange envelope

in his hand. He handed it to Campion, who tore open the flap and glanced at the contents. As he read, a sharp exclamation escaped him and he became paler than before. He passed the telegram silently to Marlowe. It ran:

COME AT ONCE STOP BODY FOUND STOP BIDDY

CHAPTER XV

The Exuberance of Mr. Kettle

BIDDY met them at Ipswich Station in Judge Lobbett's big Daimler, the chauffeur driving.

"I knew you wouldn't mind my bringing this," she said somewhat unexpectedly to Marlowe as they came across the station yard.

"My dear girl—" Marlowe looked at her in amazement. "I want to know all about it. Where did they find him?"

Biddy stared at him. "I don't understand," she said.

"We're talking about the body," said Campion. "You wired us."

The girl's bewilderment increased. "I wired you we'd found a clue," she said. "There's no trace of Mr. Lobbett himself."

Marlowe drew the telegram from his pocket and handed it to her. She read it through and turned to them, her cheeks reddening.

"Oh, my dear, how you must have been tortured all the way down," she said impetuously. "This is Kettle. His daughter found the clothes, and he's so excited about it he's gone nearly insane. I think my wire to you ran more or less like this: 'Come at once. Important clue. Meet you four-thirty train.' I wondered why you wired me."

Marlowe wiped the perspiration off his forehead and he and Campion climbed into the car, one on each side of the girl.

"Now about this discovery," said Mr. Campion. "Just what is it? What did Kettle's daughter find?"

"She found Mr. Lobbett's clothes," said Biddy; "the suit he disappeared in, I mean. They were soaked with sea water and torn, and I'm afraid there's blood on them, Marlowe. But that doesn't mean he's dead, does it?" she went on eagerly, and Campion, glancing down, saw that she had laid her hand upon Marlowe's arm.

"Not necessarily, of course."

Campion's voice was slightly irritated. "Where did Miss Kettle make this interesting discovery?"

"Up the Saddleback Creek. The clothes were left by the tide, she thought. I wired you at once. As a matter of fact, we were frightened, Isopel and I. She's all right now. She's awfully brave. Giles is with her now, so I thought I'd come and meet you. I'm glad I did. I never dreamed Kettle would send a crazy wire like that one."

Marlowe looked bewildered. "I thought," he said, "that a postmaster could get into serious trouble for a thing like that."

"So he can," said Campion grimly. "Something tells me that he's going to get it. Didn't you fill in a form, Biddy?"

"No, I took it in to him on a piece of paper. I expect my scribble was partly to blame. You know how I write when I'm excited." She smiled wryly at Campion. "You've no idea how dithery he is. He's only a silly old man, Albert."

Mr. Campion did not reply, but his expression was dubious.

Giles and Isopel were waiting for them at the park gates when they arrived. They got into the car and went back to the house together. Isopel was clinging to Giles, and in spite of the excitement of the moment it flashed through the minds of the others there that an understanding of some sort existed between them. There was a faint hint of subdued elation in their manner towards each other.

When they reached the house Cuddy and Mrs. Whybrow

were standing in the hall, distinctly flurried and unmistakably curious.

"It's in here, sir." Mrs. Whybrow could not repress the words, and she motioned Marlowe with a large bony hand to the little morning-room which gave off the hall. Cuddy did not speak, but she stood there, her hands folded under her apron, moistening and re-moistening her lips with the tip of her tongue, while her quick eyes took in every detail and noted each expression.

Campion followed Marlowe into the tiny white-panelled room, where on the round table stood a large tin tray, on which was a suit of clothes still wet with sea water. Marlowe glanced at Campion, a sharp quick look, full of apprehension.

"It's his suit, sure enough," he said. "He was wearing it when he went into the maze, you remember."

Campion nodded. A gloomy expression had come into his eyes. He thrust his hands deep into his pockets and stared darkly at the tray with its contents.

"Nothing in the pockets, I suppose?" he said.

"No, nothing at all," said Isopel. "The clothes must have been rifled before they were discovered. All the pockets were pulled inside out."

Marlowe was still turning over the muddy flannel. "Hullo!" he said, and held up the waistcoat, in which there was a jagged little hole surrounded by dark ominous stains. Mr. Campion came over to the table and bent over the garment. He made no comment, and Biddy nudged him.

"Don't torture them," she whispered. "What does it all mean?"

His reply was silenced by a commotion in the hall outside.

"My good woman"—Mr. Kettle's voice reached them, raised in protest. "My good woman, show me in immediately. I am needed in there, and I 'ave every reason to suppose that my presence is awaited eagerly."

"I ain't showin' anyone in without Master Giles's word. You ought to be 'shamed o' yowself, Kettle, forcin' your way in 'pon a bereaved family. They don't want to see you now." Cuddy's voice, shrill and contemptuous, answered him.

"Shall I go and send him away?" said Biddy.

Campion glanced at Marlowe. "If you don't mind," he began, "I think it would be an idea if we interviewed old Cleversides ourselves."

Marlowe nodded. "Certainly, if you think there's anything to be gained by it," he said, and opened the door. "Come in, Mr. Kettle, will you?"

The unprepossessing postmaster shot one delighted glance at the angry Cuddy and stalked into the room with the air of a conqueror. He was clutching his bowler hat, and was still in his overcoat which he had put on to hide his apron.

" 'Ere I am, sir," he said to Marlowe. There was a faint tinge of colour in his flaccid face. "I saw the car turn into the drive and I put on me 'at and run after you, sir. I knew you'd be wantin' the truth. My daughter, sir, she found the remains, as you might say." He had been speaking all the time in a breathless whisper. His eyes were watering and his lips twitching with excitement.

"Is your daughter here?" said Campion with unusual peremptoriness.

"No, sir." Mr. Kettle assumed an air of parental indignation. "Wot?" he said, with great dignity. "Think, sir. 'Ow could I subject the poor girl to look on once again that 'orror that 'as turned 'er from a 'ealthy woman, sir, to a mere wreck of 'er former self?"

In spite of the anxiety of the situation there was something extremely laughable in Mr. Kettle's rhetorical outburst.

He lent an air of theatricality to a scene that would otherwise have been too terrible.

"No, sir, she is not 'ere," he continued. "And I may add, sir," he went on with gathering righteousness, "that she was in such an 'elpness state, sir, such a nasty 'opeless condition, sir, that I left 'er to mind the post office and come myself. I would like to mention also, sir," he added, fixing a malignant eye upon Giles, "that although I 'ave offered myself to be the messenger, no one 'as, as yet, sent for the police. It will look very suspicious, sir, when they do come. Although you are the son of the dead man, sir"—he swung round upon Marlowe on the words—"it'll look nasty."

"What dead man?" said Mr. Campion, coming forward. He had developed a magisterial air that contrasted very oddly with his appearance. "Have you got the body?"

"Me, sir? Oh no, sir." Mr. Kettle was not in the least abashed. "When we find that I dare say we'll know who killed 'im."

"Oh yes?" said Mr. Campion with interest. "How was he killed?"

"With a dagger, sir." Mr. Kettle made the startling announcement in a breathless whisper.

"How do you know?" said Mr. Campion.

Mr. Kettle rested one hand upon the table and assumed the attitude of a lecturer. "I 'ave the detective mind, sir," he said. "I form my theories and they work out in accordance."

"That's rather nice," said Mr. Campion. "I must do that."

Mr. Kettle ignored him. "To begin with, let us start with the discovery of this clue." He waved his hand towards the table. "My daughter, sir, an innocent girl, unsuspecting, goes for a walk, sir. This is the seaside, she thinks; why shouldn't she walk there?"

"No reason at all," said Mr. Campion. He was standing with one hand on Marlowe's shoulder, and the American's keen, clever face wore an expression of enlightenment.

"Well, she went along the beach—that is, on the edge of the saltings—on the sea wall, in fact. Imagine 'er for yourselves, careless, free—"

"Oh, cut the cackle," said Giles. "Tell us what happened."

"I'm speakin' of my daughter, sir," said Mr. Kettle with dignity.

"You're also speaking of this lady's father," said Giles. "You'll say what you know, and then clear out."

A particularly nasty expression came into Mr. Kettle's white face.

"You're the wise one, sir," he said. "I shall be a witness at the inquest, don't forget. It's going to be very significant, I may say."

"I'm sure it is," said Mr. Campion soothingly. "Suppose you tell us about those deductions of yours."

The postmaster was mollified. "My knowledge is based on these instructive facts, sir," he said. "Look at this jagged hole, right over the region of the heart. Was that made by a knife, or was it not? It was, sir. See those stains all round? If you don't know what that is, I can tell you. It's blood—'eart's blood, sir."

Once more Giles was about to break out angrily, but this time it was Isopel who restrained him.

"What does that show, sir? The victim was stabbed to death with a knife. Then again, these clothes are soppin' wet with sea-water. What does that show?"

"That they've been in the sea," suggested Mr. Campion.

"Exactly, sir, you've 'it it in one. Therefore, you see, it's as plain as the nose on your face, sir, if you'll forgive me the liberty, that Mr. Lobbett was taken out in a boat, stabbed through the heart, and thrown into the water."

"Where he undressed," said Mr. Campion, "being careful to remove his braces. So far I think that's perfectly clear. However, there are several other little matters that'll have to be explained before we go any further or call in Scotland Yard. In the first place, there's this knife thrust. Rather a curious incision, don't you think? A little hole nicked with a pair of scissors and then made larger with a table knife. And then these bloodstains. The poor man seems to have bled from outside his clothes. The inside, you see, is pretty clean. But the gore on the outside is sensational. I wonder who's been killing chickens lately?"

Mr. Kettle sat down on the edge of a chair, his face immovable. Mr. Campion continued.

"There is something fishy about this—a whole kettle of fishiness, I might say. Someone's been playing the fool with you. I should go back to the post office."

Mr. Kettle got up, picked up his bowler hat, and walked quietly and unobtrusively out of the room. A few moments later he passed the window, going down the drive, still with his eyes fixed straight ahead of him.

Campion turned to Isopel and Marlowe and spoke with genuine contrition. "Will you forgive me for making you listen to all that?" he said. "But I had to do it to find out how much the local Sherlock knew."

"Then what do you make of these?" Marlowe indicated the soaking garments.

"An extraordinarily bad fake on somebody's part," said Mr. Campion. "I never saw such amateur work. This isn't your New York friends: it looks more like home product to me. I suppose you haven't been offering a reward by any chance?"

"No," said Marlowe. "But you can't get away from it, Campion," he broke out. "That's the suit he was wearing."

"I know," said Mr. Campion. "That's the only thing that makes it interesting. Our friend Kettle, whatever he is, is no prize exhibit, sleuth or crook. I think if you'll excuse me I'll go down to the village and make a few investigations."

"Are you going to interview Kettle again?" Biddy spoke curiously.

"I hardly think so," said Mr. Campion. He smiled at her cheerfully. "He's not the only interesting character in the place. I do believe the wheels are going to go round at last."

CHAPTER XVI

The Wheels Go Round

GILES and Isopel were sitting in the window-seat in the morning-room, holding hands.

The sunlight poured in upon them, and the village of Mystery Mile was as peaceful as if nothing untoward had ever happened upon the whole island. They were alone. Biddy was at the Dower House, and Mr. Campion off once more upon his investigations in the village.

The rustle of car wheels outside on the drive startled the two, and Isopel, who caught a fleeting glance of a putty-coloured body and crimson wings, turned to Giles looking utterly dismayed.

"Oh, my dear," she said. "He's come back!"

"Who? Your father?" Giles was ever more physically than mentally alert.

"No. That was Mr. Barber."

The young squire bounced to his feet.

"Good Lord!" he said. "What cheek that chap has! I'll kick him out."

He advanced towards the door, but it was open before he reached it. Mr. Barber, complete with satchel and the most important smile imaginable, appeared upon the threshold.

"Mr. Paget," he said, holding out his hand. "Let me be the first to congratulate you."

Giles, taken completely off his guard, reddened and glanced sheepishly at Isopel.

"I don't know how you knew—" he began. But Mr. Barber was still talking. "My boy, I have the proof—the proof positive. The thing's genuine. I should like to arrange for the sale with you."

It was only at this moment that Giles realized that he had been mistaken and that Mr. Barber was not talking about the all-important subject of which his own mind was full.

Isopel slipped her arm through his. "It's the picture, dear," she whispered.

"Of course I'm talking about the picture," said Mr. Barber testily. "Come and see it for yourselves." He bustled out of the room as he spoke, leading them into the big cool drawing room on the other side of the house.

The exquisite period room was seldom used, and a faint musty odour of decayed tapestry and dusty pot-pourri met them as they entered.

The portrait hung over the mantelpiece: a long-dead Mistress Paget, who smiled at them with foolish sweetness from out of her monstrous gold frame. She wore a diaphanous scarf over her golden hair, and one slender hand caressed a little white dog who nestled in the folds of her oyster-coloured gown.

Mr. Barber was visibly excited. "As soon as I saw it," he said, turning to them, his eyes watering profusely, "I said to myself, 'This is the moment of my career, this is the moment for which I have always longed. Here is an undiscovered Romney, one of the finest I have ever seen.' Now I must see Judge Lobbett immediately and make my report. I'm afraid my poor little Cotmans sink into obscurity beside this master."

"Look here," said Giles, managing to get a word in when Mr. Barber paused to breathe, "this is all very fine and large, but you don't seem to understand. We can't be bothered with little things like this just now. You don't appear to have grasped the fact that Mr. Lobbett has disappeared. You were in New York not long ago—you know the seriousness of the fuss there was there. Well, now, he's vanished—see? Naturally we can't consider doing anything till he's found."

"Disappeared?" said Mr. Barber, the fact apparently dawning on him for the first time.

"Yes," said Giles irritably. "And his blood-stained clothes were found in a pool yesterday."

The effect upon Mr. Barber was extraordinary. His mouth fell open, his eyes bulged, and he sat down suddenly upon the edge of a chair as if his feet would not support him.

"I didn't believe you," he said blankly. "I thought you were all joking with me. So many people are afraid of anyone who might want to sell them a picture. I thought Mr. Lobbett was away on some visit. When Mr. Campion and young Lobbett gave me the slip in London they were joking. Campion jokes so often. This is terrible—terrible! Where are the police?"

Giles hesitated, and then spoke stiffly. "We decided that there was no need for them at present."

Mr. Barber raised his eyebrows. "Oh, then, I see you know where he is?" he said. "You thought it would be best for him to disappear for a little while?"

"Certainly not," said Giles, who was beginning to wish profoundly that he had never entered into the conversation at all. "But we've the finest—er—private detective in the world investigating for us."

Mr. Barber appeared to be quite as much bewildered as before. "Oh, I see," he said. "But in these circumstances, for whom am I acting? I mean," he added a little helplessly, "what is my position here?"

The easy-going good-tempered Giles relented. "Oh, that'll be all right," he said cheerfully. "Suppose you go back to town to-morrow and send me in a list of your expenses?"

"But the Romney?" said Mr. Barber, his voice rising to a squeak.

A hint of the long line of independent landowners behind

him was apparent in Giles just then, as he stood squarely under the picture, his brows contracted. "It's hung there for the last hundred years, and it can stay there a year or so longer if necessary," he said. "I've told you, sir, that I can't be bothered about it now."

"But it's worth a fortune," objected Mr. Barber. "Anything up to forty thousand pounds."

"I don't care what it's worth," said Giles stubbornly. "I shall have to wait until all this is settled before I think about anything else. I'll write you then. Will that do?"

It was evident that Mr. Barber felt that he was dealing with a lunatic. "You must forgive my insistence," he said with dignity, "but the commission on forty thousand pounds is considerable. If you would allow me to take the picture—"

"No, I'm hanged if I will," said Giles, his irritation returning.

"Then let me take more photographs. There are so many people who will be interested." The expert's tone was supplicating. "I can prepare the market. Surely, surely you will not forbid me to do that?"

"Oh, do what you like," said Giles, "only don't move the picture."

He put his arm through Isopel's and was leading her out of the room when they met Marlowe in the doorway.

His dark handsome face was more than usually serious.

"Seen Biddy?" he asked.

"She's down at the Dower House," said Giles. "Anything I can do?"

"No. That's all right." Marlowe did not stop, but hurried on his way, leaving the young man engrossed in Isopel and Mr. Barber standing before the Romney, his pudgy feet well apart, his hands clasped behind his back, and upon his face an expression of rapt, almost idolatrous, admiration.

Fifteen minutes later found Marlowe striking across the park, where he encountered Mr. Campion. The pale foolish-looking young man came along thoughtfully, whistling plaintively to himself.

"Hullo," he said cheerfully when he caught sight of his friend. "I've just thought of something. Listen—

> As Sir Barnaby Rowbotham died,
> He turned and he said to his maid,
> The Albert Memurrial
> Is the place for my burrial,
> The first on the left, just inside.

There's uplift for you. It's the message that counts. Send fourpence for our free book."

Marlowe did not appear to have heard. "I say," he said, "have you seen Biddy?"

Mr. Campion looked hurt. "No soul for Higher Things," he murmured. "No, I've been sleuthing about the village again, and I believe that I have lighted upon something." He paused. "You're not listening to me," he said regretfully.

"No," said Marlowe. "I'm sorry, Campion, and I don't want to make a fuss, but I can't find Biddy anywhere. She's gone."

"Gone?"

Marlowe glanced up to find Campion staring at him. His vacuous face was transformed by an expression of puzzled consternation and incredulity.

"Absurd," he said at last. "How long have you been looking for her?"

"All the morning," said Marlowe. "The fact is," he went on, the words blurring a little in his embarrassment, "she'd promised to meet me. We were going down to the Saddleback Creek. But this isn't—ordinary caprice. She's not that sort of kid."

Mr. Campion shot him a swift glance.

"No," he said quietly, and was silent.

"But she's gone." Marlowe, who was slowly becoming more and more excited, repeated the words vehemently. "I tell you I've been everywhere. I've asked everybody. She hasn't been seen all the morning. Cuddy says that she last saw her after breakfast when she went into the drawing-room to write letters."

"Letters?" Campion spun round on the word. Behind his spectacles his pale eyes had become narrow and hard. "Are you sure?" he said, and his voice was more serious than Marlowe had ever heard it.

"Why, yes," he went on. "Cuddy says that she went straight in to her desk first thing after breakfast. Why—"

"Come on," said Mr. Campion. He was already heading for the village at a brisk trot.

"Ought to be shot!" he said breathlessly to Marlowe as they raced over the slippery turf together. "Never dreamed they'd act so soon. Was coming back to hold a committee meeting. Taking my time over it. Certain we were safe for twelve hours at least."

When they reached the park gates he came to a halt.

"I think, just to make sure that we're not making fools of ourselves, we'll drop into the Dower House," he said. "Cuddy may have made a mistake. This looks very nasty, Marlowe."

They hurried across the green and into the Dower House, where Cuddy met them in the hall. The old woman was red-faced and annoyed.

"Have you seen Miss Biddy, sir?" she said, fixing on Campion. "She was coming into the kitchen to give me a hand with the huffikins at twelve o'clock," she said, "and here have I been waiting with my oven hot and the dough spoiling for the last three-quarters of an hour. I suppose I'd better get on with them alone."

The apprehension in Mr. Campion's pale eyes deepened.

"I was looking for Biddy, myself, Cuddy," he said. "When did you see her last?" Marlowe had gone on into the drawing room, and the old woman glanced after him.

"I told Mr. Lobbett," she said; "not since just after breakfast." Her quick eyes took in Campion's expression, and she came a little closer to him. "Looks like you ain't goin' to have no chance," she said, dropping her voice confidentially. "Be more serious-like. You can't tell what's goin' to please a girl."

Campion did not smile. "May the best man win, you know, Cuddy," he said with apparent gravity.

"Yes, and I'm afraid he will," said she, wagging her head at him. "When you see Miss Biddy tell her I couldn't wait no longer."

She bustled off, and Campion hurried into the drawing-room after Marlowe. The boy was standing by the open writing desk.

"She must have been writing here," he said. "Look." He pointed to the open inkstand, the sheets of notepaper carelessly strewn about, and the empty stamp book lying on the polished wood. "There you are," he said. "Campion, if anything happens to that girl, I'll commit murder."

"That, blast you," said Mr. Campion without malice, "is the spirit. Come on."

CHAPTER XVII

"Gent on a Bike"

THE interior of Mr. Kettle's shop, which was also the post office of Mystery Mile and was licensed to sell tobacco—open for the sale of mineral waters, closing for the half-day on Wednesdays, under the Shops Act—provided one of those scenes of mingled profusion and constriction which can be equalled only by any other English village general shop. The whole place was hardly more than ten feet square, a little low room into which customers stepped down some inches from the garden path.

The wide counter divided the room in half, and over it, from floor to ceiling, the entire stock of bacon, hardware, boiled sweets, flypapers, bread, and groceries were displayed without any attempt at order.

The post office consisted of a tiny wired-off enclosure at one end of the counter, the iron rail of which was decorated with licencing notices and pension forms, and the whole place smelled strongly of camphor and acid drops, with an undercurrent of bacon mingled with paraffin and scented soap.

An open doorway at the back of the shop revealed a glimpse of a small neat room decorated with a particularly unlovely grey-and-green wallpaper, a pair of aspidistras, and a model of a white horse given away with a whisky advertisement.

It was through this doorway that Mr. Kettle advanced upon Campion and Marlowe as they stepped down into the shop.

A change in him was apparent immediately.

His pallor was even more striking than before, and there was a slightly shifty, troubled look in his pale eyes. He still wore the white apron with the carefully frayed edge in which he had come to the Manor the night before.

"What can I do for you, gentlemen?" he said, the nervousness in his voice unmistakable. Marlowe leaned across the counter, when a touch on his arm restrained him.

"Miss Paget left her purse in here, she thinks, Mr. Kettle," said Campion pleasantly. "We shall have to have all this cleared away, you know"—he waved his hand at the miscellaneous collection round him, and rambled on foolishly. "Where's the exit in case of fire? Most dangerous, all this litter about the place. Now where's that purse?"

"She didn't leave anything 'ere, sir." Mr. Kettle's voice was emphatic.

"Fine!" said Campion with sudden enthusiasm. "Now we know where we are. Is she still in the house?"

Mr. Kettle did not look at him, and Marlowe suddenly noticed that he was squinting horribly. He was standing perfectly still, his great flabby hands spread out upon the greasy surface of the counter. Campion bent a little nearer and repeated his question softly.

"Is she still in the house?"

A thin stream of saliva trickled out of the corner of Mr. Kettle's mouth, and Marlowe, who until now had been utterly bewildered, realized with a sudden shock that the man was paralyzed with terror. The sight nauseated him, but Campion was less impressed.

"Don't be a fool, Kettle," he said sharply. "We've only got to turn you over to the police. Better save a lot of bother and take us to her at once."

The effect of this threat upon the man was as startling as his terror had been. He started back from them with an

angry sound that was midway between a snarl and a hic-
cough. His fear had turned to a peculiarly vindictive type of
satisfaction.

"That's right! Bring in the police!" he said with unexpected violence. "Search the 'ouse! Turn me 'ole shop upside
down. Stick your noses into every 'ole and corner of the
place. And when you've finished that _I_ shall 'ave something
to say to the police. Where's Mr. Lobbett, eh? 'Oo 'ushed up
the parson's suicide? Why didn't you show them clothes to
the police? You daren't bring the police 'ere! You . . . !"

The outburst came to an end at last, and a transformed
Mr. Kettle stood glaring at them across the two feet of worn
counter. Gone and forgotten was his servility.

Mr. Campion seemed entirely unmoved. He stood, his
hands in his pockets, looking if anything a little more strik-
ingly inane than usual. "It wouldn't be the Heronhoe police," he said. "I think the county people would be
interested."

Mr. Kettle remained unimpressed. "No police will worry
me," he said. "I've got nothing 'ere to 'ide."

"Good!" said Campion. "Now we understand one another better than ever." He appeared to have dismissed the
matter from his mind, for his next remark seemed entirely
casual. "You sell biscuits, I see, Mr. Kettle?"

Marlowe glanced at his friend questioningly, only to find
that he was regarding the postmaster fixedly. The young
American was not prepared for the third change in Mr.
Kettle: his terror returned, and he looked at the pale young
man before him in blank astonishment.

"There, there," said Mr. Campion soothingly. "Here's a
nice old lady coming down the path, Kettle. Pull yourself
together. She'll want to be served. No self-respecting woman
will buy a stamp off you if you squint like that."

He had hardly finished speaking when Alice Broom, a
coat thrown on to hide her white apron, came rustling into
the shop. She nodded to the two young men and planked
down two coppers on the counter.

"Two pennorth o' soda, please, Mr. Kettle," she said.
"Nice after the rain, isn't it? How's your pore feet to-day?"

She was evidently in a talkative mood, and Campion seemed suddenly disposed to pander to it.

"I've been telling Mr. Kettle he doesn't look any too bobbish," he said. "What do you think, Alice? Excitement isn't healthy, is it?"

"I don't know what excitement he'll be gettin' down 'ere," she said. "I've got a bone to pick with un, too," she added, the thought suddenly occurring to her. "I sent round last night askin' for a box to keep my rarebits in. 'E wouldn't let I have un, an' I seed he this mornin' packin' off crate after crate into that biscut van."

Campion turned to Marlowe. "Another Old English custom for you," he said. "We have our biscuits here by the crate."

Alice shook her head at him. " 'E's makin' game on you, sir," she said. "Biscuts come in tins. Yes, biscuts come in tins."

She repeated the phrase with a certain amount of satisfaction, and, taking up her blue bag of soda, waddled out of the shop with a cheerful "Good-day, sirs".

Campion beamed at Mr. Kettle. "Biscuits come in tins," he said. "And Mr. Kettle returns the empty crates. That's very interesting. I shouldn't be surprised if they didn't send a special van from London for them, eh?"

Mr. Kettle moistened his lips. "I don't know what you've been 'earing—" he began desperately.

Campion grinned. "Our Albert hasn't been hearing anything—he's been seeing," he said. "Suppose we go into that artistic little room through there, where we'll sit under the portrait of the dear old Queen, God bless her, and go into the whole question peacefully and without fear of interruption?"

Mr. Kettle did not move, nor did he make any protest when Marlowe lifted the counter flap and the two young men walked into the inner room.

"Come in," said Campion pleasantly, holding the door open for him.

The postmaster followed them silently. Campion shut the door behind him and set a chair. "I don't suppose the windows will open," he observed. "What a pity, Kettle! You'd have got the smell of the chloroform out by this time. As it is, I should think it would linger for days."

Kettle did not speak, and a change came over Campion's face.

He leaned forward.

"If she's been hurt, Kettle, I'll break my rule and kill you! Now then, animal, tell us all about it."

Mr. Kettle sat on the edge of his chair, his large hands spread out on the table, and looked neither to right nor to left.

"Come on," said Campion. "We know practically everything. Out with it."

Still Mr. Kettle remained silent, his mouth twitching. Marlowe took a step forward. "You'll tell us here and now," he said, "or I'll smash you to pulp."

"No need," said Campion. "What is he now? I see I may as well repeat the procedure to you, Kettle. We'll start at the beginning. A suit of clothes came into your hands, and you thought you'd be clever with them. You were—my hat you were. So thunderingly clever that you set not only us but your own dirty employers buzzing round your head. I gave you credit for so much stupidity, but what I didn't believe was that you'd be fool enough to tell your own people about it yourself." He turned to Marlowe. "That's where I miscalculated the time. Now," he went on, returning to his victim, "you got orders to kidnap the first one of us that came into the shop, you and your precious daughter were to chloroform him, and I suppose the rest of the business was perfectly simple."

It was evident from the look of wonderment on the postmaster's face that so far Campion had been very near the truth.

"Having captured Biddy," continued Mr. Campion, "no doubt you telephoned some apparently innocent message to Heronhoe, or wherever the van was waiting, and along came the one vehicle that wouldn't be questioned by the police on Stroud—a reputable-looking trade van. You loaded your crates into it, one of which contained the poor kid. Now then, where did they take her to?"

He had taken off his spectacles, and as he leaned across the table to the shivering man his pale eyes were bright and hard.

Mr. Kettle made an inarticulate sound; his mouth sagged open.

"If they find out you know all this they'll kill me," he slobbered at last. "Oh, Mr. Campion, sir"—he grovelled across the table, his hands plucking at the cloth—"don't let them ever know—don't let them ever know!"

"Where have they taken her?" repeated Campion.

"I don't know." Mr. Kettle was on the verge of tears: there was no doubting his sincerity. "I never seen either of 'em before. I get my orders by 'phone, in code. I wouldn't 'a' done it if I could 'a' 'elped it—reelly I wouldn't. I couldn't 'elp it—I 'ad to obey 'em."

Mr. Campion rose from the table where he had been seated.

"I believe him," he said gloomily. "I think perhaps the nastiest thing we can do is to leave him to his unspeakable pals."

"I'd tell you," wailed Mr. Kettle. "I'd tell you anything if only I knew it."

"I believe you would," said Campion contemptuously. "I'm afraid there's no doubt they've kept you in the dark all right. They're not such fools that they don't know the type they've got working for them. Come on, Marlowe. He'll keep his mouth shut for his own sake."

He turned towards the doorway, but Mr. Kettle was before him. With surprising agility he scrambled from his seat and ran round the table to bar their egress. He stood before them, a lamentable figure, his great white face quivering. He was still dribbling a little, and his small watery eyes flickered open and shut.

"Mr. Campion, sir—don't let them ever know. I wouldn't be safe, Mr. Campion. I should be a 'unted man!"

They brushed him out of their way and left the shop. He

leaned heavily on the post of the inner door and they heard his husky voice quivering after them.

"Be 'umane, Mr. Campion, be 'umane—"

Marlowe glanced at the other as they strode across the green.

"What's the next move?" he said.

"That," said Mr. Campion gravely, "is where we step on the banana skin. They've got her away, you see." He had lowered his voice, and the other man realized that for once in his life the irrepressible Mr. Campion was thoroughly alarmed. "We've got to move quickly," he went on, the seriousness of his tone belying the lightness of his words. "You never know what unladylike behaviour they might indulge in to get the information they want."

"What information could Biddy give them, anyway?" said Marlowe, who was still a little dizzy at the rate things had progressed that morning.

Campion did not reply. They had entered the park gates and were striding across the rough grass at a good pace.

Marlowe looked at his companion curiously. "How much of this yarn of Kettle's did you know when you went into the store?" he said.

Campion frowned. "Not as much as I ought to have done," he said bitterly. "And there's still a link I don't get. I told you, it was misjudging Kettle's abysmal idiocy that put me out. I knew they couldn't have got going on the job so soon after the discovery of the clothes unless they had heard about it at the same time we did; and that was only possible if our friend Kettle told them himself. As he'd made such a hash of it, I didn't dream he would. But he did, and I should think from the look of him that they had come down hot and strong."

"Then it was Kettle who doctored those clothes?"

"Not a doubt of it. Though heaven only knows how he got hold of them. The only thing that matters at the moment is Biddy," he went on suddenly, lifting up his head. "Get her back and then we can start."

"I'm with you there," said Marlowe with conviction. "What are you going to do?"

Campion shrugged his shoulders impatiently. "God only knows," he said. "The old mental machinery seems to have conked out altogether."

They walked on in silence. As they came into the house through the conservatory door which stood open they heard Mrs. Whybrow's voice raised, high and suspicious. She was talking to someone in the inner hall.

"Mr. Campion? I don't know if 'e's in, but I'll take your name if you'll give it me. Who shall I say 'as called?"

A bright unpleasant voice answered her, indescribable in its cockney self-assurance.

"Don't say any name. Just go up to 'im, put yer 'ead close to 'is ear, and say, soft-like, 'Gent on a bike'."

CHAPTER XVIII

The Unspeakable Thos

MR. CAMPION, standing in the outer hall, remained for a moment perfectly silent, listening.

"Who is it?" Glancing at him, Marlowe saw to his astonishment that his companion's face, usually pale, was fiery with embarrassment.

Mr. Campion took off his spectacles and wiped them with a tasteful line in silk handkerchiefs. "That, my unfortunate friend," he said gloomily, "is the unspeakable Thos. Thos T. Knapp. T. stands for 'tick'. This is horror piled on horror."

"Why, if it ain't my old sport Bertie!" said the voice, appreciably nearer. "I 'eard your pipe from out 'ere, my lovely."

Simultaneously with this last announcement, Mr. Thos Knapp himself appeared in the doorway, where he stood looking in on them with bright, sharp, sparrow-like eyes. He was an undersized young man with a broken snub nose and an air of indefatigable jauntiness. His clothes must have been the pride of the Whitechapel Road: fantastically cut garments, they comprised a suit of a delicate shade of purple, together with a fancy tie designed in shot silk by a man with a warped imagination, and the ensemble neatly finished off by bright yellow shoes of incredible length and narrowness.

Mr. Campion surveyed him against the venerable dark oak panelling. "Quite the little knut, isn't he?" he said pleasantly. "Take your cap off to the gentleman, Thos."

Mr. Knapp removed a large, flat, buff superstructure and smiled at Marlowe, revealing an astonishing assortment of teeth.

" 'E's a spark, ain't 'e?" he said, jerking his head towards Campion affably. "Pleased to meet you, I'm sure. Well, Bertie, I've come down for a bit of private conversation with you. Nice little place you've got 'ere. I didn't 'alf 'ave a time findin' it on my bike. I left it outside. By the way, I suppose it'll be safe?"

Marlowe, glancing at Campion, saw that he was suffering acutely.

Mr. Knapp continued confidentially. "I 'ad to pinch the bike in Ipswich or I shouldn't 'ave got 'ere at all. Wonderful quiet place. I didn't even 'ave to paint it. I often feel you and me could do something in these parts, Bertie."

"How did you know I was here?" said Campion.

"Ah!" Mr. Knapp put his head upon one side and spoke with exaggerated caution. "You may know, Bertie, that from time to time I come across bits of information." He glanced at Marlowe questioningly.

Campion nodded. "That's all right," he said. "One of us."

"Is that so?" Mr. Knapp shook hands with Marlowe once more.

"On the American side," Campion explained easily. "But what I want to know is how you found me here."

"Now then, now then, not so eager," said Mr. Knapp playfully. "As matter o' fac', Magersfontein Lugg put me on to you. And a very good job 'e did, too. I've got something that will interest you, Bertie."

Campion shook his head. "I'm sorry, Knappy," he said, "but nothing that isn't directly connected with the job I'm on at the moment ever interests me."

"Well!" said Mr. Knapp indignantly. "Well! Bit free,

aren't yer? Bit free? Wot d'yer think I come down 'ere for? Fifteen miles on a ruddy bicycle. Are you teetotal in this 'ouse?"

Marlowe grinned. "Bring him into the study," he said. "I'll get some beer." He went off, and Mr. Knapp looked after him appreciatively.

"A nice chap to work with, I should think," he said. "You're always lucky, you are, Bertie. Lovely place, nice people, food and drink *ad lib*. It isn't as though you was smart or anything. It's luck, that's what it is."

"Now look here," said Campion desperately. "Out with it. What's the information? Remember, if it's any more of your filthy Rubinstein tricks I'll chuck you out as I told you I would. I'm not interested, see?"

"All right," said Mr. Knapp, "all right. What about this beer? I only 'appened to 'ear something directly connected with you and this 'ere Lobbett business, so I come all the way to see yer—just as a friendly act."

Mr. Campion's interest was now thoroughly aroused. "Hold on a moment," he said. "This sounds more like it."

"Wot did I tell yer?" said Mr. Knapp. "You an' me 'ave worked in the past, Bertie. We're after the same style, we are. We understand one another."

Mr. Campion made no comment, and at this moment Marlowe's voice from the other end of the corridor so distracted Mr. Knapp that he was completely uncommunicative until he found himself seated at the heavy oak table in the library, a glass at his side and a stone jug at his elbow.

"That's right," he said, wiping his mouth after a copious draught. "When I die, don't forget, Bertie—wreath of 'ops. Now, I dessay I'm 'olding you up. You know my terms, old sport."

He nodded to Campion, who signed to him to continue.

"Well, then, we won't go into my methods before strangers"—he winked at Campion—"but yesterday afternoon I 'appened to over'ear a very curious conversation."

"On the telephone?" said Campion.

"Natcherally. Private line wot I was interested in. Never

got much off it before—only recently been installed. But wot I 'eard was this—roughly, you understand."

He paused, and produced a small shabby notebook. "I cops in 'arfway through, you get me, so I didn't 'ear the beginning. There was two voices, one soft and smooth as you like, and the other sounded like it was disguised. Assumed foreign accent, I reckoned. This last one seemed to be the boss. 'Wot?' 'e was sayin', 'that man's a fool—get rid of 'im. Who sent the clothes?' Then the other chap says, 'There was no message, only the 'andwritin' on the label.' Then the boss says, 'Well, that's the man you want, isn't it?' "

Mr. Knapp looked up. "This didn't seem no use to me," he continued. "And then, quite sudden, the boss says, ' 'Oo's this Albert Campion?' and the other chap says, 'I'll find out about 'im.' Then of course I was interested, but they didn't say much more after that. All I 'eard was the boss say, 'If it was the girl's writin' get 'er up an' put 'er through it. You can arrange that. She must know somethink. As soon as you 'ear anythink, communicate with me in the usual way,' says the voice. Then 'e rings off."

Marlowe looked at Campion, but his eyes were hidden behind his glasses and his face was expressionless. "Look here, Thos," he said, "where did you hear all this?"

Mr. Knapp shook his head and appealed to Marlowe. "Artful, ain't 'e?" he said. "Before we go any further I want to know just 'ow interested you are in this. 'Ow do we stand?"

Campion sighed. "Thos, you make me writhe," he said. "How much do you want?"

Mr. Knapp, who had appeared somewhat dubious until this moment, now rose to his feet. "I'll tell you wot," he said, "I'll be a gent too. I'll come in with you. I can be a good sport when I like. I've often wanted to work with you again, Bertie," he went on, somewhat lugubriously. "Do you remember—?"

Mr. Campion coughed. "We won't go into that now," he said. "Let me point something out to you. Unless you know where these people were speaking from this information is no more than we know already."

"Wait a minute," said Mr. Knapp. "*Wait* for it. That's wot they tell you in the army. That is just exactly wot I do know. And I'm makin' you a gentlemanly offer—wot I wouldn't if I didn't know you, and realize that you'd treat me right whatever 'appened. I'll come in with you. When we're successful you coughs up and you coughs up 'andsome. "Ow's that?"

"Fine," said Mr. Campion. "But what do you imagine we're up to?"

Mr. Knapp hesitated. "Seems I'm doin' all the talkin'," he said. "But since I know you, Bertie, I'll say that one of yer little party 'ere is about to be took off to 'ave a particularly nasty time. If not already done. Is there a young woman down 'ere?"

Marlowe spoke before Campion could stop him. "As a matter of fact," he said, "Miss Paget has already disappeared."

"Ho?" said Mr. Knapp, his eyes flickering. "So you wasn't comin' across, Bertie? Well, I'll treat you fair, if you don't me. Fifty quid for that address, and another fifty when we get the girl back. Then I'll 'elp you, fer the sake of old times. Saved my ruddy life, 'e did once," he added conversationally to Marlowe. "Stuffed me down a drain and kept me there till danger was past. I've never forgot that. Now what do you say to that, Bert?"

"Since we're all on the make," said Campion slowly, "I'll give you a piece of information for your first fifty and the second fifty cash down when we get the girl."

"Wot information?" said Mr. Knapp cautiously.

"A little matter of 'snide'," said Campion lightly. "I think you ought to know about it."

All the bounce left Mr. Knapp. "I'm on," he said softly. "Come across. That's my old man, you know. Break 'is 'eart if anythink 'appened to that business."

"That's right," said Campion affably. "You're the heir, aren't you?"

"Come across," said Mr. Knapp doggedly.

"They're watching the building. I'd get your grandfather to move if I were you. Etching presses are very suspicious."

" 'Ow do I know you're not kiddin'?"

"Well, you can always stay and find out," said Campion carelessly. "But there's a new flower-seller at the end of the street, and an invalid man spends most of his time in a wheel chair on the balcony of the house opposite."

"I see," said Mr. Knapp thoughtfully. "I see. Gawd! 'Ood a' thought of that after all these years!" He seemed lost in contemplation. Campion brought him back to earth.

"Suppose you give us the address."

"Thirty-two Beverley Gardens, Kensington, W8." He spoke without hesitation. "It's a nice little 'ouse. Swell part. I 'ad a look at it as I come past. Three floors an' a basement. Steps up to front door. Easiest entrance by the roof. I got it all taped for you. I was workin' it all out as I come down, just in case."

He unfolded a grubby sheet of paper from his notebook. The other two bent over it.

"Now this 'ere," he said, tapping a series of hieroglyphics with a distressing forefinger, "this gives you the 'ole plan of the roofs. This 'ouse is where I 'ang out. It backs almost directly on to Beverley Gardens. That's 'ow I come to notice the extra wire there. If we made my place the 'eadquarters— I'm on the top floor—we could nip across them roofs as easy as kiss yer 'and. They won't think of keepin' an eye on the roof, but I see a couple o' heavy blokes watchin' the place as I come past and I dessay there's 'arf a dozen others inside. Money no object, it looked to me. I know the plan o' the house, too," he went on, "because all that row is built on the same idea and the last one's empty. I gave it the once-over in case there was any decent fittings left behind. Now just 'ere there's a skylight which looks like wot we want. That gives into a sort of boxroom—the smallest of two attics. Outside that door there's the stairs that goes down on to the first landing. After that—"

He was interrupted by Giles, who thrust his head round the door. "I suppose you know lunch has been waiting for half an hour?" he said. "Where's Biddy? I thought she was with you, Marlowe."

He stopped short at the sight of Mr. Knapp. Campion

beckoned him into the room and closed the door behind him. "Look here, old boy," he said, "we've got to get up to London as quick as we can. Don't get the wind up, but they've got Biddy."

It was some moments before Giles comprehended. Campion explained all they knew of her disappearance, and gradually the slow anger kindled in the boy's eyes.

"My God, someone'll pay for this," he said. "I'll thrash that little whelp Kettle within an inch of his life."

Campion frowned. "My dear old bird," he said, "we shall need all the spitefulness you can muster this evening. Get her back first, argue afterward. Our friend here seems to have been doing a spot of borough surveying on our behalf. By the way"—he turned to Knapp—"I suppose you've got all the necessary penknives and whatnots?"

Mr. Knapp's expression was eloquent. "Wot d'you take me for?" he said. "I got all my uncle's stuff after 'e was pinched. Wot we want"—he ticked the items off on his fingers—"is a couple o' jemmies, a small 'ook ladder, and 'arf a dozen life preservers, assorted sizes. A good old-fashioned outfit. I 'ate these new stunts. A blow-lamp's useful sometimes, but the rest is muck. Wot surprises me, you know, Bert," he went on, suddenly changing his tone, "is that these people should kidnap anyone. It ain't their line by a long chalk."

Campion swung round on him. "Who do you think they are?"

" 'Oo do I *know* they are," said the visitor. "A new lot—blackmail, shouldn't wonder. The chap tells fortunes—a bloke with a red beard."

"Anthony Datchett?"

"Is that wot 'e calls 'imself?" Mr. Knapp was unimpressed. "Something like that. The only thing I thought was funny was 'im goin' in for this sort of thing at all. Seems to me 'e's doin' a job for someone, same as I'm doin' a job for you."

"Answered in one," said Campion. "As far as intelligence is concerned you're coming on, Thos."

"That's right, flatter me," said Mr. Knapp, without enthusiasm.

"What I can't understand," broke in Giles explosively, "is why they took Biddy. There were all the rest of us about —why pitch on her?"

"That's easy," said Knapp. "I told these chaps that at the beginning. She sent a parcel of clothes by post, wot was mucked about with. Which is, I take it, wot they want to know about."

The three others exchanged glances.

"Clothes?" said Giles. "He must mean Judge Lobbett's clothes—the suit Kettle said he'd found. Biddy sent them away by post?" He sat down heavily in a chair and looked at them blankly.

"I deliberately refuse to consider that question," said Marlowe. "Find her first."

CHAPTER XIX

The Tradesmen's Entrance

MR. CAMPION'S council of war was made unexpectedly stormy by Giles. Until now he had borne the nightmare experiences of the past few days with comparative equanimity, but the latest development was too much for him: it seemed to have aroused every spark of obstinacy in his nature.

"Look here," he said. "I'm sorry to be uncivil, but it does strike me as being very fishy that the moment my sister disappears up comes Mr. Knapp with the details for rescuing her all worked out pat. How do you know that he's not in with these people?"

"Now, calm yerself, calm yerself," said the accused one soothingly. "An' don't interrupt me, Bertie," he added, waving a hand to silence Campion. "This gent's asked me a straight question; 'e's entitled to a straight answer. Fishy it may look, but it ain't really. And why? I'll tell you." He came over to the young man and caught him by the lapel with a slightly greasy thumb and forefinger. "Magersfontein Lugg an' me 'as been pals for some years. Union of bonds, as you might say." He winked at Campion knowingly. "Last week 'e come to me an' 'e said 'Our friend Bertie'—'e works for Bertie: cleans the 'ouse up an' gives the place a tone—

'Our friend Bertie,' 'e says, 'is off on some very nasty business. 'E 'asn't told me nothing, but you, bein' a knowin' one, might keep yer eyes open.' So I 'ave."

He stood back from Giles and grinned as though he felt he had completely allayed any doubts in the young man's mind. Giles, however, was unimpressed.

"That's all very well," he said, "but what could you do?"

"Oh, I see!" Mr. Knapp's tone was more intimate than ever. "P'r'aps I'd better introduce myself. I used to work for the Government on the telephone repairs. Then me an' the Postmaster-General, we 'ad a bit of a tiff an' I retired from public life an' service for a spell. When I come out I thought I'd make use of my electrical knowledge, an' I've worked up a very tidy little connection. You may not know it, but all over London there's 'undreds of private wires, some of 'em straight, some fishy." He paused. "Now do you get me?"

"No," said Giles.

Mr. Knapp grinned at Marlowe and tapped his forehead significantly. "That's where 'e wants it," he remarked pleasantly. "Well, I'll tell you. It's the easiest thing to listen on to a wire, if you knows the way. You'd be surprised at the stuff I pick up. Filthy goin's-on in 'igh life wot you wouldn't believe."

Without speaking, Giles looked at Campion, who smiled in spite of himself at his friend's expression.

"Well," continued Mr. Knapp, "me bein' on the lookout, it ain't really surprisin' that I 'appened to 'ear something of interest. I come down as quick as I could, 'opin' to be a prevention rather than a cure. But since things 'ave 'appened as they 'ave 'appened we're doin' what we can to make the best of it. Take my tip, old son, and leave the arrangements to Bertie—'e's got the kind of mind for a do of this sort. I remember once—"

Mr. Campion interrupted him hastily. "Keep your jokes for your profession," he said. "Now look here. The proceeding is, I take it, something like this—"

"If you know the address of the house, why not call the police in?" said Giles.

"Because, oh heart—and head—of oak," said Campion

gently, "we don't know if Biddy's there, in the first place, and in the second, they're bound to have some perfectly good get-away. The only thing to do to prevent the poor kid from being longer in their hands than we can help is to get her out ourselves if she's there, and if she isn't to scout about till we do find her. We're evidently on their track, anyhow."

Giles folded his arms and stared gloomily before him.

"All right, get on with it," he said. "What do you suggest?"

Mr. Campion perched himself on the table, where he sat with his knees drawn up a little, peering round at them through his spectacles.

"We shall have to go carefully from the very beginning," he said. "You see, according to Knapp, ever since yesterday afternoon Mr. Datchett and his chorus boys have been making investigations concerning our Albert. This is more serious than it looks. If, for instance, they discover some of his pet names, they will, I fear, be on the watch for us pretty closely. They may even have someone watching us here. I don't think Kettle will be much good to them any more, but there's bound to be someone else on the road just over the Stroud. Therefore we must not parade ourselves. The simplest thing, I fancy, is for us to appeal to old Baa Baa Blacksheep, who I see is still with us. You three will set off to town battened under his dust cover at the back. There's no need for you to go the whole way like that, of course. They'd never suspect him, so if we could get him to take you all the way to Knapp's we'd be fairly safe." He laughed. "You'll have to forgive this heavy stuff, but I assure you it's really necessary. Isopel will have to come with us. We daren't leave her here. I think the best place for her is my flat; it's over a police station, you know. I'll drive her there myself in my own bus, so that anyone on the look-out for us will only know that Isopel and I have gone off and Mr. Barber has returned to London. That's straight enough."

"Then they'll think that all the rest of us are down here?" said Giles.

Campion beamed at him. "That's the idea. Of course

they may not be watching, but it's as well to take the precaution," he said. "Now, that's all set, then, if you people agree to it."

Marlowe nodded. "I'm with you," he said. "Isopel and I have put ourselves completely in your hands all along and I believe you'll pull us through."

Campion grinned. "For these kind words, many thanks," he said. "There's only one snag in it," he went on seriously, "and that is our little picture-postcard expert. He's not quite a Deadwood Dick, but he might be persuaded to give us a hand."

"I think I can manage him"—Marlowe spoke confidently. "I'll go and talk to him. I'd like to see Isopel too."

He went out of the room, leaving the others still conferring.

"I see the idea, Bertie." Mr. Knapp pushed the jug of beer away from him regretfully. "You take this other girl to safety an' pick up the one or two things you'll need at your place, an' I'll manage this bunch. I'll 'ave 'em all primed up. I don't like workin' with amateurs, but there's nothin' like beef in a rough 'ouse. My old ma'll be up there, you know. She'll give us a 'and with the get-away if necessary. There's not much she don't know."

Mr. Campion looked sceptical, but he did not speak, and presently Marlowe came into the room with Mr. Barber. The expert was puzzled.

"Certainly," he said, "I will give anybody a lift to London, but why ride under the dust cover? I do not understand. It is so—so'—he hesitated for the word— "inconvenient."

Campion spoke soothingly. "We're in a very inconvenient situation, Mr. Barber, and if you could help us we should be enormously obliged to you."

"That's the ticket," said Mr. Knapp fatuously. "An' if I was you, my old bloke, I'd 'urry up an' do all you can fer us," he added, changing his tone. "That's a warnin', mind."

Campion kicked him gently and returned to Mr. Barber. "Take no notice of him," he said cheerfully. "He thinks he's acting for the talkies, that's why he's all dressed up."

"Film acting?" said Mr. Barber eagerly, as if he had at last found a clue to the situation, but as no one responded he sighed and repeated his offer. "Gentlemen, I do not understand at all, but I shall be delighted to do anything I can for you."

"So I should 'ope," muttered Mr. Knapp. "Now I reckon the earlier we start the better. So pull yer socks up, mates." He moved over to the table and tipped up the jug. "There's plenty left 'ere," he added cheerfully. "We might take it with us. Anybody got a bottle about 'em?" He caught Campion's eye and dropped the jug hastily. "Sorry, I'm sure," he said somewhat sheepishly, and followed the others out of the room.

Mrs. Whybrow received careful instructions from Giles. She was not to go into the village, no one was to know that they were not all still in the house. She was a sensible woman and took her instructions placidly. None of the Manor servants had as yet realized that Biddy had disappeared.

Campion packed the three men, Giles and Marlowe with Mr. Knapp, into the back of Mr. Barber's car, and fastened the canvas dust cover down securely.

"No need to stay like that once you get the other side of Ipswich," he said. "The police won't stop an out-going car on the Stroud. Mr. Barber, we shall be eternally grateful to you."

The old man bent towards him and spoke in a confidential rumble. "My dear sir," he said, "if you could persuade Mr. Paget to consent to allow me to handle the sale of his picture, the gratitude would be entirely mine."

He drove off, and Campion turned to Isopel. She was standing waiting for him, wrapped up in a fur coat, although it was summer. She looked very small and terrified standing there, her white face peering out from the dark fur of her high collar.

He smiled at her. "Scared?" he said.

"No." She shook her head. "Not any more. That part of me has gone numb."

He frowned. "That's bad. Do you think you could do

something for me? I want you to drive this car from here over the Stroud. I shall do a neat impersonation of a parcel at your feet. There's no danger. I just don't want anyone in the village to know that I've left the house."

She nodded. "Why, surely."

Mr. Campion doubled himself up at the bottom of the tiny car. "She's the easiest thing in the world to drive," he murmured. "There's one gear that I know of. Any other handle you pull you get your money back."

The girl smiled faintly. She climbed in beside him and tucked him neatly out of sight beneath the rug.

"Biddy says you always talk like this, Mr. Campion," she said. "What happens when you have to be serious?"

The muffled voice from the rug sounded pained. "Then I sit on a large block of ice. You've probably seen pictures of me in the illustrated papers."

The journey from Mystery Mile to the Ipswich road passed without excitement, and Mr. Campion emerged from his hiding-place. "Now I'll take her," he said. "I've had music hall offers for the act I'm about to perform," he remarked cheerfully as he climbed into the driving-seat. "You've managed her marvellously. I've never known her to move for a woman before. It's a sort of jealousy, I think."

Isopel did not appear to be listening to him.

"Mr. Campion," she said, "you're not talking about this —this terrible thing that has happened to Biddy because you're afraid of frightening me. But don't think about that, please. I want to do all I can to help. Marlowe is in love with her, you know. I think they fell for each other when they first met."

The little car was racing along the main Woodbridge— Ipswich road, and the young man did not take his eyes off the giddy stretch before them.

"You mean they'd probably want to marry?" he said.

"Oh yes, I think so. Isn't it funny that he and she should feel like that when I and—"

She paused abruptly, and Mr. Campion did not press her to continue. She sat back in the car, a thoughtful look in her dark eyes. Suddenly she turned again.

"I suppose," she said jerkily, "that no one knows about—about the red knight, do they?"

"Don't forget your promise." The words were spoken lightly enough, but there was no mistaking the sincerity beneath them. "No one, no one in the world, must know anything about that."

She caught her breath. "I'm sorry," she said, "but sometimes I feel so terribly afraid."

"Don't worry. I'll get her back if it's the last thing I do." The vigorous determination in his voice surprised her, and she turned to him. But Mr. Campion's face was as pleasantly vacuous and inane as it had ever been.

They reached the city in record time, and he made for a garage on the east side of Regent Street.

"I hope you won't mind," he said, beaming down at her as they emerged into Piccadilly Circus, "but I'm afraid I shall have to take you into my place by the tradesmen's entrance. You never know at a time like this who may be watching the front door. This is another dark secret, by the way. I think I'll have to insist that you stay at my flat," he went on. "It's the one really safe place in London for you. There's a police station downstairs. I'm only taking you in the back way so that no one will see me. I don't want an ovation from the populace."

He piloted her across the road and down one of the small turnings on the opposite side, and paused at last before what looked to Isopel like a small but expensive restaurant. They went in, and, passing through a line of small tables, entered a smaller room leading off the main hall where favoured patrons were served. The little place was deserted, and Mr. Campion approached the service door and held it open for her.

"I must show you my little kitchenette," he said. "It's too *bijou* for anything."

Isopel looked round her. On her right was an open doorway disclosing a vast kitchen beyond, on her left a small narrow passage leading apparently to the manager's office. Campion walked in.

A little grey-haired foreigner rose to meet him. It was

evident that he recognized the young man, but to the girl's surprise he did not speak to him. He led them silently into an inner room and threw open a cupboard doorway.

"I'll go first." Campion spoke softly. With a great show of secrecy the little foreigner nodded, and, standing back, disclosed what appeared to be a very ordinary service lift which was apparently used principally for food. One of the shelves had been removed, and Mr. Campion climbed into the opening with as much dignity as he could muster.

"See Britain first," he said oracularly, and pressed the button so that, as if the words had been a command, he shot up suddenly out of sight.

Isopel opened her mouth to speak, but the little foreigner placed a finger on his lips and looked about him with such an expression of apprehension that she was silenced immediately. Within a minute the lift reappeared, a big blue cushion in the bottom of it. A voice floated down the shaft. "Always the little gent. My second name is Raleigh. *Houp,* Elizabeth!"

The mysterious foreigner helped the girl into the lift as if he feared that at any moment they might be attacked. The journey was not so uncomfortable as it looked, and as she felt herself being drawn up into the darkness, Isopel's sense of the ridiculous was touched and she began to laugh.

"That's fine," said Campion, helping her out into the small dining-room of his flat. "Was old Rodriguez too much for your gravity? He's a wonderful chap. He owns that restaurant, and makes a damn good thing out of it—the old robber! The only way I get him to let me use the lift as an entrance is by pretending it's a case of life or death. He has a secret thirst for adventure, and my little goings and comings by the back door give him no end of a thrill. He feels he's taking part in a crook story or something. As a matter of fact, a previous tenant here had the lift put in to have his food sent up. Rodriguez is a nice chap, but he will act his part, which becomes a little trying at times. Now look here," he went on, conducting her into the other room. "You'll be quite all right here. Lugg, I fancy, is already at the scene of operations, but you'll have Autolycus to keep you company.

You'll have to watch your jewellery, that's all. It's living with Lugg that does it."

He was bustling about the room as he spoke, selecting various odds and ends from a Sheraton bureau at the far end of the room and a deep cupboard by the fireplace.

"If you get hungry, just shout down the lift. If you get scared, just shout out of the window. If anyone should call, don't open the door. Especially not to an old gentleman with an aerial to his top hat and natty black gaiters. That's my wicked uncle. You can see everyone who comes in the mirror on the inside of the door. It works on the periscope principle. All done with a few common chalks."

Isopel and Autolycus, who seemed to have struck up a happy acquaintance, watched him as he pottered about the room. For some moments the girl seemed on the verge of speaking. At last she found her courage.

"Mr. Campion," she said, "don't let Giles do anything silly—or Marlowe either, of course," she added hastily. "You'll look after them?"

"As if they were my own sons, madam," said Campion, beaming at her. "Both young gentlemen will be under the direct care of the Matron."

She laughed, but her eyes were still anxious. "You see," she burst out suddenly, the colour suffusing her face, "you don't know how dreadfully worrying it is to be in love."

Mr. Campion crossed over to the lift. She could see him through the open doorway from where she sat. He climbed in with great dignity, and sat there, looking ineffably comic, his knees drawn up to his chin, as he regarded her owlishly from behind his spectacles.

"That's all you know, young woman," he said solemnly, and shut the hatch.

She heard the lift rumble down the shaft.

CHAPTER XX

The Profession

THE glories of Pedigree Mews had departed for ever. The dirty row of broken-down stables with two floors of dwelling-rooms above was almost ripe for the condemners' notice. There were not even children playing in the uneven brick sink which formed the street, and the whole place had a furtive and surly aspect.

It lay at right angles to the blind alley which was Beverley Mews on the one side, and Wishart Street, which wriggled down into Church Street, Kensington, on the other. A dangerous and depressing spot.

Mr. Campion glanced up and down the row. There was not a soul in sight. Number Twelve A was a dilapidated doorway in the corner between the two mews. The stables under the building were apparently unused.

He pushed open the door, which was cold and greasy to the touch, and entered into a narrow passage smelling horribly of damp and cats. In front of him was a square patch of light revealing the tiny yard of the house, probably even more execrable than the passage itself. Just before the yard entrance he stumbled upon a dirty flight of stairs which wound a narrow way up into the building. Here the odours became more intense and were mingled with others even less attractive. Mr. Campion ascended gingerly, keeping clear of the walls. As he reached the top floor, which consisted of two rooms, the doors of which formed two sides of a tiny square landing, he heard the unmistakable voice of Thos T. Knapp himself, clearly intent on being hospitable.

"Mother, make room on the bed for Mr. Barber. 'E don't look 'appy in the corner there."

Campion paused and whistled softly. The door was opened immediately, and Mr. Lugg came edging his way out. He was even more gloomy than before, and he regarded Mr. Campion appraisingly.

"Think you're clever, don't you?" he remarked in a throaty rumble. "When you're goin' into a really nasty business, 'oo do you get round you? Two ruddy amateurs and somethin' out of a carpet shop. Gawd, you should see wot's goin' on in there." He clicked his tongue against his teeth contemptuously. "*Don't* lean against that wall," he added hastily. "It's *me* wot looks after yer clothes, don't forget."

"Look here," said Campion mildly, "this nursemaid impersonation of yours is getting on my nerves. Why did you get Knapp into this when I told you not to?"

"It was done afore you spoke." Lugg was not in the least abashed. "The day you gets plugged is the day I lose my job. I'm lookin' after you, see? I believe you've beat me this time, though," he added lugubriously. "S'pose I bring Thos out and we 'ave a talk in the other room? There's an atmosphere of 'appy-go-lucky in there wot neely makes me sick. I never could stummick a fug."

Without waiting for a reply, he put his head round the door and made an inarticulate sound. Mr. Knapp appeared at once.

" 'Ullo, Bertie," he said pleasantly. "We ain't 'arf got a little party in 'ere. My old ma says she feels she's got all 'er sons round 'er again."

Mr. Lugg raised his hand. "Pleasantries is over," he said. "Take 'im into the other room, Thos, and we'll 'ave a talk."

"Righto." Mr. Knapp threw open the door of the second room. "Plenty of time—'opeless to try anythin' in this light.

This 'ere is wot I call my workshop. Nice little place, ain't it?"

The room into which he conducted them was about ten feet square, low-ceilinged and as dirty as the approach had suggested. There were two long trestle tables which practically filled it, and upon these was piled the most amazing collection of electrical junk Campion had ever seen. There were odd pairs of earphones, vast quantities of wire, electric plugs, a home-made switchboard, and any amount of other odds and ends, all more or less in direct connection with Mr. Knapp's unpleasant hobby.

"There you are," he said, throwing out a hand. "All give me by the Government in unconscious recognition of my services. There's one of the old Bell telephones over there—come from Clerkenwell—interestin' relic. 'Ere's a later War Office mouthpiece—they do themselves proud there."

"Stop yer reminiscences," said Mr. Lugg. " 'Oo do you think you are? A retired admiral? This 'ere's business. I expect trouble, I don't mind tellin' you. I see yer 'ouse is Twelve A. Thirteen that ought to be by rights."

"Shut up," said Mr. Knapp with unexpected bad temper. "There's a thirteen 'igher up the street. Bloke's in quod."

"I hear you've got Mr. Barber in the next room," said Campion. "What's the idea? Have you any objects of virtue up here, Thos?"

"I 'ate jokes about sex," said Mr. Knapp sententiously. "No, I brought 'im up 'ere because I thought 'is car might be 'andy if we 'ad to 'urry off. I'll leave it tickin' over quietly in the stables downstairs. I couldn't very well keep it and not 'im. When dealin' with gents you 'ave to be a gent, so I says, 'Come up an' see Mother'. 'E's not 'appy in there, but Mother'll keep 'im quiet. She's as good as a bull pup."

"Cut the guff," said Mr. Lugg. " 'Oo the 'ell cares, anyway?"

Mr. Knapp pulled himself together. " 'Eave yerself over this 'ere bench an' take a look out o' the window. D'you see where we are? No? Well, that's the end 'ouse of Beverley Gardens, that is. Now run yer eye along." He was holding Campion firmly by the shoulder as he spoke. "Stand well back so as no one don't see you from the window. Now that 'ouse with the blue curtain to the top window—see it?— that's the 'ouse we want. It's not much of a climb," he went on. "This 'ere ledge outside 'ere goes straight along till we get to the flat roof of the shop. Mother can do it easy, so you ought to."

"Then there's a spot of mountaineering," said Campion.

"That's right," said Mr. Knapp. "I see you come in yer crawlers," he added, looking at the young man's plus-fours. "That'll be easy enough. I got me ladder 'ere. There's plenty o' rubber shoes about, too."

"I brought mine with me," said Mr. Lugg, taking a pair of mysteriously constructed rubber clogs from a brown-paper parcel which he carried.

Mr. Knapp looked at him with undisguised amusement. 'Gawd! You don't use them old things, do you? I ain't seen those since I was a nipper. Wotcher, Spring'eel Jack!"

"Think yer clever, don't you?" said Mr. Lugg. "These are an heirloom, that's wot these are."

Campion turned away from the window. "When do we start?" he said. "As soon as it gets dark? Round about half-past ten?"

"That's about it," said Mr. Knapp. "Nearly everyone's out o' doors or at any rate downstairs about that time."

"I think we'd better join the lady," said Campion. "And I tell you, Knapp, you'd better keep your exuberance down a bit. Those two kids in the next room are both deeply interested in the girl, so don't let them do anything silly if you can prevent it."

"Am I likely to?" said Mr. Knapp with contempt. "I'm in, too, ain't I? I've showed 'em the plan o' the works an' they seemed quite intelligent to me. Oh, well, it won't be the first time you an' me's been in a rough 'ouse, Bertie, will it? Do you remember, Lugg, you an' me in that 'ouse in Chiswick? Old girl three flights up—titled party, I believe she was—kept 'anging over the banisters screamin' like a train. 'Rapine!' she shouts. A great big cop was sittin' on my chest, but I couldn't 'elp laughin'."

Mr. Lugg snorted contemptuously, and Campion pushed his way into the other room.

At first sight the happy-go-luckiness to which Mr. Lugg had alluded was painfully apparent. This room, only a foot or so larger than the one they had just left, served the Knapp family as a complete domicile. In spite of the heat of the day, the window was tightly closed, and a saucepan boiled upon the decrepit gas stove. It was impossible to see clearly across the room for tobacco smoke and certain bedraggled pieces of laundry which were suspended from an impromptu clothes-line from the gas bracket to a hook in the ceiling. A large iron bedstead blocked one corner of the room, a smaller one prevented the door from opening properly on the other side, and the mother's and son's complete wardrobes were hung up along the farther wall.

In the midst of this discomfort Mrs. Knapp presided affably over a worn and impatient gathering. She was a vast florid person clad in an assortment of garments, each one of which attempted to do only half the duty for which it had originally been intended. Her scrawny reddish hair was drawn tightly into a knot at the back of her head, from which several escaping strands fell over her disordered bodice. Her face was chiefly remarkable for some three or four attempts at a beard which grew out of large brown moles scattered over her many chins.

She was seated upon the larger bed, and beside her, dignified but uncomfortable, was the unfortunate Mr. Barber.

Giles and Marlowe greeted Campion with relief.

"Thank heaven you've come!" said the American. "Isn't it time we started?"

"My dear old bird, I'm palpitating for the fray," said Campion emphatically. "But it's absolutely no use starting in the daylight because we shouldn't get there. We shall have to wait for some considerable time longer."

"This is damnable," said Marlowe. "Poor kid, you don't know what they may be doing to her. It makes me mad." He ground his heel savagely into the floor.

"You sit down, matey, an' 'ave a friendly game o' cards." Mr. Knapp was doing his best to be reassuring. "I'd go an' 'ave a mike round for you, but it's too light as yet. We can't do anythin'."

"Suicide to go out now," added Mr. Lugg sepulchrally. "We professionals, we know."

Giles was sitting on a piece of newspaper carefully spread over the boards, his knees drawn up to his chin and an utterly dejected expression on his face. "Gosh, I shall be glad when we can start," he said feelingly.

"You won't, once the time comes," said Mr. Lugg with disquieting solemnity. "We're goin' to be for it to-night. I've got that feelin'."

Mrs. Knapp turned upon him and emitted such a stream of blasphemies that everyone except her son was startled.

"Mother's superstitious," said Knapp. "She don't like premonitions."

The lady, having recovered her serenity, smiled at them toothily. It was at this moment that Mr. Barber staggered to his feet.

"I do not wish to appear unsporting," he said, "but really I think I had better go. I feel that I shall not be of any further service to you."

The Knapps turned upon him as one person.

"You stay where you are. If you go now you'll give the 'ole show away. We've 'ad enough nobs knockin' round 'ere as it is," said Thos. "Mother, pass the gentleman yer bottle."

Mr. Barber was forced back to bed, where he sat looking round in helpless misery. Mrs. Knapp took no notice of her son's last remark, much to the Oriental's relief, and a sticky pack of cards was produced.

"Nothink like poker," said Mr. Knapp. "An' remember, gentlemen, this is a friendly game."

"It seems almost a waste of time," said Mr. Lugg, drawing up a broken-backed chair.

Marlowe moved over to Campion. "You're sure this is the best thing?" he murmured. "I feel ready to burst."

Campion bent towards him, and for a moment he saw the seriousness in the pale eyes behind the big spectacles. "It's our only chance, old bird," he said. "We're going the moment we've the least hope."

Marlowe glanced at him sharply. "You expect serious trouble?"

"I expect a small war," said Mr. Campion frankly.

CHAPTER XXI

Mr. Campion's Nerve

"ARGUE as much as you like, Mother," said Mr. Knapp. "Five queens is five queens. If these gentlemen will accept the fact that some o' the old pack 'ave got mixed in we'll say no more about it. Personally, I think the time's gettin' on."

"That's right," said Mr. Lugg. "I'll be gettin' me boots off."

The atmosphere of the small room, which had been steadily thickening for the past two hours, was now positively sulphurous. Mr. Barber, after several unsuccessful attempts to make a graceful departure, had resigned himself to his unwholesome fate. Mrs. Knapp was keeping her eye on him.

Marlowe and Giles, who were profoundly relieved at the idea of doing something, at last rose to their feet, whilst the lady of the party gathered up her winnings unashamedly. Mr. Campion effaced himself as much as possible.

Now that the moment of action was approaching, Messrs. Lugg and Knapp took charge of the proceedings with the air of specialists. Knapp produced a couple of life preservers and gave Marlowe and Giles a few well-thought-out words of instruction.

"Just a gentle tap, reelly," he said—*"be'ind* the ear—or

over it—or above it—administered firmly and with precision. This is unless you carry guns. I don't," he explained. "Me an' Bertie, we're all against swingin'."

"I've got a gun with me," said Marlowe, "but I think this looks more useful."

"Same here," said Giles. "The less row the better, I suppose."

Mr. Campion said nothing. They removed their coats at Mr. Knapp's suggestion, tucking their pullovers into their plus-fours. The seriousness of the affair began to assume its proper proportion.

Campion removed his glasses.

"I see so much better without them," he explained, and set about changing his shoes.

Mother Knapp began to move about with feline quietness, producing rubber-soled shoes and small tots of rum and water.

"Now, look 'ere," said her son, when they had all assembled in the back room. "We goes carefully *an'* quietly, takin' our time, an' no mistakes. Keep off the skyline as much as possible, 'eads low, as a rule. Once there, I nips in first, bein' fairly light an' 'avin' a knowledge of the 'ouse. Then I comes out an' tells you 'ow the land lies, an' 'an's over my command to Bertie, as you might say."

"And I?" said Mr. Barber from the doorway. "Really I—"

Mrs. Knapp appeared behind him. "You stay with me, dearie," she said. "Till they come back. Did you see the car was started, Thos?"

"Tickin' over like a bird," said Mr. Knapp. "Don't let 'im go, 'owever 'e struggles."

All five of Mrs. Knapp's teeth appeared in a devastating smile.

"You'll stay with me, won't you, lovey?" she said, and gently drew the unfortunate Oriental into the other room.

Mr. Knapp continued. "Now then, me first, Bertie second. Then you two lads, then Lugg. Don't forget, soft on the slates an' quiet on the tiles. If you 'ear me whistle, stop dead, an' lie as flat as you can. Now, are you ready?"

"Any more for the 'Skylark'?" murmured Mr. Campion. "Lovely drying day."

Mr. Knapp raised the window gently and crawled out on to the ledge. After a moment of suspense they heard his whisper: "All clear. Come on."

"Railin's with spikes on under 'ere, shouldn't be surprised," said Mr. Lugg huskily from the background. "Gently does it."

The night was clear but moonless. There were people in the farther streets, and a rumble of traffic came to them. Nearly all the windows that lay beneath their path were dark, as Mr. Knapp had predicted.

Ahead of them to the east the lights of London made a glow in the sky. The air was warm, and the scents of the great city—fruit, face powder, petrol fumes, and dust—were not too unpleasantly mixed together.

The going was not so much perilous as awkward, after the first giddy twenty feet or so of parapet. Mr. Knapp unfolded a collapsible ladder which he was apparently used to carrying, since he managed its conveyance with extraordinary skill. On it they climbed up from the lower roofs of the shops to the flat lead-covered tops of the houses in Beverley Gardens. Mr. Lugg, bringing up the rear, left it in position for the return.

The trip was not without its thrills. As Mr. Knapp dropped lightly on to the roof of the second house in the row, a woman's voice, old and querulous, shouted at him through an open window:

"Who's there?"

"London Telephone Service, ma'am. Breakdown gang. Tracing a wire." Mr. Knapp's cheerful tone would have satisfied the most timid.

There was a satisfied grunt from the darkness, and they pushed on again. The sweat was pouring off Giles's face. Both he and Marlowe were law-abiding souls, and were it not for the all-important motive which now impelled them, neither of them would have dreamed of assisting in such an enterprise.

"It's the next 'ouse after this," murmured Mr. Knapp,

and paused abruptly, nudging Campion. "Absolutely askin' for it—this lot," he said, indicating the skylight of the roof on which they now stood. It was wide open. He bent over it and idly ran his torch round the dark room. It appeared to be a studio. The little circle of light rested upon a side table, where, beside a telephone, stood a decanter and a siphon.

"Wot a spot o' luck if we wasn't busy," he remarked casually. "Afraid we shan't be so 'appy next door."

One by one they clambered over the narrow stone coping which separated the two roofs.

"Gently does it—gently," Mr. Knapp whispered as the two amateurs climbed somewhat nervily over it. "Keep yer 'eads down. 'Ere we are, then," he went on to Campion. "I ain't actually been 'ere afore, you understand, but I got a nice pair o' binoculars at my place—a present from my old colonel. I've always felt 'e meant to give 'em to me. Now, a jemmy or a diamond, d'you think?"

"Diamond," said Mr. Lugg. "Less noisy. There's no one underneath. Sure this is the 'ouse?"

"Shut up, 'Appy," said Mr. Knapp. Now that the procedure had been decided upon he set to work with a silent and a practised hand.

The tension among the onlookers became strained, as he drew out a piece of glass on a rubber sucker, slipped in his hand, and raising the catch gently laid the window back upon the leads. All was dark and silent inside the house.

"Not a bit o' light showin' anywhere," said Mr. Lugg, who had investigated both sides of the building from the roof. "Now then, Thos, in with you. I'll see you buried decent."

Mr. Knapp made a careful survey of the interior of the room below, which appeared empty, and then, gripping the lintel firmly in both hands, swung gently into the air and dropped noiselessly into the room.

"Lie flat," commanded Lugg. "You don't know nothing, none of you. Be ready to nip off like 'ell if there's a row."

There was a soft click from the room below them, and the tiny circle of Mr. Knapp's torch was seen no more. They waited listening, every nerve strained, anxious to catch the least sound from the silent house below them. The minutes passed with agonizing slowness. Still Mr. Knapp did not return.

At last even Lugg began to show signs of uneasiness.

"Thos ain't the chap to stay in a nasty spot fer fun," he muttered nervously. Marlowe edged nearer, Giles behind him.

"Can't we go in?" he said. "After him?"

"You'll stay where you are," growled Mr. Lugg.

Campion, who was bending over the dark square of the open skylight, suddenly dodged back. *"Cave,"* he whispered.

An unnatural stillness fell over the whole party. No one breathed. At last a welcome whisper sounded out of the darkness.

"Give us a hand, matey."

Lugg and Campion thrust down an arm each, and the next moment Mr. Knapp, nimble and monkey-like in the darkness, scrambled softly out on to the leads beside them. His rapid breathing was the first thing they noticed.

"Keep low," said Mr. Lugg. "Keep low."

They were lying flat upon the roof, and Giles, whose face came suddenly very close to Knapp's, saw that he was considerably shaken.

"She's in there all right." His squeaky cockney voice was ominously subdued. It rekindled the apprehension in the minds of all his hearers.

Marlowe moved forward involuntarily, and Campion himself stiffened where he lay close to the skylight.

"They've got 'er on the next floor down," said Mr. Knapp. "I didn't find 'em at first. The bloke with the red beard is all alone in a sort of drawin'-room they've got lower down. I should say 'e'd got a lot o' electric gadgets down there. It looked nasty to me. I come back, an' as I reached the second floor I 'eard a sort o' guggly noise, an' I found there was a long room that runs the 'ole width o' the 'ouse, along the front. It 'ad a kind of 'arf glass over the door, a curtain coverin' it. That's 'ow I missed it goin' down. I nipped up on a chair an' 'ad a look."

He paused, and his voice when he continued was pitched

a tone or so lower. The suggestion of shock, coming from him, appalled them.

"There was six or seven o' 'em," he said, "all nasty-lookin' coves. Ikey Todd 'isself an' two or three of 'is pals. There's a long table down the middle o' the room. The girl's sittin' at one end of it, tied into a chair. They're all askin' 'er questions, one after the other—old-fashioned police methods. An' sittin' on the other end o' the table, 'is legs crossed, was that dirty little Chink Ropey, the bloke the beak speechified about. 'E's got a fishin' rod in 'is 'and. I couldn't quite see wot 'e'd got on the end of it—looked like a needle or something. 'E was wavin' it about in front of 'er eyes, looked 'e'd scratched 'er face with it once or twice already. Take a ruddy Chink to think of a thing like that. Made me sick to look at it."

After the first chill of horror which his story produced upon his hearers, each reacted to it after his own way. Lugg and Campion knew as well as Mr. Knapp the sort of men with which they had to deal: men who fought without rule or decency, men to whom broken bottles and razors were the handiest weapons.

Giles and Marlowe, on the other hand, merely realized that the girl who was extraordinarily dear to them both was being subjected to a particularly ghastly torture in a room beneath their feet.

Before any of the other three had time to prevent them, they hurled themselves one after the other down into the attic and charged into the house like a couple of bulls.

Lugg and Knapp clutched at each other.

"Shall we nip off?" said Knapp nervously. "They've done it now."

Even the redoubtable Lugg hesitated. As a man of experience he knew what the mêlée below stairs was likely to resemble.

"Wot's that?" Knapp, already nervy, almost screamed. The two men, swinging round, were just in time to see a slight figure drop silently over the coping on to the next roof.

"It's Bertie," said Mr. Knapp, " 'ooking it."

The faithful Lugg was shaken to the core. Then, as the noise below suddenly broke into an uproar, he caught his friend by the collar and thrust him into the attic.

"Come on," he said. "Lost 'is nerve for a spell. See it 'appen in the war. We've got to take blasted good care we don't lose ours. Now then, pile up them boxes for a bloke leavin' in an 'urry. I told you wot'd come of bringin' amateurs. Last man up locks this 'ere door."

As he spoke he was moving about with incredible swiftness, dragging the odd lumber in the room to under the open skylight, to facilitate an exit.

Somewhere beneath them Biddy screamed. The sound touched the last spot of chivalry in Mr. Lugg's unsentimental heart.

"Come on, Thos," he said. " 'It anythink you see, and 'it like 'ell—s'long as it ain't me."

CHAPTER XXII

The Rough-house

MESSRS. LUGG and Knapp descended the narrow stairs to the second floor with considerably more caution than their immediate predecessors had shown, although this care was now slightly ridiculous, since the noise proceeding from the room below contradicted any idea that the occupants were listening for a further attack.

As they reached the landing they saw their objective immediately. The room was brilliantly lit, and crowded with people. They crept along the passage, keeping out of the shaft of light from the doorway. As they approached, a man staggered out and collapsed over the banisters, and the noise within the room increased in fury. Somewhere in the throng a voice was swearing continuously in a high-pitched stream, the monotonous tone sounding clearly above the deeper voices and the crashes of overturning furniture.

" 'Ere goes," whispered Mr. Lugg, hitching his trousers and grasping his life preserver. "I ain't 'eard any shootin' yet."

"They daren't risk it 'ere," muttered Knapp, sliding along the wall behind the larger man to the doorpost, round which he peered.

Giles and Marlowe had evidently charged straight

through the surprised gangsters and made for Biddy. At the moment when Lugg and Knapp arrived, the girl was still bound to her chair, and the two young men, although remaining beside her, were not making any further progress towards getting her out. They were both badly cut about. Giles's cheek was laid open to the bone, and Marlowe was laying about him with his left hand, his right arm hanging limply at his side.

Clearly they had only managed to get into the room by the suddenness of their attack. The angry gangsters had only just collected themselves.

An immense Jew standing with his back to the doorway suddenly raised his voice above the din. "Put 'em up quick, both of you. Sit on 'em boys."

He stepped back a pace, his gun levelled, and Mr. Lugg, seizing the opportunity, darted into the room and caught him a vicious blow just above the ear. He grunted like a pig and sprawled forward.

Knapp made a dive for the gun, but a heavy boot descended on his wrist and the revolver was snatched out of his grasp. The next instant the butt descended vigorously on the back of his head, and he went down without a sound.

The prompt despatch of his partner stirred Mr. Lugg to fury. Flinging out his left hand, he brought down a heavy picture frame over the sprawling figures, which, while it did no appreciable good to the cause, added most successfully to the confusion.

"The Guv'nor'll be up in a minute," shouted a voice. " 'Old 'em till then! 'old 'em till then! 'E'll deal with 'em. 'Tain't the police."

"The police'll be here any minute, you blighters!" yelled Giles. He was growing visibly fainter every second from loss of blood, but he was still game and struck about him savagely.

Even as he spoke a man closed with him and they rolled on to the floor together. From the other side of the room Lugg saw the Chinese, an evil little figure in a rusty black suit, edging slowly towards Biddy. His intent was obvious.

With the girl in danger, he could easily reduce the others to reasoning terms.

Mr. Lugg made an effort. He dodged under the arm of the man nearest him and caught the Chinese round the ankles.

Even so, the position of the rescue party seemed hopeless. There were still two gangsters without immediate adversaries, one of whom had a gun, and Biddy remained fastened in her chair. Marlowe was fighting like a maniac in spite of his injured arm. The sweat was trickling into his eyes, and his black hair hung over his face in damp strands.

But in spite of his stand, and although Mr. Knapp showed signs of reviving, it did not seem that the battle could continue for long.

It was at the precise moment when Ropey the Chinese was kneeling upon Lugg's outstretched arms and was slowly but surely forcing his neck back, and strangulation seemed certain, that without sound or warning all light in the place disappeared.

"Switch don't work," said a voice out of the darkness. "Look out! There's somethin' comin' up the stairs."

The Chinese left Lugg like a shadow, and the old lag, finding himself under the chair in which the girl sat, set to work to unfasten the bonds, his fingers moving deftly in the darkness.

Fighting ceased momentarily, and there was a general movement towards the door. There seemed to be the sound of many feet coming up the stairs.

"Is that you, Guv'nor?" A strangled voice from the room spoke eagerly.

"In here, officer, in here." The voice was unrecognizable, and at the same moment a torch shone into the room.

"The police!" shouted someone, and there was a stampede to the doorway. The first man out sprawled and went down like a log.

" 'Ere," said another voice, "there's only one of 'em. Out 'im!"

The last words were drowned by a small explosion—not very loud, but curiously ominous in sound. The torch went out, and almost immediately everyone in the room became aware of something insidious in the atmosphere which choked and suffocated them.

Someone attempted to light a match, and a startled exclamation broke from him. "Smoke!" he shouted. "Fire!"

"Pull yourselves together," shouted a second voice. "Someone's foolin' us. It's the Guv'nor."

The fumes became more and more intense. Giles, staggering to his feet, heard a whisper that put new life in him:

"Return tickets ready, please. Get the girl out, you fool."

The voice was unmistakably Campion's, and at the same time a flying chair crashed against the curtained window. A tinkle of glass sounded in the street below.

Giles felt someone brush past him. He stretched out his hand and touched a silk sleeve. He seized it with an exclamation.

Lugg's voice growled at him softly under the tumult.

"You come on quick. I've got 'er."

The overpowering smoke had now suffused the landing and the floors above and below. The natural instinct of the gangsters was to get downstairs, as the quickest means of access to the street. The raiding party, on the other hand, made for the roof. Under cover of the confusion escape was comparatively easy.

In the boxroom Giles and Lugg found Mr. Knapp as they came struggling up with Biddy.

"I was waitin' for you," he said, with an attempt at his old cheerfulness. "I ain't 'arf 'ad a sock on the 'ead. That was Bertie down there, Lugg."

"Shut up, and get the girl out on the roof." Mr. Lugg was in no mood for conversation. His face was glistening with sweat, and his eyes were shifty with apprehension.

Giles looked round him dizzily. "Where's Marlowe?" he said weakly. "We must get him out. I'll go down again." He turned to the door unsteadily, but on the last word his voice trailed off and he sank down on the boards.

"Now there's two of 'em." Mr. Lugg's tone had returned to normal. "First of all, lock this 'ere door. The others must look after theirselves. We'll clear this lot away. Stop 'im bleedin', if you can. We don't want a trail be'ind us."

Knapp sniffed. "Gawd! wot a picnic," he commented. "Come on, then—up we go."

Meanwhile, downstairs chaos continued. The smoke had made the first room uninhabitable, and the darkness which persisted all over the house was made thicker and more impenetrable by the fumes.

Terrified men had broken windows and burst open doors in the hope of diffusing the suffocating clouds. No one understood in the least what had happened.

Marlowe, staggering along the upper landing, cannoned into a man who was standing by the open window. He started back.

"Wait for the wagon," said a voice softly out of the darkness. "Wait for the wagon and we'll all take a ride."

"Campion!" Before the word was out of his mouth a hand was placed over his lips. All around them in the smoke there were scufflings and any amount of profanity. Retreat was impossible. The whole house seemed to be in a turmoil. Added to the seven men who had been in the long room there were now reinforcements from below, coughing and shouting in the choking vapour.

"Don't let 'em get away!" The shout was from downstairs.

"We're cut off," whispered Marlowe. "We shall suffocate."

Campion kicked him softly, and at the same moment at the far end of the street below a fire bell's hysterical clangour echoed noisily.

"Fire!" The cry seemed to rise up from all parts of the dignified street. Campion and Marlowe, gasping for air at the open window, saw the engines pull up, the brass helmets moving with magnificent swiftness.

"Fire!" The cry was spreading to the house.

Campion touched Marlowe on the shoulder. "Emergency Exit," he murmured, and swung lightly out on to the sill. Marlowe followed him more slowly. This new development was entirely unexpected.

Their appearance on the window-ledge caused a sensation among the crowd gathering in the street below. From outside, the fire appeared to be a very serious one. Great billows of smoke poured out of every window and ventilation grille. Mr. Campion looked down at the yellow clouds with a certain pride. "Not bad for an amateur show," he said. "I've often speculated on the chances of crossing the smoke bomb with the common stink variety. What an offspring! But I forget," he went on with sudden seriousness. "Register 'Fireman, save my child'; this is too much like 'The Boy stood on the Burning Deck'. Put some pep into it. Quiver a bit; go quaggly about the knees, but for the love of Mike don't fall!"

He began to wave frantically, and the crowd below made reassuring signs. Just as the ladders were shifted into position there was a movement behind them. Campion swung round and caught the face that loomed out of the mists towards them with his rubber truncheon. The face did not reappear.

"Look out," said Marlowe, and leaned back as the top of a crimson ladder hovered in mid-air and came down within a foot of them.

"Tell them the end is not yet," said Campion. "Off we go."

As they descended, the sound of crashing glass and woodwork floated up to them from below. The door and windows of the lower floors were apparently securely bolted, and firemen were breaking in.

So great was the excitement at this incident that their arrival on the ground floor did not do much to increase it.

All the same, a small portion of the crowd pressed about them, and the fireman who collected them at the foot of the ladder inquired anxiously if there were others inside.

Mr. Campion's reply set the hopes of a spectacle-loving public ablaze.

"House crammed full," he said seriously. "More smoke than fire, I imagine. It's a man's club, you know—a lot of retired military men—all sticking to their posts or something."

"You wasn't one of the brave ones," said a miserable-looking little man in the crowd. "I don't blame you neither. Fool'ardy, I call it."

Campion glanced back at the house. The hoses were pouring water into the darkened building, the firemen were already entering.

"Hullo!" he shouted suddenly. "What's that they've got there? A corpse?"

Marlowe turned to look with the rest of the crowd which surged forward, but he felt himself firmly grasped by the upper arm and forced forward through the oncoming mass. The arrival of a couple of policemen pressing back the tide finally covered their escape.

As he reached the open street Campion's voice sounded in his ear.

"Now, since we've rung the bell pretty effectively, old bird," he murmured, "this, I think, is where we run away."

CHAPTER XXIII

And How!

THE scene in Mr. Knapp's back room was not unlike a dressing station when Marlowe and Campion arrived.

Giles, still very white and shaky, was receiving experienced first aid at the capable hands of Mr. Lugg, while Mr. Knapp was examining a lump upon his head in an oak-framed mirror, whose usefulness was considerably lessened by the fact that the words "Bass's Bottled Ales" were printed across it in large letters.

Mrs. Knapp was bending over Biddy, administering small quantities of rum in an egg-cup. Mr. Barber alone remained where they had left him. The expression upon his face was inscrutable. He had evidently resigned himself to a situation which was completely beyond his comprehension.

Campion was frankly relieved to see them back. His entry was hilarious, and they all turned towards him with an eagerness which told of the anxiety they had felt at his prolonged absence.

Biddy rose to her feet and came towards them. "Oh, I'm so glad," she said breathlessly. She took Campion's hand, but her real interest was plainly centered in Marlowe.

"You're hurt!" she said, all her anxiety returning. He gri-

maced at her and smiled. "It looks worse than it is," he said
lightly.

With her help he wriggled out of his coat and displayed a
nasty wound in the forearm. The others gathered round
him.

"I'll see to that," said Lugg. "An' you lie down, miss.
You don't look any too good. Now then, Pretty," he went
on, turning to Mr. Knapp, "leave off titivating an' give us a
'and."

"Lay off," said his friend bitterly. "I've got a lump 'ere as
big as a 'en's egg. Still," he continued, brightening, "it was
worth it. Not 'arf a bad show, it wasn't, Ma. You ought to
'ave been there."

"Blow me if I know wot 'appened," said Mr. Lugg conversationally as he applied a great swab soaked with iodine
to Marlowe's arm. "Where did you two young feller-me-lads
get to at the end? I nipped straight off with the girl as the
Guv'nor told me." He turned to Campion. "I wasn't 'arf
glad to 'ear you when you come up. What 'appened to you
an' this young spark 'ere? 'Lugg,' I said to myself, 'you're
out of a job,' I said."

"I'm afraid it was my fault," said Marlowe. "I went back
to scrag that damned Chink. He'll never be the same man
again," he added with some satisfaction. "I thought I'd
killed him at first, but he crawled away in the end. I suppose
you came after me, Campion?"

"Not exactly," said that young man modestly. "I
couldn't help staying to see the fire engines. You've no idea
what a torchlight tattoo there was after you other people
left. Marlowe and I were received like royalty."

"Fire?" said Mr. Knapp, looking up. "There wasn't no
real fire, was there?"

"Wasn't there, by heck?" said Giles. "I thought we were
going to be suffocated."

Marlowe grinned. "That was him," he said, pointing at
Campion.

"I did it with my little smoke bomb," said Campion
proudly. "This room, begging your pardon, Knapp, was
nothing to it."

"Wot beats me," said Mr. Knapp, ignoring the last remark, "is 'ow the bloomin' engines got there so quick. There
ain't no fire station for some way that I know of."

"That," said Campion again, "was me too. As soon as
these young hopefuls got up their Charge of the Light Bri-
gade, what did little Albert do? He nipped off."

"I know," said Mr. Knapp. "I seen you."

"Quite," said Campion, putting on his spectacles once
more and surveying the little man through them coldly.
"And with your sordid mind, Thos, you doubtless conceived
the idea that I had quitted. But no, you wronged me, Jasper
Strange. I dropped through that open skylight in the next
house which you found for me, and I picked up the telephone and I said, 'I'm so sorry to trrrouble you, but I'm
afraid there's a fire at Number Thirty-Two. The building is
well ablaze. Could you send someone round to see to it?'
The people at the other end seemed quite impressed and I
came back. I dropped in just in time to see the two old
contemptibles go into action. It occurred to me that there
was too much light about the place, so I toddled downstairs
to see about it. On the way I met old Gingerbeard. After a
few short words of greeting I showed him my trick with the
truncheon. He fell for it, and I went to do my electrical
work. There seemed too many wires in the cellar, so I
pruned a few round the penny-in-the-slot machine. Then I
ambled back doing my celebrated imitation of the British
Police Force. The rest was quite simple," he added, beaming
upon them fatuously. "I dropped my little Kloos bomb. Up
went the fire balloon. You showed the lady out, and Marlowe and I stayed for the washing up. Any questions?"

"Albert, you're wonderful!" Biddy, standing with her
arm tucked into Marlowe's, spoke admiringly. "You all are.
If you knew how terrified I was—I—"

Campion placed a finger on his lips and glanced at the
Knapps. Biddy comprehended, and turned the phrase off.

"I was glad to see you," she said. "I don't know yet
where we are or how we got here."

"Seems to me," said Mr. Lugg, inspecting Giles, "that I

shall 'ave to take this youngster off to old Doc Redfern. A spot o' stitchin' is wot 'e wants."

Giles and Biddy exchanged glances, and Campion, guessing the question in their minds, spoke reassuringly. "The best man you could have," he said. "He makes a specialty of this sort of thing."

"A good man? 'E's a bloomin' marvel," said Mr. Lugg pugnaciously. "If it 'adn't been for Doc Redfern, I'd be walkin' about in four separate bits. I'll take 'im right off now. See you round at the flat. You come along, mate. 'E's a beauty specialist, that's wot 'e is."

"Perhaps," said Mr. Barber, rising at the first opportunity, "I had better give the rest of you a lift to Mr. Campion's flat."

He spoke so hopefully that Marlowe grinned. No one had taken much notice of him since their return, and it was almost with surprise that Campion turned to him.

"That's a fine idea," he said. "I'm afraid we've given you an awful lot of trouble, Mr. Barber, but you see, we've had a bit of trouble ourselves."

The Oriental looked at him as if he thought he were an idiot, but he moved towards the door, and the others followed him.

Campion stayed behind to talk to Knapp. When he came downstairs at last, the others were already packed into the car. Giles and Lugg caught a late taxi in Church Street.

"Good night, all," shouted Mr. Knapp from the window.

As Mr. Barber's ornate car passed the top of Beverley Gardens the engines were still drawn up outside Number Thirty-two.

"Still playing Snakes and Ladders, I see," said Campion cheerfully. "I wonder what explanation they'll give the authorities. That ought to trouble Mr. Datchett, I fancy."

"Datchett?" said Biddy quickly. "The fortune teller? Is that who it was?"

"Mr. Datchett it was," said Campion grimly. "About the worst type imaginable—a society blackmailer."

"Of course, our friend Thos is—" began Marlowe softly.

Mr. Campion grimaced at him. "What do you want to bring that up for?" he said, and they drove on in silence.

By tacit consent no word was spoken of Biddy's adventure. Campion seemed to wish to keep the matter as much to themselves as possible.

It was about one o'clock when they reached the dark entrance beside the police station.

"Thank you, no." There was a note of complete finality in Mr. Barber's reply when they asked him to come in. "You will forgive me, but I feel I should like a Turkish bath." He hesitated, and looked at Biddy. "I had hoped to obtain your brother's consent to my handling the sale of his picture," he said wistfully.

Biddy stared at him. Had she not been so exhausted she would have laughed. This sudden explanation of his presence in the midst of such an extraordinary adventure touched her sense of the absurd.

"I think I can promise you that will be all right," she said. "Thank you so much for all you've done for us."

Mr. Barber beamed. "I shall hold you to that promise," he said. "You have no idea of the value, the exquisite state of preservation, the—"

Campion touched his arm. "Not now, old boy," he said wearily. "Go to bye-byes. Nice long day to-morrow."

Marlowe and Biddy were already climbing the stairs. Mr. Barber seemed to be on the verge of saying something, but hesitated and changed his mind. Then, raising his hat, a gesture which seemed absurd in the circumstances, he drove off.

Campion turned into the doorway and walked slowly after the others. He had not passed unhurt in the fight, nor had he any illusions that the game was approaching a finish. He climbed leisurely, his face was lined and sweatmarked: the ordeal of the last few hours had left its mark.

When he arrived, Isopel, white and tired from her long vigil, had already got the door open.

"You've done it!" she said hysterically. "Oh, Biddy, thank God they've got you back! Where's Giles?" she added nervously as Campion closed the door behind him.

"He's all right," said Marlowe reassuringly. "Lugg will bring him round in a moment."

"Bring him round?" Her eyes widened. "He's hurt?"

"Not badly." It was Biddy who spoke. "His cheek's cut. Oh, Isopel, they were marvellous." She threw herself down into an armchair and covered her face with her hands. "Now it's all over," she said, "I do believe I'm going to cry."

Marlowe perched himself on the arm of her chair and put a hand on her shoulder soothingly.

"Food," said Mr. Campion. "When depressed, eat. Full story of the crime in the later editions. Isopel, have you had any food?"

The girl shook her head. "I—I wasn't hungry."

"That makes it more difficult. Rodriguez has gone home to roost long ago. We must see what Lugg eats." He disappeared into the back of the flat. All this time he had studiously avoided Biddy, and it suddenly dawned upon Isopel what he had meant when he made his slightly comic exit down the lift shaft.

"What a gastronomic failure the British Burglar is," he remarked, reappearing. "A tin of herrings, half a Dutch cheese, some patent bread for reducing the figure, and several bottles of stout. Still, better than nothing. There's some Benedictine in that cupboard by you, Marlowe. The whisky's there, too, and there's a box of biscuits somewhere. Night scene in Mayfair flat—four herring addicts, addicting. Of course, a wash isn't a bad idea," he went on, looking down at himself. "Isopel, look after Biddy in my room, and we'll see what we can get off on the towels in the bathroom, Marlowe. Our hostess was doubtless a good mother, but as a housewife she was a menace."

"I'll say you're right," said Marlowe. "With all due deference, I guess I'll have to burn these clothes."

"It was a bit like that," Campion agreed. "I've got a spot of gent's natty suiting in the next room if you'd care for it."

Giles and Lugg returned about an hour later, when they had washed and fed. The boy was bandaged pretty thor-

oughly, and Isopel fluttered about him in a manner which
he found most gratifying.

Mr. Lugg looked round the flat in disgust. "You 'ave bin
'avin' a picnic, ain't you?" he remarked. "Washin' for one
thing, and eatin' my best bit o' cheese for another. A cheese
like that lasts me thirty days without the op. Good job me
an' the young un 'ad a bit at a coffee stall, otherwise cheese
rind an' 'erring juice'd be our portion, as the Scriptures 'ave
it."

"The time has come," said Campion, ignoring him,
"when we gather round Biddy and hear the worst. Look
here, old dear," he went on, looking at the girl, "I haven't
let you talk before, and I don't want you to talk now if it's
going to knock you up any more. We're as safe here as
anywhere for the time being."

The girl looked at him gratefully. "I'm all right," she
said. "I've been telling Isopel in the next room, and I must
get it off my chest to you all, or I shall think that I went
mad and imagined the whole thing."

"Stupendous," said Campion. "Imagine we're a Sunday
paper. Spare us nothing. Not a single gruesome detail," he
went on. "Everything is of importance. Don't leave out anything. Everything you remember."

They had drawn round the girl, who was lying propped
up on the Chesterfield. Marlowe sat on the back of the
couch, Isopel on the floor beside her, Campion straddling a
chair before her, and Giles and Lugg on either side of him.

Biddy looked at them helplessly. "The awful part of it
is," she said, "I can remember so little. I'll tell you all I can.
I went into the post office at home."

"That was this morning," said Giles. "Or rather, yesterday morning, now, I suppose."

She looked at him blankly. "It must be longer ago than
that," she said. "Why, I—"

"Never mind," said Marlowe gently. "I guess we know
what happened at Kettle's."

"That's more than I do," said Biddy. "It seems so long
ago. I remember he told me he had something to show me if
I would come into the inner room for a moment. I went in,

of course—naturally. Then I think someone must have jumped upon me from behind, and I can't remember anything else at all until I woke up feeling most dreadfully sick in a sort of box. I thought I was in a coffin. I was terrified. It was like all the bad dreams I'd ever had. I kicked and screamed, and they let me out. I was in a room—it must have been in that house you came to. I was feeling horribly sick, and I had a filthy taste in my mouth. I was still doped a bit, I suppose."

Marlowe made an inarticulate sound, and she smiled up at him faintly.

"I'm better now," she said. "And, oh, I'll tell you something, Albert," she went on hurriedly, "they weren't the right people. I mean, they weren't the people who got Mr. Lobbett. They were a different lot. They thought I knew where he was. That's what they kept questioning me about. They wouldn't believe that I didn't know anything."

"Hold on a moment," said Giles. "There's something here that's got to be cleared up, Biddy. What made them think that you knew?"

There was an unconscious movement among the group round the girl on the couch. This question, which had been forgotten in the excitement of the past few hours, now returned to their minds with redoubled importance. Looking at Biddy as she lay there, it seemed impossible to connect her with any duplicity.

She frowned at them. "I couldn't quite make that out," she said. "It was something about my handwriting."

"See here," said Marlowe, "it's up to us to explain to Biddy all that we know. Remember, we've only got Knapp's word for it, but he says he overheard a 'phone message which said more or less in effect that you had posted a parcel containing the suit Dad was wearing when he disappeared. Kettle opened the parcel and conceived the idea of his clever little trick which failed so badly. That's roughly why you were kidnapped."

Biddy shook her head. "I'm none the wiser," she said. "I sent no parcel. And yet Kettle could hardly mistake my handwriting—he's seen it so often."

"Well, did you write anything?" said Giles. "Who have you written to lately?"

Biddy remained thoughtful. "No one," she said at last. "I paid a few bills by post. Unless—oh, Giles—it couldn't be George? He couldn't—"

Campion became interested immediately. "George couldn't what?" he said.

"George couldn't write," said Biddy. "Amongst other things. But, Albert, he couldn't be mixed up in this. That's fantastic."

"Couldn't write?" said Marlowe. "That's fantastic, if you like."

"Oh no," said Giles. "I don't think there's anyone over fifty in Mystery Mile who can read or write. The Education Act hasn't been in very long, really, you know."

"But I did write something for George," said Biddy. "You see, poor old St. Swithin used to write all his letters for him—make up his bills and everything. He came to me with a sticky label. I remember when it was—it was the morning after Mr. Lobbett disappeared. I remember that because I was so tired. It seemed to me absurd that anyone could be thinking of ordinary things, like sending off a parcel."

"That's fine," said Campion. "Do you remember the address?"

"Yes," said Biddy. "It was sent to Mrs. Pattern. That's his daughter, the one who married the garage man and went to Canvey Island. I send her things sometimes. He told me he was sending her some roots."

"A funny time of year to send roots," said Giles.

Biddy nodded. "It is," she confessed. "But of course I didn't notice it at the time. The whole thing seems crazy even now. He can't know anything about it, Giles—we've known him all our lives."

"The old devil probably found the clothes and sent them off without saying anything. That's about it," said Giles. "All the same, he'll have to explain himself pretty thoroughly."

"Even so," said Marlowe, "wouldn't this chap Kettle

know who sent the parcel? George must have posted it himself."

"That doesn't follow," said Giles. "He used to take all the letters from the Manor, and the Dower House, too, for that matter. He called for them when he passed. He's done it for years. It's one of his jobs."

"That's about the explanation," said Campion. "Carry on, old dear. How long were they cross-questioning you?"

The fear returned to the girl's eyes. "It seemed days," she said. "I can't tell you how long it was really. It was that awful little Chinaman who frightened me most."

An expression of satisfaction appeared in Marlowe's face. "He'll never do it again," he said. "I don't understand, Biddy. Were they at you the whole time?"

"Yes. I was tied up when they took me out of the box. I felt most desperately ill. I think I fainted."

"What did you tell them?" said Campion.

"What could I tell them? They wanted to know where Mr. Lobbett was. I didn't know. I told him we thought he had been kidnapped, and they laughed at me. They made all sorts of threats and promises. Oh, I can't tell you about it—it was horrible."

For a moment she seemed about to break down, but controlled herself. "I never understood before," she burst out suddenly, "how real it all is. St. Swithin's death left me numbed and stupid, I think. When Mr. Lobbett disappeared and that absurd message arrived, and then the clothes turned up, my mind didn't seem to register at all. There hasn't been time to think how awful it all is. But then, when they were questioning me, I suddenly grasped how desperately serious they were. Do you realize, all of you, that either their leader, whom I didn't see, or Mr. Lobbett, is bound to die? It's a death game."

Although this thought had come to them all at different times, Biddy's point-blank acknowledgement of it startled them considerably.

Campion got up. "That's what I've known all along," he said in a tone utterly unlike his usual flippancy.

"They didn't get anything out of me," said Biddy, "be-

cause I didn't know anything. But if I had"—she looked
round at them, the colour coming into her face, her brown
eyes wide and honest—"I would have told. Courage and
decency and all that wouldn't have made any difference. I
was just scared stiff. I was frightened they were going to kill
me or put my eyes out or something. You do understand me,
don't you?"

"Perfectly," said Marlowe. "And you're quite right, too.
Campion, we can't bring Biddy and Giles into it any longer.
We—"

Giles interrupted him. "We're staying. I'm speaking for
Biddy, I know, but I think we understand one another."

"We're staying," repeated the girl. "I insisted on being in
it. Albert wanted me to go away. I feel quite brave, now
you've rescued me," she added, laughing nervously.

Mr. Lugg, who had absented himself during the latter
part of the conversation, now returned. "I got a mornin'
paper," he said. "It's just past three. 'Mystery Fire at Kensington' is our little do. Listen to this:

> "The Kensington and other Fire Brigades were called
> out last night to a mysterious outbreak which oc-
> curred at 32, Beverley Gardens, W.8. Two interesting
> and unusual features are reported. The dense clouds
> of smoke which were thought to be caused by fire
> were apparently produced by chemical means. The
> second mysterious feature is that several men, all of
> the lower class, were removed from the house in an
> unconscious condition not altogether caused by the
> fumes. The police are investigating the incident.

"Couple o' inches, that's all we get," said Mr. Lugg. "A
lovely show like that—a couple o' inches. Wait until the
News o' the World publish my life. *'I was drove to it,'* says
famous crook."

He threw the paper down contemptuously. Marlowe
picked it up and was turning to the stop press when a picture on the back page attracted his attention. He studied it
intently.

"Good Lord!" he said suddenly. "I thought that was Dad for a moment. Some scientist guy, I suppose."

Campion bounded to his feet and was beside him in an instant.

"Where?" he said, snatching the paper with altogether uncalled-for excitement.

"Here," said Marlowe, pointing over his shoulder at the photograph of a man evidently caught unexpectedly, glancing back as if at some sudden sound. The caption was not particularly enlightening:

Giant Diplodocus in Suffolk—Our special photographer, with long-distance camera, manages to catch a glimpse of archaeologists at work. Great secrecy is still being maintained by the Hon. Elwin Cluer over the remarkable discovery in his grounds at Redding Knights, near Debenham, Suffolk.

"It's infernally like him," said Giles, joining the other two.

"Like him," said Mr. Campion, stammering. "Don't you see, my babes in the wood, the ultimately improbable and ghastly has occurred on this blessed night of all nights?"

"It's damnably like him," said Marlowe.

"Of course it is." Mr. Campion was shouting in his consternation. "It *is* him. I put him there."

CHAPTER XXIV

"Once More Into the Breach, Dear Friends"

FOR some moments after Mr. Campion's startling announcement no one spoke.

"You'd better explain, Albert," said Isopel at last.

"I suppose I had," Campion agreed. "We shall have to get a move on pretty quickly, too. We shan't be the only people to spot this disgusting example of newspaper nosery. This rag has a couple of million circulation. I'm desperately sorry, all of you," he went on hurriedly, as they sat staring at him. "I've added to the anxiety of the past day or two, but it couldn't be helped. It wasn't that I didn't trust you, of course, but I wanted you all to live up to your parts. I didn't know what steps they'd take to get information from us, and I wanted to be quite sure that you were all genuinely in the dark."

"But he disappeared in front of us," said Biddy. "I was with you. You were talking to me."

"He helped," admitted Campion. "He and George really did the thing between them. A good old-fashioned put-up job, in fact. You see," he went on, turning to Marlowe, "things were getting too hot. I've explained why I didn't let you in on it. Look here, I'd better begin at the beginning.

"They pinked us the first evening you got down—Datchett turned up. I didn't recognize him, and for the moment he put the wind up me. I thought he might be the Big Bezezus himself. Then poor old St. Swithin shot himself, for which, by the way, I trust Mr. Datchett will shortly interview Lugg's distinguished patron at the Old Bailey. I was in the dark over that—I am still, up to a point. It's quite obvious now that this chap and his pals are being employed by Simister, and for a very good reason. This chap had just the outfit that the Big Noise needed. He seems to have a collection of informers all over the country—gossips, small agents, servants, and the like. Kettle was one of them. That sort of reptile provided him with his best clients. They collected the evidence; Datchett collected the blackmail. Not a certificate 'U' production."

"I don't quite get this," said Marlowe. "Did that fortune teller try to force the old minister to double-cross us?"

"That's about it," said Campion. "He probably realized that Kettle would be precious little help to him, apart from spotting us in the first place, and he wanted St. Swithin to give him the goods from inside."

"And St. Swithin shot himself rather than do it?" said Giles.

Campion hesitated. "I'm afraid," he said at last, "that it was a pretty substantial threat which Datchett held over him. I fancy the poor old boy must have been sucked dry long before this. It was obviously some sort of exposure that he feared and he had no means to buy himself off any longer."

"But what could he have feared?" said Biddy. "It's absurd."

"We can't tell what it was, old dear"—Campion spoke gently—"but what I do know is that his last thought was to help us, and he did it in a most effective and practical manner. He sent us sound advice which arrived in the rather melodramatic fashion that it did only because he was so desperately anxious that only the person who was directly concerned should understand it."

"That was you," said Giles.

Campion nodded.

"I wasn't any too quick on the up-take," he said. "The messages didn't come in their right order. Yours, Biddy, 'Danger', should have come first. That was to break any illusions we may have had about Datchett as a fortune teller. Then there was Alaric Watts—one of the most interesting old men I've met for a long time. When in doubt, I fancy, St. Swithin appealed to Alaric Watts, though he never took his principal trouble to him. And then, of course, there was the red knight. I didn't get that until I went over to see Watts. He's a bit like something out of the Old Testament, a superior minor prophet. He solved my little troubles while I waited. It appears that he has a great pal next door who is an old fossil monger. In his somewhat hefty back garden the early Britons built a church, bits of which he ferrets up from time to time. While they were on one of these pot-hunting expeditions they dogged up a toenail as big as a dining table, which cheered things up all round. The press got wind of it, and old Cluer—that's the man I've been talking about—barricaded himself in and made a kind of fortress of the place. No one was allowed in or out without their G.F.S. badge.

"St. Swithin, God bless him, knew all this, and it had probably occurred to him before that it was just the place for anyone who wanted to avoid publicity for a bit. He dared not see us again, for fear of losing his nerve. That's why he wrote."

"But why did he send a chessman?" said Marlowe.

"If you'll look at that paper over there," said Campion, "you'll see. The name of the estate next door to Alaric Watts is Redding Knights. There's a stream there where the old tin-hats used to have a wash and brush-up, I understand. That was St. Swithin's only way of telling us without writing the name, which might conceivably have been seen by anybody. That explains why I wanted you all to be as secret as an oyster about it."

"Good Lord, you knew the whole time!" said Marlowe, sitting down and wiping his brow.

Giles looked at Isopel. The girl coloured faintly and met his glance.

"I knew too," she said. "Albert told me the next morning."

"Toujours le Polytechnic," said Mr. Campion hurriedly.

"How on earth did you manage it?" said Biddy.

"It was the little grey books that did it," said Campion. "After half an hour's reading my head swelled up. Within two hours I had qualified as a motor salesman, whereas before I used to sell pups. After three days—"

"Chuck it!" said Giles. "How did you do it?"

"The ordinary Bokel Mind," began Mr. Campion oracularly. "Deep, mysterious, and replete with low cunning though it is, is nothing compared to the stupendous mental machines owned by those two losses to the criminal world, George Willsmore, and 'Anry, his brother—who pips him easily in the matter of duplicity, by the way. In all my wide experience I have never come across two such Napoleons of deceit. They staged and arranged the whole affair, whilst I looked on and admired. Such technique!

"I persuaded your father," he went on with a hopeless attempt at seriousness. "I put the whole case to him. I pointed out that if I had a clear field and him out of danger, there was just a chance that our friends might be persuaded to show their hands. They have, up to a point, but not far enough. The old boy was very sporting, and, as I said, George and 'Anry did the rest. The remarkable disappearing act was nothing like as difficult as it looked, thank heaven! You must remember, both time and place were prearranged. 'Anry discovered the dead yew, and devised the whole scheme. George was waiting for your father inside the maze. Mr. Lobbett's tour was personally conducted by him. They toddled down that ditch which you discovered so inopportunely, Giles, only instead of going on to the road they ambled along the side of the field and into a sort of dyke, rather deeper than usual, I understand, which runs diagonally through the hay field. The grass, being pretty high then, together with the depth of the dyke, hid them completely. From that they got quite easily into the mist tunnel without being observed. There's a hut down there, isn't there, Giles? Well, he changed there, since yokel garbage was absolutely necessary. 'Anry's wife's brother from Heronhoe was waiting in a rowboat just where the mist tunnel runs into the creek. It was high tide, you remember. He paddled your father down the river to a strip of coast where our good friend Alaric Watts was waiting for him in a car. There you are—quite easily done. 'Anry fixed the note on Addlepate's collar. That was your father's idea. I confess that, knowing the animal, I was dubious about that part of the scheme, but it worked all right."

Giles was looking at him in undisguised horror.

"George and 'Anry got Mr. Lobbett into a boat where the mist tunnel runs into the creek?" he said. "I didn't know anyone would dare it."

Campion eyed him curiously.

"I don't get you."

Giles shrugged his shoulders.

"It's the most dangerous bit of 'soft' on the coast," he said. "The sea's encroaching every day, so it's impossible to mark it. I'm always expecting that old hut to disappear."

"I didn't know that," said Campion quietly. "I've underestimated those two. They're Machiavellis. Anyhow, they got him away safely, all right. George's one lapse occurred in that matter of the suit. He had orders to destroy it, but having a son-in-law who is a Brummel of Canvey Island, his frugal mind suggested that the clothes might come in useful for him. That's how the rather serious misunderstanding which led to Biddy's abduction occurred."

"Kettle simply untied the parcel, then?" said Marlowe.

Campion nodded. "I imagine he was going through all our correspondence at the time. I chatted to George on the subject. He swore to me that he'd buried the clothes in the mud. Kettle, he insisted, must have dug them up again. That story didn't wash, but it put me straight on to Kettle's track; however, like an ass, I wasn't fast enough. I imagined, somehow or other, that our little postmaster might be useful to us. I thought if we could depend on his reading our letters we might supply his friends with the most incredible information. What I didn't get fixed under my golden curls was to just what abysmal depths of idiocy he could sink. See how it happened?"

"Sounds like a bit o' the Decameron to me," said Mr. Lugg unexpectedly. "Without the fun, as you might say."

"It is a bit of a mouthful," said Giles, "coming on top of everything else. What's the next move? We're all pretty well dead-beat, and I state here and now that the girls are out of it for the future."

"Quite right," said Campion. " 'Over my dead body,' as Lugg would say."

"I'm all for that," said Marlowe.

The two girls were too tired to protest. Biddy, despite her excitement and anxiety, was already more than half asleep.

"I suggest," said Mr. Campion, "that I go down to Redding Knights straight away. I think we've got about four hours' start. That's why I haven't been hurrying. Oh, they're sure to get wind of that photograph," he went on, answering Giles's unspoken question. "That's one of those certain things. Half the crooks in London probably know there's a reward in a certain quarter for information about the judge. But they won't spot it till about eight o'clock. I'll set off right away, then."

"I'll bring a couple o' pennies down for yer eyes," said Mr. Lugg, "And I'll see you laid out proper."

"You'll stay where you are," said Mr. Campion. "You're going to be a ladies' maid for a day or two. A mixture of ladies' maid and bulldog." He turned to the girls. "You couldn't be safer in Wormwood Scrubs."

"That's right," said Mr. Lugg. "I'll get my 'armonium out to-morrer. Give 'em a spot of music to cheer 'em up."

"Must you all go?" Biddy looked at Campion imploringly.

Giles interrupted his reply. "Marlowe and I are going with Campion," he said stubbornly.

"That's so." The young American nodded. He went over to Biddy, and for a moment they spoke together.

"I say, there's one thing," said Giles suddenly, looking up. "Are you going to do all your rescue work in your giddy two-seater?"

"Don't insult her," said Mr. Campion. "I've had her since she was a tricycle. Still, I hardly think she's fit for Flying Squad work. You will now shut your eyes, and Uncle Albert will do one of his pret-ty con-jur-ing tricks, kid-dies. Lugg, I think this is just about the time to catch Brother Herbert, don't you?"

Mr. Lugg became supercilious immediately. "Very likely," he said, adding gratuitously: "Sittin' up 'arf the night, excep' on business, is my idea of a vice." He went to the telephone and gave a Mayfair number. After listening for some moments his expression changed to one of bitterest contempt, and he held the receiver some distance from his ear. "Mr. Rudolph would like to speak to 'is brother," he said. There was an indistinct reply, and Mr. Lugg's scowl darkened and his little eyes glittered with sudden anger. "Yus, and look nippy about it, my young gent's gent," he said bitterly; then, turning to Campion, he mimicked a voice of horrible refinement: " 's Lordship is 'avin' 'is 'air curled and may be some moments comin' to the phone."

"Hair curled?" said Campion.

"I dunno. Cleanin' 'is teeth or somethink silly." Mr. Lugg evidently had no use for the nobleman in question. " 'Ere 'e is, sir."

Campion took the phone, and the others suddenly noticed that in spite of his unquenchable gaiety his pallor had increased and his eyes were weary behind his spectacles.

"Hullo, Sonny Boy," he said, grinning into the instrument. "Did she accept you? It'll cost you seven and sixpence. Better buy a dog. Yes, boy, I said *dog*. I say, where's the Bentley? Could you send her round? No, Wootton can leave her here. Oh, and by the way, Ivanhoe, now you're sober you might point out to the family that you can only disinherit an offspring once. One offspring—one disinheritance. Make that quite clear. Yes, I know it's four o'clock in the morning. You'll send the bus at once, won't you? Yes, the business is looking up. I'm going to buy some braces with your crest on if the present boom continues. Cheerio, old son. I shall expect the car in five minutes. Good-bye."

He rang off. "Once more into the breach, dear friends,"

he said, smiling at them. "We'll take some brandy in a flask, Lugg. Look after the ladies. Don't let them out. We won't be more than a couple of days at the most."

"Two young females in this 'ere flat," said Lugg. "Well!"

"Shocking!" agreed Campion. "I don't know what my wife would say."

Marlowe stared at him. "Good Lord, you haven't a wife, have you?" he said.

"No," said Mr. Campion. "That's why I don't know what she'd say. Get your coats on, my little Rotarians."

CHAPTER XXV

The Bait

THEY drove all through the dawn: out of the deserted roads of the city into the narrow flint ways of Essex, and from Essex into Suffolk.

Marlowe and Giles dozed in spite of themselves in the back of the great Bentley. Campion sat at the wheel, his natural expression of vacant fatuity still upon his face.

But throughout that long drive, in spite of his weariness, his mind was working with unusual clarity, and by the time they turned into the drive of an old vicarage, whose walled garden was further protected by high yew hedges at least three feet thick, he had come to an important and somewhat startling decision.

They stumbled out of the car, sleepy and dishevelled, to find themselves outside an old house, ivy-covered and half hidden by towering cedars. There was an air of darkness and shadow in the big garden, of privacy undisturbed for centuries.

An old man admitted them to the house, accepting Campion's explanation with quiet deference.

"Mr. O'Rell is having breakfast with the vicar, sir," he said. "Will you come this way?"

"That's your father's *nom de guerre*," murmured Campion to Marlowe. "I wanted to call him Semple MacPherson, but he wouldn't stand for it."

They followed the man into a long room which ran all along one side of the house. The outside wall had been taken down to allow space for a long creeper-covered conservatory, and it was here, sitting at the top of the stone steps leading down to a sloping lawn, that they found Judge Lobbett and his host at breakfast.

Old Crowdy Lobbett sprang up at the sight of them. His delight at seeing his son again was evident, but on seeing Giles's bandaged face he turned to Campion with considerable anxiety.

"Isopel and Miss Paget—are they all right?"

Marlowe answered him. "Quite safe now, Dad. But Biddy had a terrible experience. Things have moved some."

The old man was eager for explanations, but Alaric Watts came forward and he paused to introduce him.

The Vicar of Kepesake was an unexpected-looking little old man. He was very small, with a large head, the high wide brow of a scholar, and an exceedingly trim white Vandyke beard and moustache.

He greeted them cordially, but it was evident that his interest in affairs of the modern world was a very abstract one compared with his real passion, the secrets and customs of the past.

He insisted that they should sit down to eat, and would have immediately embarked upon a diatribe on his latest archaeological discoveries had not the seriousness of their situation overruled any ordinary deference on the part of his visitors.

They ate, and Marlowe, once he realized that it was safe to speak before the old vicar, sketched a rough outline of the affair in Kensington.

Crowdy Lobbett listened to him with growing excitement. At the end he rose to his feet and strode restlessly down the room.

"This is terrible!" he said. "Terrible! Always others. I seem to escape myself, but wherever I go, whoever comes in contact with me seems to suffer. I spread this danger like a plague."

"Oh, well, we're all right for the present," said Giles, with an attempt at cheerfulness. "Marlowe and I aren't really hurt, and Biddy and Isopel are perfectly safe for the time being. It's what's going to happen next that's worrying us."

Old Lobbett turned inquiringly to Campion, who had been unusually silent ever since their arrival. The young man smiled at him.

"We've been spilling so many beans for your sake that we've forgotten the pork," he said. "It's the morning papers that have brought us down here." He produced the back page of the famous daily from his pocket and handed it to the judge.

An exclamation escaped the old man as he saw the photograph Campion indicated, and he handed it to the vicar.

"Disgusting!" said Alaric with sudden heat. "Disgusting! It's an ichthyosaurus, not a diplodocus. They'll be calling it an iguanodon next. Cluer will be furious about this."

"Anyhow, it's a darn good portrait," said Mr. Campion. "That's the real trouble."

The seriousness of this new development was by no means lost upon Crowdy Lobbett.

The worry of the last few months had told on his nerves badly and this last blow shook him considerably.

He had been lulled into a false security by the peace of Kepesake and by the absorbing interest of his new friends and their discovery on the closely guarded estate which abutted directly upon the Vicarage garden and itself comprised practically the whole of the parish of Redding Knights.

He turned to the three of them. His very blue eyes had grown darker, and the lines were deepening upon his still handsome old face.

"It's no good," he said. "This can't go on any longer. I made up my mind here, where I had time and peace to think it out, that if this last scheme of yours failed, Campion, or if the danger threatened any of you youngsters, I should face this thing alone and take what was coming to me. It's the only way to buy immunity for those about me."

Campion let the other two finish their outbursts against this suggestion without making any contribution towards it. At length his silence became noticeable, and they turned to him. Giles was angry.

"Good Lord, Campion, you're not saying that you agree with this ghastly idea?" he said. "We wouldn't stand it for a minute, sir," he went on, turning to the judge. "We're in it now. We'll see it through to the end. You're with us in that, aren't you, Campion?"

Campion shook his head slowly, and was about to speak, when the vicar interrupted him.

"No doubt you would prefer to discuss your affairs without me," he said softly. "I shall be in my study when you want me." He went quietly out of the room; as the door closed behind him Giles and the father and son turned towards Mr. Campion once more.

That young man was still seated at the breakfast table. The effects of the night's work had told upon him physically. There were dark shadows in his pale face, and behind the heavy glasses his eyes were inexpressibly weary. But his spirit was as effervescent as ever, and his voice, when he spoke, had lost none of its light-heartedness.

"This rather ticklish question," he began, "has been dragged up before I meant it to be. I hoped to be able to hand in my report, so to speak, before I dished out any proposals. Natheless, as they say in the writs, since the matter has now come to a head, let's dot it. I think, if you don't mind, sir," he went on, glancing at the judge, "a review of our transactions to date is clearly indicated. There're one or two facts that are important and must be properly filed for reference."

Judge Lobbett, who had now become accustomed to the young man's somewhat misleading business manner, signalled to him to go on.

"First of all," said Campion, "the root main-spring big idea. Old Airy-fairy Simister, who, as we all know, is anxious to remain a kind of Machiavellian Mrs. Harris, has a theory that you have a line on his birth certificate. So you have, but since it's written in Esperanto, or something, you can't read it. He doesn't know what you've got hold of, and realizes that he wouldn't recognize it if he saw it." He paused and glanced round at them. "Any boy who does not follow that, please put up his hand. All got there? Good! I'll carry on. He realized it was impossible to kidnap you in New York without running undue risk, so he hit on the ingenious little plan of scaring you out of action, or at any rate into a conversational stage, by carrying on a small war all round you. That proving unsatisfactory, he invented a sensational killing on board ship that would quite possibly have burned your clothes and any odd marriage lines you had about you to unrecognizable shreds. The untimely end of my poor Haig finished that idea for him. Now we come to Mystery Mile." He talked on hurriedly, peering at them anxiously through his heavy spectacles.

"There, as we know, we were spotted straight away, and poor old St. Swithin got it in the neck, more by luck than judgment on Simister's part, I fancy. There's a mystery there we haven't fathomed yet, by the way."

He paused for breath.

"All clear here," said Marlowe.

Giles nodded more slowly. "Ye-es," he said. "I see."

Judge Lobbett was bending forward intently. The fact that he was listening to a man half his age with such grave eagerness showed that he was nearing his last hope. Campion continued:

"To return to little Albert," he said. "How did the famous sleuth go to work? First of all he gained the confidence of our client here. How did he do this? He detailed to Mr. Lobbett senior the facts appertaining to the putting-away of Joe Gregory, a gentleman who crossed upon the same boat unspotted by anyone or anything except his own dirty soul and myself."

The judge turned to Marlowe. "That was so," he said. "Until Campion convinced me of that I thought he was some young adventurer who had got hold of you. I could not help being impressed by what he told me. You see, the moment you commissioned him—that is to say as soon as it was his business—he put them wise at headquarters that an undesirable alien had come over very cleverly disguised. I don't suppose you remember hearing about Gregory. I sent him down for a good long term some years ago. He was one of Simister's men. When I found that out it impressed me very considerably."

"Thousands of these splendid testimonials at our head office," murmured Campion, and continued: "It was through this, then, that Our Hero and the Guv'nor got down to business on the disappearing act. Mr. Lobbett agreed with me that our best chance was to make them show their hand a bit. This was done by our sensational vanishing performance at the maze. So far so good. The clever detective's splendid ruse worked sensationally, apart from one or two nasty bloomers which resulted in Biddy's adventure.

"Then, as the movies have it, 'Chance with her Fateful Finger, Like a Cheap Loud Speaker, Bellowed our Little Secret to the Waiting World', and now you and little Albert are in the *bouillabaisse*."

"You really expect them any minute, I suppose?" said Marlowe.

"Hardly," said Mr. Campion judicially. "We learned a good deal *via* Knapp and Biddy. In the first place, we discovered that Old Holy Smoke, the Voice in the Dark, was using our friend Datchett and his neat little organization, plus a pretty selection of the toughest thugs in London—always excluding Lugg, of course. That is to say that we know exactly who our enemies are with the single exception of our little Sim himself, who, by the way, is probably some well-known and respected person, like the Premier, or Mr. Home, of the Home and Colonial—someone who doesn't want to spoil his social prestige by a hanging in the family or anything equally crude."

"You don't think he's got any of his own men over here?" It was Judge Lobbett himself who spoke.

"It all depends on what you mean," said Campion. "I'm not sure whether Mr. Datchett isn't one of his own men myself. Certainly, however, he is second in command at the moment. And that is where we come to our second slight advantage. If ever anyone had his headquarters and staff mucked up neatly, thoroughly, carefully, and completely, that man is Mr. Datchett. He himself is probably not yet convalescent. That gives us time, anyway. It also gives us the blessed possibility that the Big Bezezus himself will turn up to make a personal affair of it. It's well on the cards, I think."

"Still I don't get your idea," said Marlowe, cutting in. "What's your plan of campaign?"

Campion hesitated and looked at the judge. "You said just now," he began, "that you'd a mind to go out and see what was coming to you. Since, quite obviously, you meant what you said, I feel you'll understand me when you hear what I've got to suggest. I want you to come back to Mystery Mile with me. I choose Mystery Mile because it's our own ground, so to speak. As they can't bring an army down there to wipe us out, we'd have more chance there than anywhere. We should be alone. They'd attack *us*. We shouldn't be endangering anyone else, for I'm certain Simister's not the man to go yokel baiting. So we have a comparatively fair chance to bring the thing to a head and finish it off, once and for all. Either we get them or they get us. Any development will be pretty speedy, certainly sensational, and probably final. What do you say?"

A gleam had appeared in the old man's eyes. This was the sort of proposition that appealed to his forthright personality.

"I'm on," he said.

"So am I," said Marlowe.

"You can count on me," chimed in Giles.

Campion shook his head and blinked at them nervously. "Sorry," he said to Marlowe, "but your father and I go alone or not at all. That's the scheme."

"Yes, that's final," said old Lobbett. "See here, Marlowe, I'm in this because I can't and won't help it. Someone's got to look after Isopel. It's not only because you're my son and a man likes to feel that there's someone carrying on if anything happens to him, but you've got work to do. You've got Isopel and all my affairs to look after."

The boy looked at him helplessly.

"But I can't let you and Campion go alone into this, Dad. Why Campion?"

"Oh, orders taken for this sort of thing daily," said the irrepressible young man airily. "You seem to forget my professional status."

"That's so," said the judge. "You and Paget, Marlowe, are out of it."

"Rot!" said Giles. "I'm coming, even if I only go back to live in the Dower House as I've a perfect right to. None of you know your way about Mystery Mile as I do. I'm the man you want. I've two arms still useful, which is more than Marlowe has. My head never was much good, anyway."

Mr. Campion looked thoughtful. "There's something in that," he said.

"What about your sister?" said old Lobbett.

Giles hesitated and glanced at Marlowe. "I think she'll be all right," he said.

Lobbett looked sharply at his son. "Is that so?" he said. "Then you cut back to the city as soon as you've had a rest. What do you say about young Paget, Campion?"

"I don't see that we can prevent him coming," Campion said slowly. "It's a far, far better thing, and all that, you know, Giles."

"I'm coming anyway," said Giles stubbornly. "That's settled."

"I don't like it," said Marlowe. "Campion, if you don't bring this thing off I'll never forgive myself for being out of it."

" 'Efficiency' is my watchword," said Mr. Campion. "Who arrested Jack Sheppard? Who convicted Charlie Peace? Who trailed Palmer the Poisoner? Who brought Jack the Ripper triumphantly to Justice? Who stopped mixed Ping-Pong in the Polytechnic? Don't heckle me, I only ask you. Who? For the next thrilling instalments see *Polly's Paper*, twopence every Tuesday."

"That settles it," said Lobbett. "Now, Campion, what's the next move?"

"Sleep, Nature's sweet restorer," said the young man quite seriously. "The learned cleric must be prevailed upon to put us up to-day. We'd better arrive at Mystery Mile at night. I think we're safe here until then and a deal longer if necessary. Marlowe, you'd better rest, too. We'll put you out at the nearest railway station on our way."

"Hell to you!" said Marlowe, "I don't think I shall ever sleep again."

"Amateur," said Mr. Campion happily. "I shall slumber like a babe."

There was no difficulty about accommodation in the old Vicarage. Within half an hour the adventurers were established in a great old-fashioned bedroom whose stripped beams and plaster walls were cool and silent.

The Reverend Alaric Watts, once the young men were safely above stairs, suddenly revealed those attributes of a minor prophet to which Campion had alluded, displaying in addition the tactics of a thirteenth-century general expecting a siege. His entire household, consisting of two old women servants who had both been with him for the past forty years, his gardener, and the man who had opened the door, were galvanized into strenuous action.

The dining-room where Crowdy Lobbett sat writing to his daughter was literally barricaded. Food and conversation were passed through the hatchway to the kitchen, while the gardener's son, a humourless cross-eyed youth locally accredited with great strength, was detailed to sit outside the door where the young men were sleeping.

The great garden gates were shut, and when the three awoke they found that a repast had been prepared for them which would not have dissatisfied a small mediaeval army going into battle.

Campion was almost hysterically amused. It was the first time that any of them had ever seen him laugh wholeheartedly. On discovery of the gardener's son he returned to his bed and appeared for some moments to be in danger of total collapse. At last he recovered, and after thrusting his head out of the door and commanding in a voice which shook the household: "Boy! Bring me my battle axe!" he dressed himself and returned to normal.

It was nearly nine o'clock when they finished their meal. There were no reports of any strangers in the village, and Campion became thoughtful.

"They must have watched the flat," he said. "I thought there was a man there. Quite likely they had a bit of a hangover from last night. We may not see a sign for a day or two."

"I wish I was in this," said Marlowe for the hundredth time. "My arm isn't nearly as stiff as I thought it would be."

His father turned upon him. "We settled that this morning, son," he said. "You pack right back to the city and take this letter with you to Isopel."

"You're out of it," said Giles. "You've got this battle ration under false pretences. I hope someone turns up before the effects of it have worn off. I feel primed up to hit something. God help Kettle if nothing more serious arrives."

"There's a train for you, Marlowe," said Campion, "at Woodbridge at half-past ten. We shall get back to Mystery Mile about an hour later, allowing for detours. Are you all ready?"

They nodded. The realization of the seriousness of the expedition returned to their minds, and although Campion remained as flippant as ever, the others were more quiet under the tension.

Alaric Watts unbarred his gate and let the great Bentley creep noiselessly out. He stood looking after them for a moment, a little black fantastic figure in the gathering darkness. Then he returned to his fortress and his studies.

They stopped only a minute to put Marlowe down at Woodbridge. The narrow awkward old town was almost deserted, and there were few travellers in the London train.

Marlowe and his father, who had been sitting in the back of the car in close conversation, merely shook hands.

Giles bent towards the younger man. "Look after the kid," he said, and added awkwardly, "All my love to Isopel if anything happens."

Marlowe nodded. "I envy you, old boy," he said sincerely. "Any message, Campion?"

"Tell Biddy, 'Smiling, the boy fell dead'," said Mr. Campion. "Should I do so, of course. Tell her she can have Autolycus," he added more seriously. "Lugg, too, if she likes. The woman could hardly hope to forget me if she had those two about the house."

On the last word he trod on the gas and swung the car round out of the tiny station yard towards Mystery Mile.

It was at that precise moment that back in the Vicarage at Kepesake the Reverend Alaric Watts pored over an ultra-late telegram which the postmaster had only just brought over himself, "to oblige".

It was addressed to Campion, Redding Knights. It had been delivered at the Hall, and Cluer had sent the postmaster over to the Vicarage.

The old vicar had hesitated before he read it, but as the postmaster volunteered the information that it was urgent, he finally slit open the flimsy envelope.

RETURNING MYSTERY MILE STOP [IT RAN]. COME TO US AT ONCE STOP. URGENT. BIDDY. YSOBEL.

Alaric Watts turned to the postmaster. "The post office makes funny mistakes," he said testily. "The lady spells her name I-S-O-P-E-L."

"That's 'ow it come, that's 'ow it was sent." The man spoke stolidly. "If there's a mistake, it was made by the sender."

Although he did not know it, the postmaster of Kepesake and Redding Knights was amazingly justified in this observation.

CHAPTER XXVI

One End of the String

THE Bentley crept slowly towards Mystery Mile by devious routes. Campion knew the county well. As they drew nearer, the faint cold smell of the sea reached them. The night had become extraordinarily dark, but it was close and thundery, and the sense of oppression which hung over them all was intensified by the heavy atmosphere.

Crowdy Lobbett bent forward and touched Campion on the shoulder. "Now that Marlowe is right out of it," he said, "I shall be prepared to tell you everything I know. You understand that?"

Campion promptly pulled the car into the side and stopped. He turned round in his seat and faced the older man.

"You've no notion what a good idea that is," he said. "If you don't mind, I think here is the time to let us have it. We need every ounce of help we can get." He switched off the headlights and composed himself to listen. "We appreciate the fact that you have only kept this thing dark out of consideration to us," he went on quietly. "But now I think the time has come to make all clear."

The judge nodded in the darkness. "That's how I see it, he said. "Now I'll tell you, and you'll see just how awkwardly I've been placed. I don't know if Marlowe told you that all through my career as a judge in the States I've had a reputation for my handling of these Simister gangsters. I've been a thorn in their flesh ever since—well, for the last fifteen years. Most of their work was carried on in my district and they came under my jurisdiction. And each and every one of them, I don't mind telling you, got it extra strong. There's been a great feeling for many years that they ought to be stamped out. To tell you the truth, we could never find out who this alleged Simister is. All we know is that there is an unknown head, and stamp out the subordinates as we liked, we could never make any impression on the mainspring of the business."

He paused. "That was the thing that we were always trying to find out about them—the identity of this mysterious leader. So far, you understand," he explained hastily, "I had only annoyed them. I was no real source of danger. But then one day I got hold of something which looked like a clue. It was after I had retired. The police had what you would call over here, I suppose, a standing committee, especially appointed to investigate this lot. As an authority on these people, I was invited to join it. We had special facilities for the questioning of prisoners and the like. Nothing came of it for some time, and it became pretty clear that the men we got hold of knew nothing material at all. Whoever squealed, however high his position in the gang, he could never tell us anything about the man at the top. Yet they were much more scared of their mysterious leader than we were, and quite as much in the dark.

"Then this thing I'm telling you about happened. There was a man in the state jail named Coulson—not the ordinary type of criminal, a man of education. He was doing a term for implication in a very nasty case of dope smuggling in which several policemen had been shot. They couldn't send Coulson to the chair, but they kept him locked up on what was virtually a life sentence. He was a Simister man: we knew that from a little rat who was also caught, and who squealed.

"While in prison Coulson developed internal trouble

which turned out to be cancer. He was dying in the penitentiary infirmary when I was approached by the committee to visit him, which I did. He was particularly anxious to die in his own home, wanted to spend his last days with his wife. I went into the matter and found that he was too far gone to do any more harm, so I obtained the necessary release and struck a bargain with him."

He peered through the darkness at them. They were listening intently.

"It's no use going into details," he said. "Just like all the rest of them, he couldn't tell me much, but he swore to me that he had something which he believed was a clue to the identity of Simister himself.

"At last, after a lot of trouble and persuasion, I got hold of it. As soon as I saw it I thought he'd been making a fool of me. But he was so earnest, so sincere, that I was gradually forced to believe that the ridiculous thing in my hands was in some sort of way a line on our little problem.

"Coulson died, and either through his widow or a fellow gangster, Simister must have heard that he gave me something.

"I'm sure that was all they knew." He spoke emphatically. "As you suggested, Campion, it's perfectly obvious that they don't know what they're looking for. But from that day to this they've been pursuing me. You may think me foolish for keeping this to myself, but in the first place I couldn't be sure whether I'd got anything at all. I wasn't keen on getting myself laughed at, and then, of course, there was the indubitable danger it brought with it." He was silent for a moment or so, and Giles and Campion pondered over the extraordinary story they had just heard. "Looking back on it," Lobbett remarked suddenly, "I feel I've been rather an obstinate old fool, but I don't see how I could have behaved very differently. You see, our committee was like every other committee: it had its section of fools. I was pestered by these folk to tell if I had found out anything, and I realized that once they got hold of it my precious information would leak out. Simister would cut the string, and my end of it would be no use to me. Things being as they were, I couldn't tell one without telling another, and I decided I'd do the job myself. It was too big a chance to be wasted.

"You're the first people who have heard as much as this, and if it brings serious harm to you—well, you offered to come, Campion, and you insisted, Paget. That's how it stands."

"Fine!" said Mr. Campion. "But what does your little *billet doux* consist of?"

The judge moved in his seat. "A kid's fairy-story book," he said.

Giles stirred.

"In the blue suitcase?" he said.

"Marlowe told me he opened it," said the old man. "Yes, that's so. I bought the whole series—there was a list of them in the back of the first book. I've read every word of those books, hunted for every kind of cipher, and neither I nor your great expert, MacNab, could make anything of it."

Campion stared at him through the darkness. "Good Lord, was it one of those we saw?" he said. "We'll push back at once. I'd no idea you'd left your clue at Mystery Mile."

"It was the safest thing to do," the old man pointed out. "While it remained there among the other books it was impossible for anyone to tell which was the key copy unless one knew. If I'd been caught with that one book the inference would have been pretty obvious. That's why I used to carry it like that with all the others. It was the safest way I could think of. It was too big to strap into my undervest."

"All the same, I think we'll get on," said Campion. "I'd like to have a look at it before anything happens. A bedtime story with a point, for once. I must have a go at it. I got seven-and-six for an acrostic once."

He started the engine and they drove off with more speed than before. The night had now reached a pitch of darkness unusual in the summer months. The sky was thick with clouds and the air was sultry in spite of the cool tang of the sea which reached them every now and again.

This, combined with their sense of approaching danger, made the drive a thrilling and unnerving experience. The whole countryside seemed to be stirring. Birds and animals slept uneasily in the heat and there were rustlings and little squeals from the roadside as they passed, and strange cries from the woods as the night birds prepared for the storm.

They reached the Stroud unchallenged. Campion glanced at Giles beside him. "No police on the road. What's this— economy? or has someone been busy? I wish my Seven Whistlers were still operating. I think we'd better push on."

Giles breathed heavily through his nose.

"Nothing else for it, now," he said. "If this storm doesn't break pretty soon I shall explode. It may hang like this all night. They do down here sometimes. It always makes me feel like murdering someone."

"That's the idea," said Campion cheerfully. "I fancy you're going to get your chance." He swung the car round the bend and they mounted the long low hill to the village.

There was a slight ground mist, and the fields were dark. Here, too, the uneasy rustlings could be heard from all sides, and from the marshes came the sudden cries of the saddlebacks stirred in their sleep.

The village was in darkness as they passed by the silent little cottages and turned into the Manor gates. The park, with great trees towering over the narrow drive, seemed unfamiliar, ominous, and uneasy.

"Lights," said Giles suddenly. "Lights in the drawing-room, I think. What are they up to?"

Campion shut off his engine, and the car rolled on a few yards and stopped. He jumped out on to the grass and spoke softly.

"I think we'd better approach with caution," he said. "I'll go and reconnoitre outside that window. It may be nothing, of course."

He spoke lightly enough, but it was plain that he was by no means satisfied that all was well.

For a few moments he was lost in the darkness, and there was no shadow across the shaft of light from the drawing-room window, which gilded the green boles of the elms. At length they heard his voice again quite close to them, whispering in a tone unusually agitated.

"We're for it," he murmured. "We've gone and put our little necks into it like bunnies in a snare. Look here."

They followed him across the lawn, treading softly on the springy turf. The silence in the house was terrible, though the lights still glared out unwinkingly. They crept up to the drawing-room window and peered in.

The sight within was an extraordinary one.

The room was brightly lighted. From where they stood they could just see the Romney. The beautiful girl with her sweet, stupid smile simpered in her frame, and before the picture, sprawled out in a little Louis XVI armchair, was Mr. Barber. His great head was thrown back, disclosing the thick bull throat beneath his beard.

"Who the heck is that, anyway?" murmured the judge. Campion explained.

"Is he dead?" Giles heard his own voice break as he whispered.

"I think not," said Campion. "He's breathing pretty heavily. He looks as if he'd been drugged."

Judge Lobbett craned forward a little too far, and his shadow fell across the stream of light. Campion jerked him back.

"Come round here," he whispered. He led them round the back of the house to the kitchen windows. There, too, the lights were burning. Once again they peered in.

Mrs. Whybrow sat at the kitchen table, her head resting on the boards, her arms hanging limply at her sides.

"Good God, they've got her too!" Giles ejaculated.

"Comfort me with chloroform," said Campion cryptically. "Wait a minute, and I'll go and play peep-bo round the house. I'm afraid we've come and settled in the very middle of it. Look here, Giles, I'm going to bring out that blue suitcase if I can lift it. Meanwhile, should I not return said Our Hero, you, Giles, will not obey your natural ass instincts and attempt to clear off in the Bentley, but you will use the only other exit which is not known to everybody, and that is *via* the mist tunnel. George and 'Anry have had orders to have a boat there ever since the search for Mr.

Lobbett was abandoned. I never knew when we'd need it. In the words of the immortal Knapp, 'Good night, all'."

The judge caught his sleeve. "The book you want is called *Sinbad the Sailor and Other Stories,*" he said.

The fatuousness of the title at such a moment was not lost on Mr. Campion. "That sounds like me," he said. "In view of the scene in the drawing-room it really ought to have been *The Sleeping Beauty.*"

He disappeared noiselessly round the side of the house. Giles and old Lobbett flattened themselves against the wall and waited. The boy was breathing like a horse, and his heart was thumping so loudly that he felt he must shake the foundations of the house.

Lobbett was calmer, but he was by no means impervious to the excitement of the moment. He drew a gun out of his hip pocket and waited.

Still there was no sound from the house. The minutes went by. Giles was quivering with impatience, and the wound in his cheek had begun to throb.

All sense of time left them. It seemed hours since Campion had disappeared. At last a board creaked in the house and Giles started violently. Next moment someone dropped lightly on the ground at their feet.

The judge whipped up his revolver, but it was Campion's whisper which greeted him out of the darkness.

"The Sleeping Beauty good and proper inside, the Babes in the Wood outside," he murmured. "Rummiest job I've ever seen. The chauffeur, Mrs. Whybrow, and the two maids, to say nothing of old Cleversides Barber, all laid out in different rooms. Ether, I think it is. I didn't hang round them much. It serves old Barber right for overzealous attention to business. He seems to have put up a bit of a struggle. There's a chair or so overturned. The others seem to have gone out like so many candles. I don't understand it. There's not a soul moving in the house." He lowered his voice still further. "I've got the book. Now, then, it's your one chance. Down the mist tunnel."

Giles did not move. "It's suicide in the dark like this," he said. "You don't know that 'soft', Campion."

"I've got a storm lantern I pinched out of the kitchen. We'll light it when we get down there," said Campion. "It's hopeless to go back by the car. That's their bright idea, I fancy."

Judge Lobbett nodded towards the window. "What about those people in there?"

"I know," admitted Campion. "All the same I don't think they're in any real danger. Our friends are evidently not going to hurt them or they'd have done it before now. We're in a trap and we must get out of it as best we can. It's not safe even to try to get back to the village."

All round them the dark garden was whispering. They had no idea where the enemy might be hidden. They could hardly hope that their coming had not been eagerly awaited. No one could have missed seeing their headlights as they came across the Stroud. Perhaps even now they were being observed, perhaps at any moment the attack would come.

Neither Giles nor Judge Lobbett had doubted for an instant the wisdom of Campion's remark when he had pointed out that the enemy were probably guarding the way back. Mr. Datchett and his followers were clearly not the only subordinates their mysterious enemy possessed.

They obeyed Campion without question.

"Carry on, Sergeant," said Giles. "I don't like the navigation scheme, but we'll have a shot at it."

"Hang on to Uncle Albert, then," said Campion. "This isn't going to be a pleasant country walk. The snake-in-the-grass stuff is on our programme."

They set off, Campion leading. Their progress was slow and nerve-racking. Every sound startled them. Every moment they expected something to leap at them out of the darkness.

Campion paused constantly to listen, but the house behind them was as silent as ever.

When they entered the maze he produced a torch and Giles took the lead. They found the gap and struggled out into the dry ditch on the farther side. The heat and breathlessness of the air had become intolerable. It felt as if a great hot compress had been placed over the little isthmus.

Giles was bathed in sweat, and even old Lobbett breathed uneasily.

Campion alone showed no outward sign of excitement. He padded along stealthily, keeping up a fair pace.

The hay was still standing, and they turned down into the deep channel of which Mr. Lobbett had made use before. The ditch was quite dry and their passage was easy.

They dropped out at last into the mist tunnel.

This wide dip in the saltings, which had been at one time an old river bed, was now quite dry and covered with short wiry grass, very slippery to the feet. Now, as ever, it was half filled with a fine white ground mist, only discernible in the darkness by its dank, marshy taste and smell.

"This place is pretty ghastly in the daytime," muttered the judge. "It's like the Valley of the Shadow of Death at night."

"Keep it pleasant, Guv'nor, keep it pleasant," quavered Mr. Campion, unexpectedly shrill.

"Look out," Giles's voice was quiet. "We're getting near now. Keep close in."

All around them the saltmarsh sucked and chattered horribly, and still farther ahead the disturbed sea birds wailed disconcertingly at uneven intervals.

Presently Giles stopped. "It's not safe any farther without the lantern," he said. "Your little torch isn't strong enough. I tell you, Campion, this is quick mud we're coming to. You can sink up to your waist, up to your neck, or out of sight altogether, and nothing but a couple of horses and a cartrope can save you."

They paused and lit the lantern.

"Now," said Campion, as he replaced the glass in its wire shield and the lantern gave out its uncertain yellow light through the fine mist, "Speed, my old sea dogs. All aboard for Paris, Dijon, Lyons, Macon, Victoria, Clapham Junction, Marseilles, and the Gates of Gold. *En voitures.*"

The flippancy sounded bizarre, almost terrifying in the fetid, breathless atmosphere.

"We're in luck," said Giles. "The tide's more than three-quarters' way up. Keep well in, keep well in."

They were standing nearly opposite the little hut where so few days before old Lobbett had changed his clothes before joining George in the rowboat. The grass had come to an end, and all around them was the mud, squelching and gurgling as the sea came nearer and nearer.

"Up to here you're safe." Giles spoke emphatically. "From now on, for God's sake look out. This is the hard side. All round the hut on the sea side the 'soft' begins. It stretches across here unevenly. It shifts, you know, but I'm afraid we've got to risk that."

Campion was peering forward into the circle of light thrown by the lantern. There was a thin white line on the mud a few feet ahead showing dimly through the mist. It was the oncoming tide.

"How high does this come?" said Campion, indicating it.

"Up to where the grass stops," said Giles. "It stops just short of the hut, except in September in the neap tides. Can you see the boat?"

"There it is," said the judge, preparing to step forward.

Giles jerked him back. "You've got to feel it step by step now," he said. "Hold the lantern high, Campion."

The boat was rocking gently, just clear of the bottom, only a few yards out.

Giles ripped off his shoes and stockings. "I'll have more chance if I find the 'soft'," he explained. Then he stepped forward gingerly, trying each step with the utmost caution.

Campion glanced back over his shoulder. Far back among the trees he fancied he saw moving lights.

"Hurry," he whispered softly, "hurry."

Giles went on steadily. Once he started back, plunged, and righted himself. He reached the boat and clambered in.

"It's all right if you walk straight at me," he said. "Come on. I daren't bring her in nearer or she'll ground."

Campion gripped the older man's arm. "Off you go," he said. "Just set your mind on the boat and get there. Tell Giles to make for Heron Beach, or if he can't in this light to get out into the stream and stay there."

It was not until the judge had completed his unsteady

journey to the bobbing rowboat that he realized that Campion was still standing on the bank, lantern in hand.

"Come on," said Giles, raising his voice.

"Shut up, you fool! Row out or I'll plug you—with my water pistol." Campion's whisper had a peculiarly carrying quality, although he was so far away they heard him perfectly.

"Rot!" Giles proceeded to draw in.

"For the love of Mike, get on! No heroics." Campion's voice was imploring. "You haven't a minute to spare and everything depends on it. You'll spoil everything. Trust your Uncle Albert."

"Boy, you can't do this." Crowdy Lobbett's tone was dangerously obstinate.

"Giles," commanded Campion, "pull straight if you don't want us all murdered, and stay out, whatever you hear. If that dear old stowaway of yours makes any noise, for the love you bear his daughter, dot him on the head with an oar."

Giles had known Campion for many years. So far he had never disobeyed him. This, he realized, was quite obviously the last moment at which to waver. He made up his mind.

Dipping the oars softly into the water, he pulled out to the centre of the estuary.

Campion waved the lantern to him enthusiastically. Giles's last glimpse of him was of a lank wild figure standing upon the bank, the hurricane held above his head in a ridiculous gesture.

"I loved Ophelia!" he bellowed with great dramatic effect. "It's the tobacco that counts!"

With which cryptic utterance he walked quietly back along the edge of the bank, dropped into the mist tunnel, and advanced towards the hut. He climbed the wooden steps and hung the hurricane carefully upon the corner of the door so that the light could be clearly seen for some distance. Then, taking his torch out of his pocket, he stepped in.

The hut, which was built up on piles some four feet high, contained a rough flat table, supported by one leg and a couple of hinges in the wall. On one side was a shelf set low enough to form a seat.

The young man looked round him carefully. Apart from a certain amount of odd boat tackle and an empty wooden box, the place was quite empty. The only other thing of interest was the fact that the floor boards at the back of the hut, directly under the form, had been removed, doubtless to prevent the sea from carrying it away at phenomenally high tides.

Campion sat down on the form, and placing his lighted torch beside him on the table, took out the child's book that he had brought from the house.

Sinbad the Sailor and Other Stories. He turned over the pages one by one, past Frontispiece, Dedication, Preface, and Editor's Note. The list of contents caught his eye—children's stories that he had known all his life. Anything more fatuous at a time like this it was impossible to imagine.

His eye wandered down the list. "Sinbad the Sailor," "Aladdin and His Wonderful Lamp." Suddenly his glance became fixed.

A title leaped up at him from the page. He put his hand over it and stared out into the darkness. His face was blank, his eyes dull behind his spectacles.

"I've gone mad," he said aloud, his voice strangely subdued. "It's happened at last. I'm insane. 'Ali Fergusson Baba and the Forty Thieves'."

CHAPTER XXVII

Late Night Finale

CAMPION, alone in the hut on the marshes, listened to the dying ring of his own voice, and then taking off his spectacles he wiped his face with a huge pocket handkerchief, and stared into the little haze of light which the hurricane made outside the narrow door.

Minutes passed, and he remained there looking blankly ahead of him: the silence was unbearable. Then very softly out in the darkness beyond the screen of light something moved. Instantly he sat up stiffly, listening, his head thrust forward.

At first he fancied that he had heard no more than the movement of some wild thing on the saltings, or the ominous clucking of the mud, but the sound came again, nearer this time and more distinct—footsteps on the short wiry grass.

Campion thrust the book he held into his jacket pocket. His torch followed it. He sat silent, waiting.

Someone trod softly on the wooden steps leading up to the hut; he could hear the creak of the ancient wood as it trembled under a heavy weight.

The next instant the lantern was snatched from its mooring, and a shape, ponderous and elephantine, stood in the doorway.

Mr. Barber was barely recognizable. The genial, rather stupid old gentleman had vanished, and in his place there looked out at the young man at the table something mocking and incredibly evil hiding within this monument of flesh.

"You are alone?" he said inquiringly. "You are very clever, my friend."

Campion grinned at him; his expression was if possible even more fatuous than usual.

"Spoken like a true gent," he said. "If you would sign that for me it might do me a lot of good."

The man who called himself Ali Fergusson Barber moved over to the table, where he set down the lamp and stood towering above the pale young man, who appeared dwarfed and negligible beside him.

"Perhaps it is as well," he said. "I fancy it is time that you and I had a little discussion together, Mr. Rudolph K—" He mentioned a name which so startled the young man before him that he betrayed himself with an exclamation.

The older man smiled faintly. "I have here, my young friend," he said, drawing a paper out of his pocket, "a most interesting dossier. To read it to you would be a waste of time. But I assure you it contains some very remarkable reading. You and I have both made the same mistake. We underestimated each other, Mr.—"

"Shall we say Campion?" said the young man, his vacant smile returning. "Now perhaps, since we're getting so matey, we'll go into another matter. Who the hell are you?"

The other man laughed, and just for a moment there was a trace of the old art expert in his face. The next moment it had vanished again, and he was once more this new and vivid personality.

"I am a man of integrity," he said. "I have never made the mistake of using an alias. It would be silly of me to try and disguise myself, and also very tiring. I live my own life."

Campion shrugged his shoulders. "You know your own limitations better than I do," he said. "Still, I could have suggested another name for you. Sit down and make your-self comfortable. There's a soap box over there."

Mr. Barber accepted the seat. "I suppose you've got Lob-bett away by sea, as you did before," he said easily. "That was very clever of you. I repeat, you're a very clever young man, Mr. Campion. We shall have no great difficulty in deal-ing with that old gentleman, I fancy. But my chief interest at the moment is in you."

The change in the man was extraordinary. It occurred to Campion that no disguise he might have adopted could have concealed him half as effectively as this remarkable new per-sonality, which he seemed to drop and adopt at will.

"As you have no doubt guessed," he went on, "I am a representative of one of the cleverest organizations in the world. In fact, I believe that you were once commissioned by us on a rather delicate mission in an affair at a house called Black Dudley. On that occasion you failed. What was the cause I do not know, but perhaps that explains why we took your entrance into this particular business as so negli-gible a matter. It may interest you to know that I and my superiors have now considered it worth while to offer you a position in our organization."

"Sign along the dotted line," said Mr. Campion. "Please tear carefully. Nothing genuine without this signature."

The face before him was expressionless. Mr. Barber's al-tered voice went on. "That rather irritating humour of yours —I suppose that's involuntary."

"That's a remark that might have been better put," said the young man, who seemed suddenly for no apparent rea-son to be enjoying himself immensely.

"I suppose that it is an asset," the other man remarked judicially. "But a distressing price to have to pay for busi-ness efficiency."

"In replying to yours of the fifth ult," said Campion, "I take it that you are making me an offer?"

His visitor nodded. "Exactly," he said. "This man Lob-bett is making himself a nuisance to our organization in general. He is so obstinate that he is a little difficult to han-dle. We have also reason to believe that he has, or thinks he has, a key to a secret so important that it is impossible for me to discuss it with you. Should this be a fact, he might be very dangerous. I don't need to tell a man of your intelligence any more. A settlement of this affair would be the best introduction you could possibly have, and I can assure you personally that you will never regret it."

"I suppose I should live in?" remarked Campion thoughtfully. "All found, washing done by the firm, and perhaps a Circassian or two thrown in when times were good?"

The older man folded his hands. "I appreciate your humour," he said seriously. "Your remuneration would be in no sense inadequate. I should like to point out that your alternative is complete exposure. What do you say?"

"Cheek," said Mr. Campion with sudden warmth. "Unadulterated Prep School cheek. Now I'm going to talk. In the first place, I want a complete explanation of several points. First of all, how did it happen that you were waiting for us with your neat little put-up job? And why? Bit of a bow at a venture, wasn't it?"

"Not at all. I knew my telegram would bring you. Women are a great handicap in affairs of this sort, Mr. Campion."

"Oh yes, of course." The young man spoke hastily, an inkling of what had happened occurring to him.

"I admit you were too quick for me," the other continued. "Foolishly I imagined that you would search the house for the young woman and then appeal to me. I should have been easy to revive. We had received the information that the document which old Lobbett set such store upon was a bulky affair. I argued therefore that he would have left it at the house, carefully hidden. Since it was useless for me to search for something I should not recognize, I waited for Mr. Lobbett himself to show it to me."

Although the conversation had been comparatively amicable, the atmosphere in the little hut had grown steadily more electric. Outside the breathlessness which comes before a storm had become stifling. A flash of sheet lightning lit up the marshes.

"Not bad," said Campion suddenly. "But not good either. The situation is becoming clear to me. I am to appear in the gossip columns or do your dirty work for you. I suppose you've been to Pinkertons about me?"

Suddenly he began to laugh. "All the same," he said, "even if I do appear in the What Shall We Do With Our Boys? section, I'm not sure that it won't have been worth it. You were with us all through our spot of fun last night. I shall see you to my dying day sitting next to Mrs. Knapp. I wouldn't have missed it for anything."

A slow flush passed over the Oriental's face: the first sign of anger he had betrayed. "I considered it best to let you carry out your rather childish little rescue," he said. "I knew that our people would have got any information they wanted out of the girl by that time. I also thought it valuable to be in your confidence. I, too, consider it was worth it."

Campion leaned back a little. "On the whole I suppose you're pretty pleased with yourself?" he said. "No doubt they treat you fairly well? You're not beaten or anything if you fail? But you're not going to get Our Little Albert on the staff. Now consider your own position for a bit. Here you are, chucking your weight about in the middle of a marsh, far away from home and mother. Suppose I bang you on the head and go home and say no more about it?"

Mr. Barber smiled faintly. "I don't think you'll do that," he said. "You must remember I've studied your record pretty closely. I may point out to you, quite safely, I think, that a body would be very difficult for a man in your position to explain. Your friends at Scotland Yard would hardly outweigh the record of your curious profession. On the other hand, I am a man of unblemished character, and everyone knows who I am."

"Except Our Albert," said Campion, with a lightning change of tone.

Something in his manner silenced the man opposite him, and the little hut was suddenly uncannily still.

"Do you remember a man called Coulson?" Campion was speaking softly. "The only man to whom you ever half

betrayed yourself? My second name is Morgiana, Mr. Ali
Baba."

No muscle of the Oriental's heavy face moved. "I do not
understand you," he said. "You are still making jokes."

"That's where you're wrong, my captive Helen." Campion still spoke lightly, but every second now was tingling
with suppressed excitement. At any moment the storm
might break.

"You admitted that you didn't know what sort of key the
estimable Judge Lobbett had," Campion continued. "I can
clear things up for you a bit. His precious clue is perfectly
bona fide. It's clear enough to anybody who knows you. In
fact, your name is the hidden word in the acrostic. Now, I
think, in view of everything, we're properly introduced.
How now, brown cow?"

That the man was shaken there could be no doubt. He sat
mouthing at the young man before him, and for the first
time there appeared in his wet reddened eyes an expression
which Campion had not seen in them before. It was that
expression which made it possible for him to believe the
many astounding stories he had been told about this man,
tales of utter ruthlessness, examples not so much of con-
scious cruelty as of complete disregard for anything but his
own ends.

After the first shock he pulled himself together with
amazing control.

"You are what they call over here 'Too clever by half'
young man," he said heavily. "It says in my dossier that it is
one of your peculiarities that you never carry a gun. I think
you are wise, with such a varied record as yours. It would be
interesting to learn if it is true."

"Talking of confidences," said Mr. Campion airily,
"since I see that one of us is going to cop in for it shortly,
there are several things I'd like to know. For instance, I
would like to know—as a last favour—how have you managed to keep so quiet about yourself all this time? Accounts
of you go back, they say, for the past hundred years. You're
pushing along, but you haven't come all that way, surely?"

During the last few seconds Mr. Barber had seemed to

become positively affable. Outside great drops of rain had
begun to fall. The lightning was becoming more frequent.

"I am in no hurry," he said. "Perhaps I will tell you. I
must remain here till after this storm, at any rate. But I am
afraid I must withdraw my offer."

"Spoken, I take it, as a sort of funeral oration?" said Mr.
Campion. "Let's have something from the heart."

Mr. Barber sighed. "You are either a very brave man," he
said, "or you are even more foolish than you pretend to be."

"Pure courage," said Mr. Campion modestly. "I wasn't
going to point it out, of course, but since you've brought it
up—"

Mr. Barber silenced him with a gesture.

"I am glad that this opportunity has occurred," he said
slowly, a new and almost philosophical tone in his voice,
"although I am naturally sorry to have lost such a likely
recruit. The desire to confide is very strong in a man of my
temperament, Mr. Campion. I have never before found myself in a situation in which it was safe for me to indulge this
particular desire."

Campion nodded gravely. Had he been listening politely
to a hostess telling the story of her life in a Mayfair drawing-
room he could not have appeared less aware of the imminent danger of the situation.

The Oriental was fast becoming more and more expan-
sive. He seemed to have grown into a larger, more sophisti-
cated personality than ever before. Now at last it did not
seem absurd to connect him with the mysterious figure
whose name had been a byword in police circles for so many
years.

"I am the only man," he said, looking at Campion, a
slight hint of pride in his eyes, "who ever turned my particular business into something as pleasurable as any other more
legitimate concern. That is to say," he went on with surprising contentment, "I am, as a general rule, as safe, as well
respected, and as undisturbed as any other man of my
wealth. I do not have to have lonely castles in Austria, Hun-
gary or mysterious houses in Paris. I go where I like, live as
I choose. I have a villa with a hanging garden on the Bos-

phorus, the most delightful of Queen Anne houses in Chelsea. I moved there from Mayfair when the fashion changed. My apartment in New York is one of the loveliest in that most expensive of cities. I have a positive palace in California, and my château behind Juan-les-Pins is famous throughout France. I am an authority on pictures, and I have the finest collection of Reynoldses in the world. My amusements are many. I am a respected citizen in every district where I have a house. All sorts of people desire to know me. I have many friends. And yet"—he shrugged his shoulders—"there is no one in whom I dare confide absolutely. But that is my only disadvantage. For the rest, if I made my money out of oil, coal, or motor cars, what difference would it make?"

Campion appeared impressed. "Your business is done entirely through agents, I suppose?" he said. "I can understand carrying it on, but I don't see how you started it. You are the financier of the show? You buy the brains on one side and the executive power on the other?"

"That is so." Mr. Barber nodded. "It is a great pity, my friend," he remarked, "that I should have to kill you. I find you quite intelligent. The question you raise is a simple one. My father was the original Simister."

Campion stared at him, and for a moment he seemed about to laugh.

"Good Lord!" he said, "you inherited it?"

"Why not?" The Oriental spread out his hands. "There seems to me to be nothing ridiculous in the idea that a man should leave his son a business of this kind any more than any other concern. A wholesale butcher becomes accustomed to the idea of killing a million beasts a year, whereas the sight of an animal being slaughtered might sicken him. I never take part in any of my—shall we say?—business transactions, save at the very beginning. The idea does not shock me. That is all there is to say about it. My father preserved my anonymity most carefully. When he died I carried on. I do not think that anybody, even among our own people, realized that a change had taken place. You see, the organization must necessarily be very scattered and secret. One man does not know another. That is how I have preserved my identity."

"Wonderful!" said Campion, whose eyes were dancing. "Forgive me, Mr. Barber, but have you any family?"

The old man hesitated. "After all," he said, more to himself than to the man opposite, "you will have no opportunity for abusing my confidence. No, there is no one to follow me."

"Hard lines," said Campion sympathetically.

Mr. Barber shrugged his shoulders. "I do not think so," he said. "I am very much of an individualist, and"—he laughed confidently—"I shall live to be very old."

Campion leaned across the table.

"Forgive my asking," he said. "But what's to prevent my killing you, as soon as we stop being matey? I mean, when you dot me one, why shouldn't I dot you one back? Suppose I risk being found with the body? I'm younger than you are, and probably more gifted at horseplay."

"I do not think you are so well armed." There was something terrifying in the calm satisfaction of the tone in which the words were uttered. Mr. Barber's large face was mild and affable.

"Let me explain. In the first place, Mr. Campion, I have heard that it was your custom to carry a child's water pistol manufactured to look like a genuine service revolver. I confess I was amused when I heard this. So amused that I also had my little joke. I too possess a water pistol, Mr. Campion. It is at this moment trained directly upon your face. I would like to mention in passing that I am considered a remarkable shot. I did not wish to copy you exactly, however, and my pistol maintains a particularly corrosive fluid. I understand the English magistrates are very much against its use, but the idea so amused me when I thought of it, that at the risk of its appearing a little in bad taste, I had it prepared. It is not humanly possible to stand up against such a fire, and in your confusion an ordinary bullet will finish you easily."

Campion had not stirred, but a muscle at the hinge of his jaw twitched violently.

"I didn't realize that you'd planned this *conversazione*,"
he said at last.

The man opposite him fancied that his tone had lost some
of its buoyancy.

"Nor had I," he said easily. "I had hoped that it would
not be necessary. But there was always the possibility of
your friend Judge Lobbett's discovery being serious. I knew
I should have to be prepared. However," he sighed, "there is
plenty of time yet. You may be assured, Mr. Campion, that I
shall avail myself for as long as possible of this delightful
experience of confiding the secret which I have kept for fifty
years to a man both brave and intelligent enough to recognize the size of my achievement, most especially since I can
feel that I make the statement in perfect safety."

Campion breathed more heavily.

It was not long after midnight, he guessed. Mystery Mile
would not be stirring for another five hours at least. Giles,
he felt sure, would obey his instructions. The remote chance
of anyone's noticing the lighted hut in the rainstorm was
negligible. For once in Mr. Campion's eventful life he was
almost subdued.

"Don't be afraid of boring me," he said, with a vigorous
attempt at his old flippancy. "I love these peeps behind the
scenes. Oh, by the way, before you go any farther, there's
something I'd like to make quite clear. There is no use wast-
ing your time unduly in bothering the old gentleman, in
whose employ I am, any longer. The clue he had to your
identity was a copy of a child's book—absolutely harmless
in itself—and unintelligible to anybody who didn't already
suspect you. He thought there was a code message hidden in
it, and still thinks so. The book is in my pocket now."

The Oriental's eyes regarded him narrowly. "Do not
have any illusions about my little toy, my friend," he said.
"Stand up. Put your hands above your head."

Campion obeyed him. Mr. Barber stood up also and from
under the edge of the table, where his hand had levelled it,
there appeared what was, in the circumstances, the most
dangerous-looking weapon Campion had ever seen. It was a
small glass syringe, exquisitely made, and any doubts he

might have had as to the truth of the other man's threat were instantly dispelled.

"In your left pocket, I see." The voice was smooth and almost caressing. With his left hand he removed the book deftly.

"Sit down," he went on. "May I congratulate you on your very gratifying intelligence? Now that we understand one another perfectly our conversation will be so much more pleasant."

"What little gents we both are," said Mr. Campion. "Tell me, do you do all your murders like this?"

Mr. Barber moved his left hand deprecatingly. "To be quite truthful," he said with delightful confidence, "this will be the first time that I have ever been personally implicated in any of my ventures. I work from my desk as a rule. I know everything: I am behind every *coup* of any consequence. It was only because Mr. Lobbett very foolishly wrote for an art expert that, on receiving that information, I decided to take part personally. I am enjoying the experience immensely. My one regret is that I shall be compelled to dispose of so amusing and useful a person as yourself."

Campion did not reply. His spirits seemed to have failed him. Mr. Barber continued.

"I was also not very satisfied with my agent, Datchett. I have neglected that little branch of my organization. A man brilliant in his own line, but not a good servant. I ought to have known all about you long ago."

The first faint hint of a smile appeared on Mr. Campion's face. "Stupendous!" he murmured. "A sort of departmental store. 'Don't Miss Our Bumper Blackmail Basement. Wholesale Murder, First Floor. Kidnapping and Hosiery on Your Left.'"

Mr. Barber was not listening to him. His left hand still rested upon the little green-and-gold-bound children's book. He tapped it gently with a heavy forefinger.

"Since you are being quite fair with me," he said, "I will tell you that I am fully satisfied that this was the missing clue to my identity. It recalls an incident which I had forgotten—an incident of twenty years ago. Coulson was the only man with whom I ever had direct personal dealings. I always represented myself as my own lieutenant, and I do not think he ever questioned it. To him I was a mysterious person, known only by a number, not much older than himself. That fact alone would have discredited any serious suspicions he might have had about me, since the leader of the concern was known to have been in authority for so long. I was comparatively young, and this desire to confide was very strong in me. One day he asked me if I knew the identity of Simister himself—if I had seen him. Foolishly, I confessed that I had. Ever afterwards he bothered me for the truth. Frankly, I was amused by it, and one day, when he had been very importunate, I pointed to this book which lay upon the counter of a second-hand bookshop which was his headquarters at the moment. I had been turning the pages over idly in my hands, and I fancy he thought I had brought the book with me. "There is your clue," said I. I never saw him again, since soon afterwards he was sent to the South. The incident had slipped my memory completely, which shows one, my friend Campion," he added with sudden sententiousness, "that a foolish act is much more dangerous than an evil one."

Campion nodded quietly.

"There's only one more thing I'd like to know," he said. "What had your friend Datchett got against old Swithin Cush?"

Mr. Barber shrugged his shoulders.

"How should I know?" he said. "A lot of Datchett's business shocked me. It was so small. That animal Kettle—he should never have been entrusted with anything. I was ashamed that he should be even remotely in my service."

"That's the spirit," said Campion, a shadow of his own returning. "I was interested in Swithin Cush," he added. "It seemed to me impossible that such a man should have a secret."

Mr. Barber shook his head. "A secret is never impossible," he observed. "Look at me, for instance."

"If it's not being nosey," the young man remarked slowly, "I should be very interested to know how you intend to get away with your reputation all pure and virgie and our Albert's poor little mucked-up corp lying about? I may be crude, but the question of the body has always worried me."

"That will not be difficult." The Oriental spoke confidently. "Luck is with me, and my plan was simple to begin with. After I had sent the telegram which I knew would bring you here, my agents came down here, waited until the village had retired—which, as you know, is early—and then set upon the servants and drugged them as you found them. They had orders to do that and then remove themselves. I arrived upon the scene immediately afterwards. To them, as to everyone else, I am Fergusson Barber, the art expert. I waited for you, as you found me. What more simple, then? I shall go back, change my boots, which will be necessary after this rain. I shall even drug myself."

"Don't forget the footmarks," said Mr. Campion. "They're very hot on them over here."

Mr. Barber nodded. "I had thought of that," he agreed. "But you ought to know that to follow footmarks on a saltmarsh is an impossibility. My alibi will be perfect—especially since both Judge Lobbett and young Paget saw me at the same time you did. By the way—" He paused, as if hesitant over some delicate question. "You are young. If there is—er—any errand of the heart that I can do for you, you may rely upon me."

"Manners good, but customs beastly," commented Campion judicially. "No. Sing no sad songs for me. And since we are exchanging compliments, I'm sorry you've been troubled."

"Not at all." The Turk spoke quite seriously. "I shall have a beautiful Romney as a memento of my visit. It is quite genuine, by the way—one of the loveliest specimens I have ever seen. Were there time, I should be inclined to take you back to the house and show you its beauties. I shall have it put up for sale, discredited by good authorities—it may be necessary to substitute a copy for that—and sold quite cheaply to one of my agents.

"But the time moves on, my friend. It sounds as if the

storm were clearing. Such a delightful conversation—it is a pity that it should ever have to close."

"Something occurs to me," said Campion, looking up. "I have just composed my epitaph, and since you're so anxious to help, you might see if you could get it put over my grave. No vulgar antique lettering either; good Roman Caps. Now listen carefully, because I should hate you to get it wrong."

He was speaking with intense seriousness, and the Turk was amused. His veering eyes watched the young man tolerantly, but always he held the deadly syringe ready for the first sign of violence.

"No text," said Campion. "Just this, neatly and sincerely inscribed:

Here lie I, poor Albert Campion,

don't forget to get the scansion right."

He recited the rhyme earnestly, his long thin hand beating out the rhythm on the rough table:

"Death was bad, but Life—*was champion*!"

On the last word his voice rose to a note of triumph, and with a gesture of amazing swiftness he swept the lamp from the table, dropping his head sharply as he did so.

Instantly something soft and horrible splattered over his shoulder, and the acid burning through his clothes ate deep into the flesh beneath, an almost paralyzing agony. The lantern crashed on the floor and, the draught catching it, went out, leaving the hut in complete darkness.

Campion wriggled towards the gap in the floor boards. It was his one hope. The pain in his shoulder was crippling him. He was terrified lest his senses should give way before it and he should faint.

In the darkness the man who a moment before had been chatting affably to him hovered, ready to kill.

Campion found the gap with his foot. Savagely he jerked himself towards it, and at that instant Barber fired. The gun had a silencer on it, but a flash of flame cut through the darkness. The place was too small for there to be a chance for the younger man to escape. The bullet entered his body.

The Oriental heard the stifled grunt of his victim as he slid helplessly through the opening on the marsh beneath.

Unaware of this second exit, he fired again, bullet after bullet.

The silencer was most effective. He had no cause to fear an alarm and he was determined to despatch his man.

When at last he paused there was an ominous silence in the hut.

"Clever, my friend, clever to the end!" He spoke softly, but there was a peculiarly horrible satisfaction in his tone.

Still holding the gun cautiously, he drew a match-box from his pocket, his spent torch being useless. The tiny spurt of flame flickered for an instant, and went out in the draught. He moved to the edge of the gap under the bench and once more struck a match. This time the flame lasted longer.

Campion lay upon his back on the fast-reddening grass. His spectacles had fallen off and his eyes were closed, his face livid in the momentary light. Just for an instant the Turk hesitated. He had fired five times. There was one shot left in his gun. He debated if he should use it. There was no way of making sure if the man were dead unless he went out to him.

As he knelt looking down, the little green-and-gold book which he had snatched up in his first rush from the table slipped from the pocket where he had hurriedly thrust it and fell out on to the figure below.

That decided him. He clambered carefully to his feet and crossed the hut.

In the doorway he paused, feeling for the steps. He descended carefully.

Once on the grass he attempted to strike another light, but the rain which was still falling lightly rendered it impossible. He stepped out blindly to the left, unconsciously taking the shorter way round the hut. He took a step forward, then another, the short thick grass still beneath his feet.

As he took the third step a sudden sense of impending

danger seized him, and he tried vainly to swing his weight back. A moment before he might have succeeded, but the turf beneath his feet was slippery.

He staggered and plunged forward over the three-foot drop of ragged earth into the stretch of slimy mud which lay beneath—that very stretch, paler and smoother-looking than the rest, which Giles had been so fearful of finding not an hour before. Unconscious of the imminent danger, he struggled to right himself, his only fear being that his alibi would be more difficult to establish now that his clothes were soaked with sea water and slime.

All round him the mud sucked and chattered to itself in its quiet guttural tongue. The rain continued to fall. He was alone between clay and sky.

He fought fiendishly to escape, realizing suddenly that the slime was past his waist. He beat out wildly with his arms and touched nothing but the foetid stuff. It reached his shoulders, and oblivious of any other danger he screamed aloud, calling upon Campion, straining his lungs until he felt that the village must hear.

The mud gurgled and spat. Little rivulets of water burst up through it. He slipped deeper; in a moment it must reach his chin. He forced his arms down, an instinct telling him that he might so gain a moment's respite. The stuff was closing about him, sucking him gently, firmly, and with horrible slowness into its slimy breast. He dared not scream now, lest the very movement should drag him under.

It was at that second that, far below, his foot touched the hard. He stiffened all over, a new hope returning. The difficulty of breathing was intense; as if it felt itself cheated, the mud pressed him, flattened him with its enormous weight.

Still, hope was returning, a wild, reckless desire for life, whatever it might bring with it.

The rain stopped.

Cramps were racking him, but he dared not relax the muscles that alone held him above the morass.

Far over his head the clouds parted. The tail end of the storm which had passed over them had dispersed itself. It became a little lighter.

He stared ahead of him. His eyes strained out of their sockets. His face was distorted, his mouth gaping, the veins standing out in great ridges under his pallid skin.

Not a foot away from him was a thick white line, irregular, more terrible, more relentless than the mud itself, the tide.

He watched it. Every spark of life that was left in him concentrated against this last and most dreadful foe. It retreated a little way, only to rush forward again within an inch of his face, splashing him with brine.

He forced up every fighting nerve that was in him. His frenzied scream startled the wild birds, and echoed, a cry of death, into the silent rooms of the Manor itself, acres distant across the saltings, and died away hollowly in the stillness of the early morning.

The waves retreated once more, and this time returned frothing, laughing, smothering over his mouth.

CHAPTER XXVIII

Moral

"Two teeth?" said the man from Scotland Yard with contempt. "He's got seven. Three at the bottom, four at the top. Mary and I are crazy about him. You'll have to come round and see him as soon as you can get out again."

He was sitting forward in the big chair, before one of the first of autumn's fires, in the flat at Bottle Street.

"I'll come down next week. I'm all right now." The slightly high-pitched voice was more hollow than it had been in the old days, but it had not lost that suggestion of exuberance which had always been its characteristic. Campion was almost completely hidden in the depths of his high-backed Toby chair. Only now and again when the firelight flickered did the other man get a glimpse of his face. It was still desperately haggard from his long illness. Ali Barber's bullet had pierced his lung and the mending had been slow. But his old sparkle had returned and his eyes behind his horn-rimmed spectacles were once more amused and very much alive.

His companion smiled at him. "You were damned lucky to come out of that as well as you did," he said. "You were always lucky. I don't mind telling you there was a general feeling of relief on all sides when your Turkish friend passed out."

"I'm very grateful to the boys for getting me out of it so quietly," murmured Campion with genuine gratitude. He sighed. "I was afraid I was going to get a medal."

"More kicks than ha'pence in our job," said the other. "It's something to lay to your credit, though. There wasn't a doubt that it was the right man. We've been tracing the sources of his income among other things. Marvellous!" he remarked dreamily, leaning forward and knocking the ashes of his pipe out on the hearth. "You wouldn't think it could have happened. Truth is stranger than fiction, as they say."

Campion chuckled. "You ought to start a copybook, Stanis," he said. "But I really thought I was for it that time when I fell through the floor. I recited God Save the King, sang the old school song, muttered the family motto—'No Rubbish to be Shot Here'—and passed out. Any further developments in the Datchett case?"

"Lugg told me I wasn't to talk shop."

The man from Scotland Yard looked round him nervously. Lugg, in his new rôle as hospital attendant, was a truly terrifying personage. As he was nowhere in sight the man continued softly.

"I wanted to tell you about that," he said. "He went to pieces at his trial—I don't suppose you've seen the papers. Old Livery let him have it before he sentenced him. 'Scathing Sentences', the press boys called it, and they were, too. He got the limit. I don't think there'll be any appeal either. We got all the witnesses we wanted from the Maplestone Hall affair. There was no need to go into that other business."

Campion glanced up sharply. "Swithin Cush?"

The other man nodded.

"That was interesting if you like," he said, glancing up with new interest. "In the house at Kensington there were masses of stuff dealing with all sorts of things. Wherever possible we bunged the papers back to the right owners and said no more about it. We're not out to stir up scandals all over the country. We got our man where we wanted him, and that was quite enough. But the old man had his secret all right. The last thing you'd guess in a thousand years. He wasn't a parson."

Campion stared at him.

"He wasn't a parson?" he repeated blankly. "They've pulled your leg again, Stanis."

"No. It's quite true." The other man shook his head. "An impersonation story fifty years old. I'll tell you. There were two brothers—Swithin Cush just ordained, Welwyn Cush, too poor to take the necessary 'varsity course. Round about 1880 Swithin died, apparently quite suddenly, from heart trouble. The two brothers were living alone together in rooms in Kensington. The dead man, still only a boy, had just been appointed to his first curacy in a Norfolk village. The younger man had a great friend in the daughter of the house, and it was she, I fancy, who put the idea up to him. From what we can find out he didn't intend to do it for long, but he seems to have been on his beam ends. He allowed the dead man to be buried in his name, and took his job. There was only a year between the brothers, and they seem to have resembled each other very closely. No one appears to have doubted Welwyn for a moment, and the years slipped by as they do in the country. The life was congenial to him, the vicar liked him, and he was a great favourite with the parishioners. Five or six years later he was appointed to Mystery Mile, and his history there I suppose you know much better than I do. The older he got the safer he was. The only person who knew his secret was the woman in Kensington. She died only about a year or so ago. Her name was Aggie Saunders, and very much the class of person you'd imagine." He glanced at Campion, who was sitting forward in his chair, his eyes goggling. He continued.

"It seems pretty obvious that she had expected the old man to marry her. When he didn't, although she never made any attempt to give him away but rather seems to have shielded him at every opportunity, she could not resist reminding him from time to time of the power she held over him by deliberately referring to the secret in long rambling letters to him. He replied to these imploring her not to write anything so incriminating.

"I fancy that she found that a letter on this subject invariably brought a reply from him, and therefore harped upon it shamelessly. When she felt that her time was drawing to an end she packed up all these letters of his and sent them to him, choosing, by extraordinary bad luck, the first week of Kettle's appointment as postmaster.

"Datchett must have got him to transfer because of some rather fishy business in the village near Yarmouth where he was before. Kettle simply pinched the letters, including the last one she wrote, which was all on the subject and pretty good reading, and packed them off to Datchett. From which time the poor old boy you knew as Swithin Cush couldn't have had a moment's peace. How's that?"

Campion was silent for a moment, lost in amazement. "Good Lord!" he said at last, and repeated softly, "Good Lord!"

"Blackmail is the filthiest of all crimes," said the man from Scotland Yard. "I'm glad Datchett got what was coming to him."

Campion regarded his visitor awkwardly.

"This raises a rather delicate question re Births, Marriages, and Deaths in Mystery Mile, doesn't it?" he said. "What are your people doing with the letters?"

Detective Inspector Stanislaus Oates shrugged his shoulders. He seemed almost official in his vagueness. "Whatever criticism anybody ever makes about Scotland Yard," he said, "they can't call us mischief makers. We protect the peace: that's our job. I don't fancy we shall go into it any further. It would make a lot of unpleasantness all round, and a scandal in the Church, which is always to be avoided. I'm not an authority on ecclesiastical law—I suppose it would be a case for the archbishop if it ever came out."

At the words "ecclesiastical law" Campion pricked up his ears. For the first time he realized the meaning of the mysterious phrase in Swithin Cush's letter to Giles: '*In the event of any serious trouble . . . send to Alaric Watts . . .*

who will know the correct proceeding." This was the serious trouble of which the old man had been afraid.

"Of course," the inspector went on, "I don't know yet. The authorities may decide to take the matter to the Church. I think it would only mean some sort of minor bill being passed. At present no one's moved. It's not an important thing now, but it was serious enough for him."

Campion did not speak. He realized more than anyone how serious it had been for the old man, so beloved by his bigoted congregation. He could imagine Biddy's horror, Giles's obstinate refusal to accept the truth, and he hoped sincerely that they would never have to be told. In view of everything he did not think it was likely.

"I suppose you're very satisfied?" The detective inspector dismissed the subject airily. "Apart from your wound and the old rector's death you're not sorry it happened. If you hadn't got old Lobbett and his kids down to Mystery Mile a lot of things would never have happened."

"There's something in that," said Campion, so thoughtfully that the other man glanced at him shrewdly.

"What's worrying you?" he said.

"I had such a nice death scene," said Mr. Campion unexpectedly. "I feel that the curtain's gone up and exposed me crawling off. No more fun until the next performance, Stanis, and I'm not sure I wouldn't rather be in the stalls for that."

"A spot of brandy'll put you right—that's nerves," said the other cheerfully, but he had made a mistake in his diagnosis.

They chatted for some time longer, and eventually the Scotland Yard man took his leave. Campion lay back in his chair and reflected upon the tragic story of Swithin Cush.

"As perfect a parson as ever lived," he reflected. "And a damned old fraud at the same time, God bless him!"

After some time he took an envelope from his dressing-gown pocket and reopened it. Biddy's handwriting was not of the best. It might have been a schoolgirl's letter. He re-read it slowly:

Home.
Sunday.

MY DEAR ALBERT:

Lugg tells me you're allowed out, in a really marvellous epistle which begins "Dear Madham" and ends "Well duckie, I must close now". We're coming up to see you again on Friday. Mystery Mile looks marvellous now, all the leaves turning and apples waiting to be picked. The D'arcy Spice that St. Swithin planted in the courtyard is bearing this year. They'll be just eatable when you come down, though why you ever wanted to convalesce in London I don't know.

The new rector is a dear. Four kids, and an exceptional wife (for a parson). He's going to officiate on *the great occasion*. Only a month now. Isopel's going to have a short frock and I'm going to have a long one. A real country do, with a party for the village and George and 'Anry as sidesmen. All the county will turn out.

Giles is going to get an awful lot for the Romney, it seems. It's impossible to believe that that ghastly man could have been right about anything, but I'm not going to write about him or anything connected with that dreadful time, although of course if it hadn't happened I shouldn't have found Marlowe.

I'm bursting with happiness now, but I wish you were down here with us. Giles says that we shall have to watch you or you'll come in Boy Scout uniform to the wedding, but you won't, will you? He says you turned up as a Salvation Army General when Bunny Wright married Lady Rachel. You won't do anything silly this time, promise, because I mean—oh, well, please don't, anyway.

Cuddy's daughter had her baby, quite a beauty. Mr. Lobbett (I'm beginning to call him "Poppa", which seems to be American for "Daddy", "Daddy" meaning something else) gave it the Bounty. *And* (this will please you) she wanted to call the poor little beast

"Nuptial" because of our weddings, but we persuaded her not to, so it's going to be called "Bridget Isopel" instead.

Addlepate has got a new collar because he got the old one off and ate it, or tried to, anyhow he did it in.

There doesn't seem to be anything more to say, although such heaps of glorious things are happening. I miss old St. Swithin dreadfully. He would have enjoyed this. Alice is looking after the new people at the Rectory. And do you know I do believe Cuddy is having an affair with the new postmaster who came when Kettle went. He isn't married, or at least not now. He has two children that Cuddy is always washing for him. She puts papers in her hair at nights, now, and looked quite gay in church this morning.

And you did all this, you wonderful old thing. Marlowe and I thank you from the bottom of our hearts and so do the others. We'll never forget it. All the best.

> Lots of love, old dear,
> BIDDY

There was a postscript on her letter, written in Marlowe's precise, educated hand:

Coming to town with this abandoned woman, Friday. Everything O.K. The dad wants to know where he can buy some more port like that '98 stuff in the cellar. The doc says it will give him gout. He says "What's gout?"

> Yrs ever,
> M. K. L.

The other two had signed the letter. It was a family epistle. From time immemorial Biddy's letters had been like that —frank, unconscious affairs which anyone might read.

Campion thrust the wad of notepaper back into his pocket, and glanced up to find Mr. Lugg looking down at him with lugubrious interest.

"That's a warnin'," he said. "There's a moral in that, there is. Find the Lady is a Mug's game, that's wot this 'as shown you, and don't you forget it neither."

Campion ignored him.

"Two wedding presents," he remarked. "I shall have to send you out on to the tiles again, Lugg."

"I wish you would," said that worthy with unexpected vigour. "Buy, buy, buy—it gives me the 'ump. That letter's from that girl you was rather sweet on, ain't it? A little fair-'aired girl—not much of 'er. You know," he went on with deep consideration, "wot you want, if you must 'ave a woman about the place, is a nice sensible 'omely 'ospital nurse. Someone who'll do the washin' up for us."

"Shut up, Lugg," said Campion. "What about those wedding presents? Silver, I suppose."

Lugg was dubious.

"Don't 'ave it inscribed, whatever you do," he remarked feelingly. "Can't pop it, can't sell it, no one even wants to pinch it. It does silver right in, inscribin' does. There's a sight too much of it these days. I'll think of something."

Campion remained silent for some time. "Lugg," he said at last, "suppose I retired? This profession of mine puts people off."

Mr. Lugg's expression silenced him. The old lag was staring at him, his eyes bulging, his jaw dropped.

"You're not well," he said at last. "You've 'ad a relapse. I'll mix you something."

"Stop!" Campion put up his hand. "Don't be a fool, Lugg. I'm serious."

"That's un'ealthy in itself," said Lugg, and trotted out of the room.

Campion sat down again. He took the letter from his pocket and threw it into the fire. Folding his hands on his knees, he watched it burn. Then he moved restlessly in his chair. Von Faber in Broadmoor, Simister dead—for the moment he felt like Alexander, sighing for new worlds to conquer.

At this instant Lugg returned. He appeared considerably subdued, and a little troubled. In his hand he held a card.

"Not 'arf a funny bloke outside," he said in a hoarse whisper. "A foreigner. Shall I chuck a brick at 'im?"

"I don't know," said Campion. "Let's have a look at that."

Lugg parted with the slip of pasteboard unwillingly. A glance at it brought a sparkle in Mr. Campion's eyes, and a flush of pleasure appeared in his cheeks. He swept past Lugg and threw open the door.

In a moment he reappeared with a man about his own age, dark and distinguished-looking, with a somewhat military carriage.

They were talking together with great animation in a tongue which Mr. Lugg afterwards described as "monkey talk". It was evident that they had known each other for some time.

After the first moment or so the stranger produced a letter, a massive grey-white envelope, sealed and bound with crimson tape. He bowed and withdrew a pace or two as the Englishman cut it carefully open. The single sheet of paper within was crested with the arms of a famous European royal house, but the few lines were scribbled in English:

Salutations. My dear fellow, I am in despair. State Trip to Indo-China indicated. Fed to the teeth. Could you impersonate me, as before?

Ever yours, R.

P.S.—Trouble expected, if that appeals to you. For the love of Ike (I think you call him) come and help me.

Mr. Campion folded the missive carefully, and dropped it into the fire after Biddy's. He was obviously elated. He turned to his visitor and beamed. Crossing to his desk, he wrote a few words on a sheet of notepaper and slipped it into an envelope, which he sealed carefully. Then he exchanged a few more civilities with his visitor, and the stranger departed.

As the door closed behind him Campion turned to his inquisitive aide.

"Lugg," he said joyously, "you may kiss our hand."

ABOUT THE AUTHOR

MARGERY ALLINGHAM, who was born in London in 1904, came from a long line of writers. "I was brought up from babyhood in an atmosphere of ink and papers," she claimed. One ancestor wrote early nineteenth century melodramas, another wrote popular boys' school stories, and her grandfather was the proprietor of a religious newspaper. But it was her father, the author of serials for the popular weeklies, who gave her her earliest training as a writer. She began studying the craft at the age of seven and had published her first novel by the age of sixteen while still at boarding school. In 1927 she married Philip Youngman Carter, and the following year she produced the first of her Albert Campion detective stories, *The Crime at Black Dudley*. She and her husband lived a life "typical of the English countryside" she reported, with "horses, dogs, our garden and village activities" taking up leisure time. One wonders how much leisure time Margery Allingham, the author of more than thirty-three mystery novels in addition to short stories, serials and book reviews, managed to have.